HOOD

OTHER URBAN EROTIC TALES BY NOIRE

HOOD

An Urban Erotic Tale

NOIRE

ATRIA BOOKS

New York • London • Toronto • Sydney

ATRIA BOOKS

Division of Simon & Schuster, Inc.
1230 Avenue of the Americas
New York, NY 10020

Song lyrics courtesy of Reem Raw and Robb Hawk

First Atria Books trade paperback edition August 2007

ATRIA BOOKS and colophon are trademarks of
Simon & Schuster, Inc.

For information about special discounts for bulk
purchases, please contact Simon & Schuster Special Sales
at 1-800-456-6798 or business@simonandschuster.com.

Designed by Dana Sloan

Manufactured in the United States of America

10 9 8 7 6 5 4 3 2 1

Library of Congress Cataloging-in-Publication Data

Noire.
Hood : an urban erotic tale / by Noire.—1st Atria Books trade paperback ed.
p. cm.

1. African Americans—Fiction. I. Title.

PS3614.O45H66 2007
813'.6—dc22
2007015746
ISBN-13: 978-1-4165-3303-0 (trade pbk.)
ISBN-10:   1-4165-3303-6 (trade pbk.)
ISBN-10:   1-4165-4543-3 (ebook)

This urban erotic tale is dedicated to all the Jimmys, Thugs, Pimps, Smooves, Farads, Finesses, Drekos, Sackies, and Hoods who grind on the block and face the consequences of street life every single day.

No regrets 'cause life is sacred!
Never let go of what you put your faith in!
Times get hard, gotta keep your patience . . .
Hold on till your dream comes true and embrace it!
Face it!

—COURTESY OF REEM RAW

Keep doin ya *own* damn thang!

ACKNOWLEDGMENTS

Father, thank you for allowing me to do what I do.

Nisaa, Missy, Jay, Man, Ty . . . my stinky baby . . . I luv y'all to the bone.

My fam at Noire Music Group and N.J.S. Entertainment, We next!

Reem Raw . . . your lyrics are on fiyah.
We about to take this to the next level!
Readers hit Reem at Myspace.com/NJSMusic to hear those hot tracks.

Angie, Aretha, Melissa, and the rest of my fam who puts it down
for me at NOIREMagazine.com, you have my thanks and my luv.

To the thousands of readers and fans who watch my back,
Shield me from the noise,
And send me luv and support every single day,

I luv y'all right back.

STAY BLACK

—NOIRE

SO HOOD!

This here ain't no romance
It's an urban erotic tale
Bitches, chips, and gangstas
A grimy hustle Hood knows well

Youth got stolen, manhood molded,
The streets welcomed him in
Loyal soldier, no man's doljah,
Determined to get it in

Making traps, pulling gats,
Piff, yay, and sticky green,
The love of dollas, money, power
Friends turn into fiends

Mind slippin, foes trippin,
the Hoodsta's going mental
Self destruction, soul abduction,
Grimy street essentials

Underhanded dealing
'Cause the love was just pretend
Outlandish flossing, double-crossing
What kind of G betrays a friend?

So this here ain't no romance
Hood payback is a bitch
Life shits on you twice as hard
When ya fuckin wit' a snitch!

—NOIRE

IN THE BEGINNING . . .

HAVE YOU EVER been shitted on? Nah, not no regular every day street shit. I'm talking that low-down grimy diarrhea shit. The kinda shit that no matter how much you try to make it right, it still stinks? Have you ever lived in the gutter? Slept in somebody else's piss? Crawled around with fake niggas like wet rats in a barrel? Yo, check it. Lamont be my government, but Hood be my name. Reppin the true definition of a street soldier. A general. Out there on the front lines getting it in. Doing whatever it takes. I earned my stripes chilling up in Fat Daddy's joint, a Brownsville barbershop in the belly of Brooklyn. We went to war up in that muthafucka, and when the smoke cleared wasn't but one gangsta left standing. Some called me a street savior . . . others said I was just another Brownsville boy gone bad. Whatever. I brung it and I took it too. But when it was all said and done I walked away with a lesson learned in street loyalty: Ain't no need in looking over your shoulder in this game. Because your real enemies ain't aiming at your back. They lunging straight for your heart. Ya dig?

CHAPTER 1

I'm a G-E-N-E-R-A-L!
Get it right, I'm the type that'll always prevail!
I'm a G-E-N-E-R-A-L!

THE CLUB WAS packed out and niggas was wildin. In a back room the bass thumped hard, booming through the walls and sending vibrations up through the cold cement floor. Dreko opened his legs wider and watched the white girl as she bobbed her head up and down between his thighs. Her pink lips nibbled along the shaft of his dick as he wound his fingers through her hair, then slid them down to grip her slim neck.

"Stop playin," he growled from deep in his throat. "Suck this shit right and don't be fuckin playin."

The girl giggled and puckered up, pecking his wood with tiny kisses. She took a deep breath and blew on his dick, amazed at the thick black snake she held in her hands.

"Man—" Dreko squeezed her neck painfully then slammed her face down into his groin. "Suck my fuckin dick! Fuck all them little kisses. Gimme some of that throat."

"Sorry," the white girl whispered. She'd spotted Dreko when he stepped in from the bitter cold with three other guys, and right away her pussy had started throbbing. She had a thing for muscled up, dark chocolate guys with danger in their eyes and this cat had walked up in the joint like he paid the bills.

She took his pretty dick in both hands and stuffed it in her mouth. A lot of cats liked it when she spread her long blond hair over their thighs and teased them with her lips while they watched. She always made sure they got a good look at her smooth, white skin pressed up on their black dicks. It turned them on to see that contrast, feeding those secret fantasies of dominating and fucking the shit out of a white girl.

But this dude seemed cranky and impatient. The way he held her neck in a death grip told her he wanted his head straight up. No frills and no fancy foreplay. Just suck the dick and get the damn nut. She went to work on that shit like it was her day job.

"Yeah," he moaned as she slurped away, taking his whole dick in her mouth, then spitting it out halfway, before sucking it in again. The white girl worked him over. Her best friend Lauren had been fuckin with club ballers like him for months now, but she was still pretty new to this scene and was looking for a real playa who could offer her some status.

Her family was Italian and they lived over in Canarsie. They hated black people and if her father and brothers knew she was in a club naked on her fifteen-year-old knees with a black man's dick rammed down her throat, they'd kill her ass. They'd have to catch her first, though. She'd run away from home seven times in the last few months and the pull of the streets was enough to make her stay gone forever.

She glanced up as Dreko pounded up into her mouth. His eyes were closed and there was rage mixed in with the hot pleasure on his face. He was a real youngster too. He looked a whole lot younger now than he did when he had stepped through the door looking all good under them club lights. He licked his pretty brown lips as he groaned again and she damn near lost her neck rhythm staring at his fine ass. Young wasn't the fuckin word. He was even younger than her. His goatee was barely more than peach fuzz. He was heavy in the dick though, and his tall, strapping body was all man. He opened his eyes and busted her staring. She picked up her pace and slurped his dick harder, then hummed in the back of her throat, vibrating her tonsils against his sweet, swollen head.

"Faster," he demanded. His hand still gripped her neck, tighter now as he worked anxiously for his nut. She felt his dick straining as he arched his back and pumped into her mouth. She worked double-time. Sucked his muscle deeper. Put every trick she knew into pleasing him as she anticipated how good his big black dick was going to feel pounding inside of her.

She smiled to herself as she felt his body stiffen, then shudder. He *was* young, she realized. He'd lost his head in less than three minutes and she silently congratulated herself as she felt his warm semen fill her mouth. Holding it on her tongue, she savored his salty flavor.

Above her, he pushed her away then leaned back in the chair. He laid his head back against the wall. "Damn. That muhfuckin shit felt good."

Still smiling inside, she rose and climbed into his lap, straddling his strong legs and rubbing her damp pussy on his still-hard dick. She pressed her lips against his throat then pulled his head forward, covering his mouth with hers. She parted her lips and tongued him down real deep, letting his bitter spurt flow out of her mouth and into his.

"Wha—" he snatched away, spitting out slime. He wiped his tongue on his sleeve and cursed.

She laughed. "It's a snowball," she explained. "I just gave you a little snowball."

He swung so fast she never saw it coming. Broke her nose with just one punch. The blow sent her flying backward from his lap. Her head cracked on the edge of a metal table and she thudded to the floor. Pain exploded between her eyes and every bone in her body hurt. Blood trickled from her nose and filled her mouth. A wet scream burst from her throat.

"Nasty *bitch!*" His scream was even louder than hers as he yanked up his pants and raised his foot and kicked in her face.

Her nose throbbed in agony. She tried to turn and avoid his blow and a bomb went off in the back of her head. His boot cracked her skull and the horrible sound that split the room came from her own lips. Not even the club music could cover it, and it just got louder and louder as she rolled over on her back and his boot came down again. Hard. Bashing into her broken nose and busting both her lips.

"Please . . ." she begged, flat on her back gurgling blood with her arms stretched toward him. He raged like a fuckin maniac above her. Sweat was dripping off his face and his eyes looked devil red. Cursing, he buried his boot in her stomach. She rolled over again and threw up.

"Nasty fuckin bitch," he panted as he stomped her face into the cold cement. Sobbing, she curled herself inward like a baby, her hands slippery with blood as she tried in vain to spread her fingers over her busted head. Her blond hair was sticky in her eyes and she screamed louder when her fingers pressed against a soft, dented part of her skull. The pain was so intense she gasped, nearly blacking out, cowering under the flurry of his blows, unable to escape.

He was gonna kill her and she knew it. All she could do was lay there and pray. A minute later there was a commotion and the door was flung open as a bunch of dudes busted up into the small room. *Thank you, God*, the girl thought as she lay weak and disoriented. Dreko was swarmed by five big cats who pulled him off her and tackled him to the ground.

"I will kill that dirty bitch!" he was screaming and spitting as they took him down to the ground. "Word my niggas, I'ma *kill* her nasty ass!"

As she lay naked and moaning on the cold, dirty floor, the young white girl silently thanked God again. She'd been fucking with fire on these mean streets of Brownsville and this time she had come real close to getting burnt. They dragged Dreko out of the room and he was still screaming like an animal.

Somebody threw a sweater over her tiny titties. She fought against the black pain and willed her fingers to move as she struggled to pull the sweater over her bloody head. She was up on her hands and knees, and Dreko's threats were still ringing in her ears and sending cold terror rushing through her blood.

Right then and there she made the wisest decision of her young life. These streets were hungry as hell for a girl like her. They'd eat her little ass up and shit her right out. Fuck all this. Her girl Lauren could stay in Brownsville wildin with these crazy niggers for the rest of her life if she wanted to, but if she could just find enough strength to make it outta this club alive she was crawling her white ass back home to Canarsie.

CHAPTER 2

It's priceless, never felt love like this,
Only you can bring light to my crisis,
Life just ain't worth it at all without you, swear,
I don't wanna do it at all without you, true . . .

"I'M COLD," MONROE complained for the hundredth time. The streets were deserted and his breath came out smoky in the night air. "I'm so so *so* cold, Lamont. My feet not even there no more."

It was one of the bitterest nights of the year. The young boys had been chased out of the abandoned building they'd been living in and the police were sweeping the streets and forcing the homeless into heated shelters.

Inside the torn, wet mitten they shared Lamont entwined their fingers, gripping his baby brother's hand real tight. They'd been walking the dark streets of Central Brooklyn for hours and he was frozen too. Lamont had already given Moo one of the two thin jackets he'd worn. Now he took off his skully and pushed it down on Monroe's head, but the cold was so bad that even five knit hats wouldn't have mattered.

"Just keep your other hand in your pocket, Moo," he told him, guiding the four-year-old across the ice-covered pavement. He looked down, trying hard not to slip in the frozen footprints left by pedestrians before him. His raggedy sneakers were like thin pieces of cloth. He removed his left hand from his jacket pocket and immediately regretted it. Throbbing pain stiffened his fingers as the bitter cold gripped him.

"This better?" he asked as he pulled the knit hat down lower on Moo's forehead. His little brother coughed deeply. His nose was running and his lips were cracked and dry.

Moo nodded. He was cold but he was trying hard to be brave. He saw how red Lamont's ears were as he tried to hunch his skinny shoulders and duck his bare head against the biting wind. Somehow Moo had lost his mittens so it was his fault they only had one glove to share, but Mont didn't even get mad about it.

"I'm so hungry," Moo said softly.

Lamont closed his hand around the softening brown lump in his pocket. It was supposed to be Moo's breakfast for tomorrow, but neither of them had eaten in hours and he was gonna have to give it to him tonight. They stopped and leaned against an ice-covered Mazda.

"Here." Lamont took his hand from his pocket again, ignoring the stiffening cold. He held the small potato out to Moo. "Take a couple of bites."

As hungry as he was, Moo looked at the potato and shook his head.

"C'mon, man," Lamont urged. He'd found the potato in an almost-fresh bag of trash and it was the only thing in the whole pile that the rats hadn't already either shit on or gnawed on.

Moo stared at the spindly white buds that were growing out of the skin.

"Man, them just the eyes," Lamont said, breaking off the buds and tossing them down to the ice. He wiped a fuzzy sheen of mold from the potato's skin and waited while Moo bit into it hesitantly and then chewed.

"Act like it's like a apple, man," Lamont told him. "Eat it just like a apple."

Moo ate the mushy potato quickly and the brothers walked on, this time down the middle of the street. It was safer that way. Lamont had already stuck his knife into a fiend who tried to snatch Moo from a doorway the night before, and the piss-soaked abandoned car they had been sleeping in for the last few nights was also a bust. Some fool had kicked all the windows out and crackheads had been sleeping all up in it. Pissing it up some more.

"M-m-my legs cold, Mont. My toes feel funny too."

Chin down against the ice-flecked wind, Lamont moved onward.

Monroe started to whine. "Mont, when Mama coming to get us, huh? Maybe she ain't never coming, right? She don't even come see us no more. Is the police gone shoot her like they did Daddy, Monty? Huh?"

Then Moo got real quiet like he was thinking. The moon was full. Long minutes passed where there was nothing but the whistling wind and the sounds of their small feet crunching through the ice.

Then he said softly, "Prob'bly you gone die too, huh, Monty. That would scare me real bad. You think you gone get dead one day and I'ma have to walk around out here by myself?"

"No," Lamont said quietly. The wind took his answer and tossed it toward the north. Theirs was a straight up hard-knock life. They'd slept in concrete barrels on the project playground, down a garbage ramp in Tilden, and snuck on the train and rode all the way to the Bronx and back. Twice they ran from transit cops, jumping off at one stop and crossing over and catching a train going in the opposite direction. Damn right Moo was scared.

Hood had his fears too, but they were not of anything on the streets. His greatest nightmare was that his mind might one day slip off, just like his mother's had, and so he conditioned himself to use the words in his head every single day. And even though he always looked calm and fearless on the outside, his brain was constantly on whirl: spittin lyrics, building bridges, stacking verses, humming hooks, and composing street songs that overflowed with metaphors and similes.

"Mama crazy ain't she, Mont? That's why we ain't got no house no more. Gramma said Mama buggy. Done lost her mind. Is that why Daddy's friends shot him up, Monty? Cause Mama lost all the words out her head and got crazy?"

Lamont ducked his head against the freezing ice that was starting to fall. He tried not to think about his parents as tiny shards bit into his skin and he trembled inside the Members Only windbreaker he'd gotten from the Salvation Army.

"Mama got her words back now, and Gramma don't know shit, Moo. Especially about Mama."

"But w-w-why we can't go to Gramma house? Or what about Miss Baker, Monty? Huh? Why we always walkin around so much? Miss Baker always real nice to us. Why we can't go get warm over there?"

Lamont stopped and looked at his little brother. The cold wind shoved them around and their feet slid across the ice as they struggled to remain upright. He broke it down to Monroe for the umpteenth time. "I told you, Moo. Miss Baker is sick in the hospital right now. And you already know why we can't go to Gramma's. Aunt Pat don't like us. She ain't let us in last night, and she ain't gone let us in tonight neither."

"Then we can go back to the empty house, right? Them guys with the fire cans probably gone somewhere else by now, huh?"

"No," Lamont said firmly. It had been two days since the pair of crackheads had run them into the streets and

Lamont was still mad about it. Head up and toe-to-toe, he could have given them some fight with his knife. But those fiends had gotten real stupid and started pouring gasoline everywhere, threatening to roast Lamont and Moo while they slept unless the two boys un-assed the premises.

They'd spent the next four nights sleeping on the floor in his friend Reem's bedroom. Their mothers had been friends back in the day, and Jareem and Lamont had been tight since the sandbox. Reem's mom worked two jobs and left him home alone a lot. Reem was a generous kid and a loyal friend. He let Mont and Moo in the crib and snuck them as much food as he could, and whenever his moms was home he made sure the coast was clear so they could use the bathroom.

But Moo was sick, and the cement-tiled floors of the projects were hard and cold. Reem let Moo have his bed while he toughed it out with Mont on a thin blanket they spread on the floor. Reem cut school every day while they were there, so they could plan their future as moguls in the music industry. They swore they'd cut a string of platinum albums one day, and both had verbal skills that were far superior to their ages and their environment. So the moment Reem's mother left for work he doubled back to the crib, and the three boys spent the cold days watching karate movies, playing video games, and spittin endless battle raps.

"Check it," Reem said as they looked out the window one morning. The cold was brutal, but the corner action was still rolling heavy outside of his building. Them trap boys was bundled up in layers as they ran back and forth between a steady stream of customers.

"That guy is a jake," he said pointing to a cat in a red SUV. "Them traps better shake them lookout boys up and get in they asses because somebody's about to get knocked." Reem grinned at Hood, then with a challenging look in his eyes, he started spittin.

> *Them boys standin on the corner,*
> *Heavy on the grind,*
> *Clientele swarming, demand and supply*
> *Business booming, real good line*
> *That's when I seen out the corner of my eye*
> *Dude by the bus stop—undercover on watch,*
> *Kept talking into . . . a cigarette box*
> *That's the third time that Suburban rolled by . . .*
> *I'm lookin up and it's a full moon in the sky . . .*

"That's tight as hell!" Hood said dapping Reem hard. He nodded his head and let his creativity flow. Then he cut in with his own phat lyrics and got some too.

> *Something don't feel right and I ain't trippin,*
> *Say what you wanna but it's street intuition!*
> *So much heat feels like we in a kitchen,*
> *So keep ya eyes peeled and listen . . .*
> *Cuz its about to be a showdown, whoa-down*
> *Ya better throw y'all stash on the ground!*

Cause I got a strange feeling . . .
Something's bout to happen
And I aint tryna get caught out!

The three boys were real comfortable up in that small room together, and they would have stayed there rapping and making up karate moves even longer but Moo's cough was so loud it got them busted. Reem's mom found them hiding in his closet and made them come out.

"Now Lamont," she said gently. She'd made them take a hot bath and fixed each of them a big plate of food. "You know I love you and Moo, and if there was somebody here to watch y'all while I worked I'd keep you both forever. But your Aunt Pat ain't nothing but trouble. If she found out I had y'all up in here without no papers she would do her best to see me in jail."

Mont knew Reem's mom cared about them but he wasn't just gonna sit there while she called Social Services to come pick them up. He had grabbed Moo and made a run for the door the minute her back was turned, and ever since then they'd been right back out in the cold, walking the streets.

"Well, w-w-what about the staircase then?" Monroe asked, stomping his numb feet. His big brown eyes were desperate as his small body jerked and shuddered with the penetrating cold. "We slept on the stairs before and we was okay, right?"

"Can't," Lamont said shaking his head. "Winos already got the stairs. X-fiends and crackheads got the porches

and the doorways. It ain't safe, Moo. We just gotta keep
moving, man. Okay?"

"B-b-but we already walked this way before! Two
times! Where we gone go, Lamont? Huh? Where we gone
go?" Moo was cranky and crazy tired. Not only was he
way too cold, his head hurt and his throat burned. Moving
his small legs quickly to keep up with his brother, all he
could do was whimper softly because he was too cold and
too sick to cry any real tears.

Lamont felt for his brother as he looked around at the
deserted streets. Moo had it right. They'd already walked
from one side of town to the other. Twice. He knew they
couldn't last much longer out here. They'd both probably
die. But he also couldn't decide which was worse: walking
the evil streets of Brownsville on the coldest night of the
year, sneaking into one of the crack houses that were all
around him and getting killed, or running into the police
and getting separated from his brother. He shook his head
at that last thought.

"Okay," he said, turning around and pulling Moo in the
direction they'd just left. "Let's go to Gramma's. Maybe
Aunt Pat'll change her mind. Maybe she'll let you in for a
few minutes to use the bathroom or something. We'll try,
okay?"

Moo nodded and a tear made its way down his frozen
cheek.

Lamont wiped it away, his bare fingers grazing the reddish mole under Moo's left eye. Not even the burning cold
could match the pain in Lamont's eleven-year-old heart.

He pulled the skully completely down over Monroe's face, covering his eyes and snotty nose.

"Hey!" Moo complained. He stopped walking and slid along, pulled by his brother's momentum. "I can't see nothing, Mont. How I'ma walk if I can't see?"

Lamont squeezed his brother's hand and pulled him again. "You ain't gotta see nothing, Moo. You gone be straight lil man. I promise. All you gotta do is follow me."

$ $ $

The moon shone brightly as the two boys walked hand in hand down Rockaway Avenue. They cut across the street on Dumont and struggled along the ice until they reached Van Dyke projects. Lamont paused outside of the Brownsville branch of the Brooklyn Public Library. A sign said it was closed for renovations. He pulled Moo further down the street and they entered the back of building 345 and slipped into the dark stairwell. It was just as cold inside as it was outside. Every light bulb and window had been broken out and the slippery steps were caked up with icy piss. Winos huddled around their bottles sipping liquid heat. Lamont guided Moo around a needle fiend and they climbed up to the fourth floor. The exit door squealed loudly as Lamont pulled it open, startling them. They walked down to the end of the hallway. Lamont dragged his wet feet. They stopped outside the last door on the left and he just stood there. Looking at the door and shivering.

"Knock," Moo demanded. He was cold. Starving too.

He woulda done anything to get through that door and get next to some heat. "C'mon. I'm f-f-freezing, Mont. Just watch. Aunt Pat gonna be n-n-n-nice this time."

Lamont shrugged, then knocked on the door and waited.

He knocked twice more. Three, five times, no answer. He could hear them moving around on the other side of the door. He heard the refrigerator open and slam closed. A chair scraped across the floor.

He sighed and took his brother's small, cold hand. "They sleep, Moo. Let's go."

"No," Monroe said, snatching away. He lifted his soggy little foot and kicked the door hard. He kicked it twice, then banged on it with his frozen fists.

"It's Moo, Gramma!" the small boy pleaded, tears in his eyes. "Moo! Out! Here! Let us in, Aunt P-P-Pat!"

No answer.

The child sobbed, sagging against the closed door. "Please, Aunt Pat. Let us in. We tired and it's really really really really cold out here!" Grimacing, Monroe pummeled the door again, swinging his hands as hard and fast as he could, and when that became too painful he used his elbows then went back to kicking again.

Finally a door opened. Behind them.

"Boy." A scratchy, cruel voice filled the hall as their grandmother's neighbor poked his big gray head out the door. "Quit banging on that damn door 'fore I let my dogs out on ya ass. Can't ya take a hint? Don't nobody want you 'round here. Now get goin' wit' all that damn noise."

Minutes later the boys were back outside. The wind had picked up and tiny pellets of hail were pinging down all around them.

"Here," Lamont said. He held his torn mitten out to Monroe. "Put both your hands inside." Moo obeyed silently. His face was drawn and his four-year-old eyes looked about forty.

Lamont's look was also grim. He wrapped his arm around his baby brother and together they headed back out into the streets.

CHAPTER 3

Y'all niggas got a problem . . .
How do you think you gone solve 'em?
Not like that!

A USELESS SUN shone in the sky. It gave off no heat and the bright day was just as cold as the bitter night before it had been. Corner boys were out grinding and making that trap, while Dreko stood in the lobby of his tenement building getting warm and taking a break from his lookout duties.

He slouched his lanky frame against the wall and stared out through the glass door with his hands in his pockets. The lock was busted and the handle had been broken off. The frigid wind whistled in sharply, sliding through the narrow gap where the doorframes failed to meet.

Dreko sniffed, then spit a big gob on the floor. He'd had a nasty taste in his mouth since last night when that

stupid white bitch had tongued him, slobbering his own
cum back down his throat. Rage rose in him just thinking
about it. They'd had to pull him off her ass up in Baller's
Paradise 'cause he'd been ready to dead that bitch. If he
ever caught her stupid ass out here in Brownsville again,
he would.

He was a big nigga. A menace. Already he stood taller
than some grown men and he had bulk on his muscles and
a nice long dick. And he was just going on thirteen. He
had a foul temper too, and was known to bust muhfuckas
in the head with little provocation. Especially if there was
some doe involved.

A deep scowl creased his face as his stomach growled,
reminding him that he hadn't eaten since the night before.
His moms had gone to work already, taking his brother
with her. All the food in the house had been locked up in
her bedroom. Even the damn refrigerator had a lock on
it. That bitch had problems with him, and she didn't even
trust him around his own brother.

She was constantly trying to turn little Drew against
him, telling him all kinds of crazy shit that wasn't true. She
walked around the house silent and cold, and at night she
took Drew into her bedroom and locked the door behind
them. He knew she kept a knife in there, but it wouldn't
help her ass if he ever decided to bust down that door.

She treated him like he was something dirty, and
just last night she'd told him if he couldn't take his ass
to school and keep his nasty hands off other kids, then he
could raise, clothe, and feed his damn self. And that's ex-

actly what he was doing working as a lookout for Xanbar and his crew.

Dreko peered out the glass door and down the block. He was supposed to be out there with Lil Jay, taking turns as lookouts on the corner. He sneered as he watched white boy Sackie Woodson run out to a car and make a transaction. Him and the rest of the crew were out there trapping hard, and Dreko wanted to be a part of that.

Instead, Xan was holding him back. Like he was a herb. Dreko glanced at his watch. He should have been back outside about fifteen minutes ago, but fuck it. If Lil Jay got cold enough or got bad enough, let him come inside this fuckin building and get him.

Dreko stared out the doorway watching people hurry up and down the street, their heads bent against the wind. Every now and then somebody walked past him either coming in or going out the building, but he never moved. Instead, he made 'em walk around him. Even the old ladies.

For the third time, a pair of raggedy-ass boys caught his eye as they walked past. One cat was older than the other one, who was really just past being a baby. Dreko stood up straighter and watched the way the bigger boy held the lil dude's hand and pulled him down the street. The whole time the cat had his eyes on prowl. Every chick who passed by with a purse was a potential victim. Dreko could see it in his sharp, intense face. The kid was eyeballing the hero shop and the storefronts too. Thinking on something to steal, Dreko knew.

There was something about the cat that intrigued him, and braving the cold Dreko threw his hoody over his head and stepped out of the building so he could watch as they moved on down the street.

"Lil bitch," he muttered under his breath as the bigger cat pushed his brother up against a wall like he was warning him not to move. That fool was gone get straight knocked. How the fuck he thought he was gonna steal something and get away while he had a youngster running beside him was crazy. Dreko woulda never brought his little brother out on a lick. Besides, he had gotten knocked enough times to know how to get down and how not to get down. And not behind no petty-ass purse snatching shit like this kid was scheming on neither. He'd been a real stick-up kid, and sometimes he didn't even have to use a gat to get what he wanted.

But he had gotten cool on all that shit. It was too risky and it didn't pay enough to be worth it. These days he schemed up grand plans of one day ruling the entire Brownsville drug trade, but for now he had to be satisfied with all this low-level action. He'd hold down his little lookout post for now, but as soon as he gained Xanbar's confidence he'd be inching up to a corner grind so he could make that trap and start kicking up that doe. Hell yeah, the boys in blue had swooped down and fucked with him a time or two, but lookouts didn't carry no product so eventually he'd landed back on the streets. Shit, he was still a youngster. Not a lot the courts would do to a cat like him unless he straight popped somebody. And still . . . even then they had to catch him before they could do something about it.

Dreko watched the lil cat with the desperate eyes for a few seconds more. Punk-ass. Muhfucka needed to leave that purse snatchin shit to the winos and the fiends and get himself a job on a lookout station. He stomped his feet a few times, then blew into his icy hands and headed back inside of his building. On the way in he bumped into a youngster named Berry.

"Yo, nigga. Don't you owe me something?"

The level of fear that came into the nine-year-old's eyes would've been heartbreaking to anyone else.

But Dreko didn't give a fuck.

"Look, muhfucka. The next time your moms feening for that pipe and you beg me to get one of my boys to spot her, you better come back with my money, you hear?" Dreko grabbed the kid's shoulders and turned him around, pushing him deeper into the building and toward the back stairs. He was about to get him some and Lil Jay was just gone have to fuckin wait.

It was quiet on the back stairs as Dreko slammed the frightened kid against the wall. The little boy shook his head, then shrank down to the ground with tears in his eyes.

"I don't wanna . . ."

Dreko smacked Berry real hard on top of his peasy head, then yanked him to his feet by his jacket.

"Yo shut the fuck up and quit whining!" He unbuckled his belt and zipped down his pants. His dick was already hard and straining.

"You know just how I like this shit. So get up on it and do it right."

$ $ $

Fat Daddy was in the barbershop getting toasted up.

A hefty, barrel-waisted man with a tight goatee, he had a chocolate dutch in one hand and a Corona in the other.

"Fuckin kids," he said glancing out the wide window of his shop. His boy Felton had a customer in his chair, and so did his seventy-year-old uncle, Chop. "This the third damn time they been past here today. Seen 'em out there a couple of days last week too. Little muhfuckas. Need to have they ass in school."

Felton looked up and stared. He was edging up Kraft, who was second in line to Xanbar, the neighborhood's most brutal drug kingpin.

"Butch, you know who them kids is. Them is crazy Marjay's boys. Miz Jones keep 'em now. Whenever evil Pat let her."

Kraft laughed, looking out the window. He was a hand-some cat, muscled up with an even row of pearly teeth. "I know them lil niggas too. My lil sons usta fuck with the big one over in Van Dyke projects. They'd knock him down and take all the little change his granny give him to go to the store." He chuckled again and shook his head. "He got smart real quick, though. Got good with his hands. Nigga started fightin back and fightin real dirty too. He stabbed Beano in the arm and head butted Ike so hard he broke a bone over his eye. He put some shit on that long-faced

nigga Bally too." Kraft rubbed his freshly trimmed goatee. "The kid is small, but he nice. I might hafta give him a
job . . . train him up to be one of my trap boys."

"Oh, yeah?" Fat Daddy mused, his eyebrow raised.
He followed the boys with his eyes. Kraft had more trap
boys than a little bit. Most of them had been kids sitting
in Fat Daddy's chair just yesterday, and today they were
the same niggas who would shoot him in the back for a
wrinkled dollar bill.

He watched as the two boys walked back and forth, up
and down the street. He swigged from his bottle as the
older boy pushed the younger one up against the wall of
a building like he wanted him to stay put. The kid gazed
at the pedestrians real hungry and desperate-like, as if
he was searching for something to steal. Fat Daddy took
a long pull from his stick and sucked it deep. He was still
holding it in when he opened the shop door and let in a
blast of frigid air.

"Hey you! Brang yo ass over here boy!"

The older kid looked up and grilled him, then moved
forward, placing himself between Fat Daddy and his
young brother.

Fat Daddy narrowed his eyes. "Don't gimme no fuckin
looks, son. Get it over here."

The kid didn't move.

"All right," Fat Daddy shrugged and made like he
was about to close the door. "I was gone give your little
brother a sandwich but I guess he ain't hungry."

The littler kid took off. He broke free from his brother

and ran toward Fat Daddy so fast it caught him off guard.

"Whoa, hold up there lil man," he chuckled. "Don't knock Fat Daddy on his ass. That sandwich ain't going nowhere."

"I'm hungry," the little boy said without shame. His face was narrow and he had a familiar little funny-colored mole under his left eye. He was just a baby, but he looked Fat Daddy right in his eye. His brother caught up with him and cursed and tried to pull him away, but the kid wouldn't budge. "I'm hungry."

Fat Daddy took the small boy's arm and pulled him inside the shop, knowing his big brother wouldn't let him come in alone. He led them past Kraft, Chop, and Felton, and into a small kitchen behind the shop.

"Come on back here. Hungry ain't no good thing to be. But you gone hafta work for your food, boy. Around here we scramble hard. Don't shit come free."

In the back, the little one stared at a pot of stew on the stove with big, greedy eyes.

"Uh-uh," Fat Daddy checked him. He handed him a roll of paper towels and a bottle of window cleaner. "Grab that broom over there," he told the big boy.

He took them back into the shop and was about to put them to work, but stopped when he saw who was sitting in his chair.

He smiled at his little girl, then bent over and smoothed her dredlocks. He kissed her forehead. She looked so small sitting in his big barber chair with her legs dangling above the floor.

"Hi, Daddy," she said grinning. Egypt was a tall, bright-eyed child. Chocolate brown with glasses and a slight overbite. She was a daddy's girl and Fat Daddy spoiled her rotten. Gymnastics, dance class, piano lessons, he drove her out to Canarsie and signed her up for every damn thing under the sun, whether them white folks wanted her in their classes or not. Her mother had died from a blood clot when she was three days old and there was nothing too good for his little girl. She mighta been a motherless child of the ghetto, but she sure had herself a daddy. One who adored her and protected her and gave her everything her sweet little heart wanted.

But spoiled or not, Egypt was a smart girl who had grand dreams of a future that just tickled the shit outta her father. Almost from the time she could talk she declared she was gonna be a doctor someday, and she'd broken every single doll baby Fat Daddy had ever bought her, just so she could tape bandages all over them and make them well again.

"Who's that?" She looked curiously at the two strange boys, then grinned and nodded at the bigger boy.

Fat Daddy looked at the kid and was startled by the expression on his face. As cold, wet, and hungry as the boy must have been, he was looking at Egypt like he'd just discovered the eighth wonder of the world.

"Nigga say ya damn name," Fat Daddy urged him. "When a female wanna know who you be, you better make yourself known."

"I'm Lamont. This my brother, Monroe."

"Moo!" the four-year-old piped up. "My name Moo."

Fat Daddy nodded. Lamont's eyes had never left Egypt's face, and for once the outspoken little girl had nothing to say. The way she stared at the boy with her mouth open had Fat Daddy wondering if something invisible was going down between them.

"All right." He stepped between them and shoved Lamont toward the door and thrust the broom in his hand. "Break that shit up." Then he muttered, "Lil nigga."

With one last smile at his baby girl, Fat Daddy sprayed some glass cleaner on the towel for Moo, then told Lamont to get to sweeping.

"Slide that broom all up in the cracks between them stations, too. Make sure you get deep in the corners and don't you miss not one goddamn hair."

$ $ $

Two hours later Fat Daddy sat in a back room wondering what the fuck he was doing bringing Marjay's kids up in his shop. All around him were boxes of shit that had fallen off the back of various trucks and had been sorted and cataloged for resale through New York City's homeboy shopping network. He had taken an old pastrami hero he'd had in the refrigerator and cut it in two. The bigger boy, Lamont, took his half, tore it in two again, and passed half to his brother. Then he scarfed his down in two big bites.

Somebody banged on the side door and Fat Daddy stood. He glanced toward the front of the shop, then reached into his pants and pulled out his piece. He went to the door and stood beside it.

"Yeah!" His voice boomed.

He listened, then unbolted the door.

A young fiend walked in looking wild as fuck. Ice chips were frosting his lopsided afro, but sweat ran down the sides of his face like he'd just run a race. He grinned at Fat Daddy as he stomped snow from his feet. "I got some good shit for ya, Fat Daddy," he said, holding out an appliance with the cord dangling from it.

"Junior, what the fuck is this? Boy what I tell you? Don't be bringing me no shit like this! What the fuck I'ma do with a goddamn VCR? Take that shit back home and plug it up for your grandmama, nigga! Next time you come to my door with some slum I'ma put something on your ass."

Fat Daddy slammed the door and bolted it, then looked at the boys.

"Fuckin crackheads. Don't nobody fuck with no VCRs no more."

Back in the shop, Fat Daddy saw that Kraft was gone. The cold had driven most folks inside their apartments, and since business was light Fat Daddy decided to give both boys a haircut. But the minute he sat the younger one in his chair, he regretted that shit.

The child stank. He had grime all over him and a horrible cough. The back of his neck was black with caked dirt, and his little red ears had sticky wax crawling up out of them.

But it was his scalp that fucked Fat Daddy up.

The boy was wearing two hats, and when he took them off and raised the kid up in the barber chair, Fat Daddy frowned and shook his head.

"Boy what you done got into?" Fat Daddy had seen some bad heads in his lifetime. He'd started cutting hair in the joint, and some of them inmates had head lice, others had sores and nasty, moldy fungus growing down they face like sideburns. But this kid had the worst case of ringworm he'd ever seen. There were round, weeping patches on his scalp with clumped hair permanently plastered down in dried pus.

It took him over an hour to wash and trim their heads, then to sterilize every damn tool at his station. He even sprayed bleach all over his barber's chair. "Can't have no shit like that growing 'round here," he muttered as he washed his hands with some of the solution.

The boys looked a lot warmer and a whole lot cleaner, but Fat Daddy knew that shit was only temporary. For one thing, they both needed something to wipe out the shit that had taken over their scalps, and for two, they needed to get ready to get the hell up outta his shop because Egypt had a gymnastics class and Fat Daddy had dollars to catch.

He thought about Marjay, then looked at the two boys again. Life was brutal for boys like them but Fat Daddy didn't have no damn soft spot for kids other than his baby girl. Shit, there wasn't no such thing as being "just a kid" no more anyway. These lil muhfuckas running the streets these days was ruthless and he'd blow a cap in one of their asses in a quick minute. The older boy looked back at him with familiar eyes. Fat Daddy knew his story well, because he knew their mama well. He knew her *very* well. Marjay had been the finest thing walking the streets of Central Brooklyn back when they were coming up. A sweet, light-skinned honey with stacked hips and a cute reddish mole on her pretty face that made folks call her Red Dot. They'd done a little something back when Fat Daddy was still that slim, handsome, panty-busta nigga called Butch from Blake Avenue.

It had started out as a childhood screw in a pissy staircase, and Marjay had cried so bad afterward that he almost felt bad about cracking that cherry. Still. She'd been a real nice girl, somebody who'd never really left his mind, and years later he caught some kind of jealous feelings when he heard she hooked up with some cop from the Bronx. They'd gotten married and had a couple of kids, then moved out to Mount Vernon. They'd stayed out there living the white-picket-fence life until her man got smoked in a suspicious police-on-police shooting, and that's when Marjay went mute and outta her mind with grief, and dragged her boys back down to Brooklyn. By the time she got her voice back she'd gotten something else along with it. A crack habit. She was lost after that. Just like the rest of the fiends.

Fat Daddy looked at his watch. These lil niggas was gone have to bounce. The smaller one was cozy and had a full belly. He had nodded off to sleep and was leaning on his brother's shoulder, wheezing like he had asthma or some shit.

"Hey now," he said. He got his nine-hundred-dollar mohair coat off a hook and grabbed their dirty jackets up too. Fat Daddy cursed under his breath. It was one of the coldest winters on record and Marjay had her kids out there dressed in some raggedy-ass windbreakers. Shit.

"Wake up now," he said. "It's time to go."

The little one sat up and opened his eyes and started coughing real hard again.

"Gotta make moves," Fat Daddy said, pushing them out of the back room and back through the shop. He hustled them over to the door and handed them their jackets. Lamont took his and put it on, but the baby boy stared up at Fat Daddy with tired old man eyes.

"But where we gone go?" he asked coughing and scratching his scalp at the same time. "Don't nobody want us."

His brother stepped between them. "Shut up, Moo. Stop all that jaw-jacking and put on your coat. We got a lotta shit to do."

Fat Daddy watched as they left the shop hand in hand. The streets were cold in this hood, but that nigga Kraft was right. The boy Lamont had something steely in his heart. As little as he was, he looked like he could handle his. But the baby boy. Fat Daddy shook his head. That little one wasn't gone last long out there. Too many sharks swimming in these icy waters to let a lil nugget like him be.

CHAPTER 4

Nobody better move!
Give up the jewels, shit's hard now!
Niggas shootin in the air like they ain't scared
to bring God down!

THE WARMTH OF the barbershop had only been a temporary comfort, and the little bit of food in their stomachs
wasn't gonna hold them for long. Lamont held Moo's hand
as they walked the neighborhood, staring into storefronts
and trying to come up with a plan. He led his brother
past the avenue and down a side street where rodents
swarmed in and out of a stretch of overflowing Dumpsters. It was dangerous down here, and most people
would rather toss their trash out the windows than risk
the wrath of the rats that ruled the alley: both animal
and human. But that pastrami sandwich Fat Daddy had
given them wasn't gonna last forever and Lamont wanted

to find something else for Moo to eat before it got dark.

They leaned into the wind as they rounded the corner, and they were less than five steps deep in the alley when Lamont realized they'd made a mistake.

"Shit!" he snatched Moo by the front of his jacket and ducked down beside one of the big brown Dumpsters, fighting hard not to fall flat on the ice.

Lamont clamped his cold hand over Moo's mouth, stifling his startled cry. He pushed his brother all the way down to the ground, dragging him into a small space between the Dumpster and the wall of the building. Lamont slipped his hand into his pocket and gripped his knife as they listened to the sounds of the lick going down directly ahead of them.

It was Postal and Dante. The two crackhead fiends who had chased them out into the streets and threatened to set him and Moo on fire. They were playing stickup kid with that dealer they called Kraft, the one who had been at Fat Daddy's earlier. Signaling Moo to hold still, Lamont peeked out from behind the Dumpster and watched the lick go down.

"Yo!" Kraft said, with a slight chuckle. "You gone wanna put that tool away, son. You fuckin with the wrong man's shit, baby. Xan a fool. You might not wanna slide up on none a this shit right here."

Postal swung his burner and Kraft folded over grunting in pain. He reached for a piece he had under his pants leg and the crazy dude checked him by pressing the Glock to his temple.

Kraft tried to stand upright and Lamont watched as Dante pulled out a knife and started jabbing him wherever he could get him. The blade was shiny and quick and this time Kraft went down to his knees, moaning and clutching his stomach.

"Bitch nigga!" Dante stood over him with bloody hands and breathing hard. He nodded toward his partner in crime. "Go 'head, Post. Get them fuckin tan goods. Them jewels too."

Lamont held his breath as they went in Kraft's pockets and under his jacket, popping the platinum off his neck. They didn't find no money, but they stripped Kraft of his shine. All the way down to the rings on his fingers.

"Yo where the fuckin money?" The fiends had gotten the product, but of course they wanted more. "Where the doe at, nigga?" Kraft took a boot to his gutted stomach and Lamont saw bright red blood seeping through his jacket.

Kraft rolled around on the ice, holding his stomach in agony. His moans were deep and miserable but his gangsta was still going strong.

"Suck my dick!" he gasped, pressing his hands deep into his bloody midsection. "You want my money?" he moaned. "Then you gone hafta suck my fuckin dick!"

The cats swung on him with their pistol and their fists, working Kraft over until he lay stretched out on his back, bleeding badly and nearly dead. Postal had just cocked his tool and aimed it down at Kraft's head when a woman screamed out of a window in a fifth floor apartment above them.

"Don't you do that!" she warned, her voice panicked and high-pitched. "I done called the fuckin cops! Get your asses outta here 'cause the cops is on they way!"

Lamont's eyes widened as Postal pointed the gat away from Kraft and raised it toward the woman in the window. She yelped and quickly ducked out of sight. Dude laughed, then aimed his hammer at the sky and popped one off, and behind him Lamont felt Moo's body shake at the retort.

Kraft moaned a little and his foot jerked twice in his death throes, and then it was all over. Police sirens sounded in the distance.

"Aw shit," Dante said, and then both fiends tore down the street heading north.

Lamont moved without the slightest hesitation.

"Stay here!" he whispered to Moo. He crouched down and was moving before the fiends were even out of sight. He crept from behind the Dumpster and immediately Moo tried to follow him.

The sirens were getting louder. Closer.

"Mont, no! Don't!"

Lamont waved him back and ran over to Kraft's lifeless body. He looked around twice, then reached down and stuck his cold hand down inside the front of Kraft's pants until he touched his dick. Snatching what he wanted, he stuck it up under his jacket. Then, with the sirens almost on them now, he yanked up Kraft's pants

leg and snatched his burner from its holster. Pocketing
the gun, Lamont looked up in time to see a curtain flut-
ter in that fifth floor window as the woman jumped back
again. Cursing, he jetted back to get his brother. *Damn,*
he said to himself as he ran and dragged Moo the best he
could. Times was bad and the game was real hard now.
*Niggas shootin in the air like they ain't scared to bring
God down!*

$ $ $

Lamont ran from the alley pulling Moo along behind him.
He was pretty sure Postal and Dante were walking and
trying to look normal instead of running like they stole
something. That would cast too much attention on them.
He was also pretty damn sure about where the two fiends
were heading and he cut through the projects trying to
get there before they did. Minutes later Lamont and
Monroe stood outside the abandoned building on Chester
Street that they had once called home. The city had come
out and reboarded up the windows, but that didn't stop
the hardcore squatters and the fiends. No sooner did the
city workers leave with their hammers than the walking
desperate were seen pulling out nails and making their
way back inside.

Lamont knew his plan was dangerous, but it was a
chance he had to take. There was a lot riding on this shit
and if he succeeded him and Moo would be set for a good
minute.

He looked down at his brother. The icy wind had tears

flowing down Monroe's cheeks, and he was wheezing real bad from running so fast.

"I want you to wait right over here, Moo. Okay? No matter what happens, don't you move. Just be quiet and wait for me, you got that?"

Monroe's eyes were big and scared and his frail body trembled, but he trusted his brother. He wiped his snotty nose with the back of his hand, then nodded obediently as Lamont showed him how to squat down between two parked cars and hide under the back fender of the bigger one.

With Moo safe, Lamont crept around to the side of the house and hoisted himself up. He pulled the window board back just like he'd done before, then swung his legs over the ledge and dropped down inside the dark, abandoned house. Huddled in a near corner, Lamont allowed his eyes to adjust to the darkness, then waited. He didn't have to wait long neither.

Dante came through the window first. His long skinny body fit through the boards easily, and his partner came through right behind him.

The moment the pair turned to walk up the rickety stairs, Lamont was on it.

Pop! Pop!

Then just to be sure, *Pop! Pop!* Again.

The hammer he'd taken off Kraft echoed in the empty house. The thud of falling bodies could be heard. Lamont's footsteps were light and quick. He had aimed for the upper back and both times he had hit his mark. He dropped the gun and went to work. It took him a few seconds to rifle through Dante's pockets as the dying man moaned and twisted around on the floor.

"Shit!" Lamont cursed when his hands came up empty. Dante gasped and pushed away from Lamont as he tried to rise up on his knees. Lamont kicked the fiend in the face, sending him down again. Still moaning, Dante used his arms to pull himself toward the stairs as he tried to escape. Lamont jumped into the air, coming down on Dante's lower back. That did it. Dante sprawled out on the floor, bright red blood gushing freely from his mouth.

Next, Lamont eyed Postal. Grabbing him by his bubble jacket, he rolled the skinny dead man over onto his back. Underneath his coat, in the large front pocket of his hoody, was the package Lamont had come for. He despised drugs for real, but he wiggled the package out and stuck it down inside the front of his pants anyway, making sure it was halfway in his underwear and wouldn't fall out.

"Pipe-head muhfuckas," he muttered as he looked into Postal's lifeless eyes. Lamont could still remember the fear that had rushed over him when they were awakened by Postal and his can of gasoline. The fiend had sloshed that shit everywhere, even on Moo's bomber coat, which is why his baby brother was walking around in just a thin jacket now. No matter what they did the smell of gasoline just wouldn't wear out of his coat, and breathing it in had just made Moo cough even harder and get sick to his stomach too.

Lamont looked at the body, then kicked it. Anybody who even threatened to fuck with his little brother deserved to die. He reached down and took Kraft's jewels out of Postal's jacket pocket, then snatched both gloves off the corpse's hands too. Dante wasn't moving no damn more either. He lay still and quiet near the foot of the stairs, dead as fuck.

Just the way Lamont wanted him.

CHAPTER 5

I'm a beast ya dig??
I'm a buh-buh-beast, my nig!
I'ma muhfuckin beast, ya dig?
On the beat,
In the muhfuckin streets, my nig!

WORD GOT AROUND fast in the hood, and Kraft's body was barely cold when news of the robbery and back-alley murder hit the corners. Dreko had caught the buzz about the two fiends who'd stuck Kraft up near the projects, and every street nigga in the area, from the lookouts to the paid niggas who worked to package their goods, was on watch. There was no doubt the killers would be smoked out like rats in a deep hole, and when they scurried out into daylight then the streets would hold court and retribution would be Xanbar's to dole out.

Dreko walked the streets alone. His boys Lil Jay and

Vandy were pulling look-out shifts on the corner they shared, and his moms had locked him outta the house again. One of their nosy-ass neighbors had been in her ear telling lies about him, and as usual Portia was always down to believe the worst when it came to her oldest son.

Dreko was heading down Livonia when he saw some static popping off, and walked up on a group of wanna be come ups from Riverdale Houses.

He paused and leaned against the rough stone of a nearby building and dug his hands deeper into his jacket pockets. Them Riverdale boys had snatched up that same lil cat he'd seen earlier in the day. The kid had pushed the small boy behind him and was talking mad shit for somebody who was outnumbered about five to one.

"Nigga, you ain't gone do shit to me," the little dude said holding his ground. Dreko saw a blade glinting in the kid's hand, and the look on his face was so cold and fearless that he wondered which one of them Riverdale boys was gonna get stuck first.

"Step up if you wanna. I'll slice you and all ya goddamn homies too."

The raw violence in his face was even more chilling than the cold.

A wicked smile curled Dreko's lips as he watched the boy get set to make good on his threat. The biggest cat in the bunch jumped on the kid, and the boy's hands moved so fast and with so much brutality that seconds later the big kid was writhing on the ground, screaming like a bitch and pressing both hands to his side.

One of his homies rushed the little dude and lifted him off his feet. Those hands moved like lightning again, and Dreko bit his bottom lip in glee as the kid locked his legs around the Riverdale dude's waist and flailed with his knife hand again and again. The boy fought deliberately and with so much fury that it was hard to tell who was the fuckin attacker and who was getting attacked. When another dude grabbed the kid's arm and tried to wrestle his knife away, the kid started wildin like a goddamn maniac. Not only did he cut them niggas wherever he could, he bit, punched, kicked, clawed, spit, and used his forehead like a bat.

By the time two grown men rolled up in a Range Rover and jumped out to break shit up, the kid had taken him an ass kicking but he'd put one on them boys too. Ere last one of them Riverdale niggas was either beat up or cut up. The kid had held his ground to the max and Dreko was impressed. The cat was obviously very violent, and above all, Dreko had mad respect for that kinda brutal street shit because violence was his middle name.

"Yeah!! Yeah!!" he yelled loudly, jumping up and down. The kid was a fuckin beast. The Riverdale boys had retreated, but the kid was still wildin. It was all them two guys in the Range Rover could do to stop him as he tried to break loose and run after them boys to get him some more. "Ay yo!" Dreko hollered.

The kid turned and put them brutal eyes on him and Dreko grinned.

"Yeah! That's how you keep a muhfucka in pocket, my nigga! Them fool bitches won't be runnin up on you no muthafuckin *more*."

The kid lifted his chin, realizing that the tall guy lounging against the building had witnessed everything and seen how he got down. He nodded, accepting the compliment while returning the respect. Dreko grinned and nodded back, his energy and his mood suddenly high. Yeah, there was no doubt about it. Dreko punched his fist into his open palm. Violence was his middle name.

$ $ $

All the edging and haircutting was done for the day and by nightfall all the community niggas was congregating up in Fat Daddy's joint. Like a lot of ghetto barbers, Fat Daddy was the kind of neighborhood icon who drew folks to him. Especially since he had some of Xanbar's boys selling blow and sticky from the back of his joint. He kept a cee-low game going and youngsters with rap skills could always get their spit on in his joint at night. Plus, Fat Daddy had connections. He was the go-to guy when you had something that needed off-loading, and if he thought he could sell it for two cents more than he paid for it, Fat Daddy would take it.

It was still freezing cold outside, but inside the lights in the shop were bright and there was a full house warming up the shop. As usual, the neighborhood shot callers had come together to discuss the day's operations, handle any ongoing problems that hadn't been solved during the day, and to plan for the next day's successful management of their growing drug empire.

Xanbar was a black-hearted killer at the top of the food chain in these parts, and his crew had flowed with him into the shop the way they always did. Tonight the talk had been about who mighta done Kraft and how they were gonna get some get back on that shit. Now that Xan had given the word to dead Kraft's killers on sight, niggas were sitting around listening to music, taking turns spittin battle rap on a cordless mic, and waiting for the deepest part of night so they could hit the streets and start their manhunt.

Fat Daddy was getting lifted. He'd worked hard all day and Egypt was upstairs asleep. He had washed and twisted her locks earlier, enjoying his daddy-daughter time as his baby girl sat on a stool between his legs and read out loud to him. It looked like every other day she was begging him to buy her two or three new books. Fat Daddy would act mad sometimes and tell her to slow down on her reading, but deep inside that shit made him swell up with pride. Him and his baby had something special going together and Fat Daddy cherished it. He cooked for her, snuggled with her, washed her clothes, and took care of her every need. You couldn't find a hustler no grimier than Fat Daddy out on the streets, but when he was at home with his daughter he tapped into the best parts of himself and loved her deeply and completely. And Egypt loved him right back the same exact way.

But late-night was a time for grown-man things, and right now Chop and Felton were out front catering to Xanbar and making sure him and his crew were comfortable. The music was blasting all the way into the back room, where Fat Daddy sat in a lounge chair playing in the pussy of a young chick he held on his lap.

He thumbed her clit, and plunged his fingers around inside of her damp cave as she squealed and puffed on some treez, inhaling the weed deeply. Fat Daddy's dick was uncomfortably hard in his pants and he wanted some of the tight pussy that was bouncing all over his lap. He withdrew his fingers and held them under his nose, smelling her funk and getting high on that shit. He wasn't about to put his face in her box but he was hooked on the taste of pussy so he licked the juices from his fingers and pushed his dick up toward her.

"Butch," his uncle Chop called out, interrupting Fat Daddy's flow. Chop was about seventy but he kept himself trim and looked less than fifty. "That boy around here again. One of them kids Felton say belong to Marjay."

Fat Daddy sat up. "Let 'em in." He smacked the girl on her ass and pushed her off his lap, pausing to smell his fingers one last time. Her pussy was strong-odored and he had to fix his dick in his pants before he could join the guys out front in the shop. He stepped into the main room just as the bigger kid was coming through the door.

The boy's eyes were cold and his face set in a hard mask. One of the neighborhood lookouts, Dreko, had the floor. He was practicing for new jack night down at Baller's

Paradise and the elder G's were nodding their heads and digging his flow game.

The kid stepped inside and ignored Dreko, violating his a cappella spit game as he stared dead ahead and walked straight up on Xanbar, who was sitting in Felton's chair.

Plap!

Fat Daddy watched as Lamont slapped a package wrapped in brown paper down on the arm of the chair, shutting everybody up, including Dreko.

Silence fell over the room and the rising aura of danger filled the air.

The boy spoke deliberately. "This you, man. Kraft's last stash."

He waited a few seconds then said, "I took it off them fiends who stuck him up. Ya nigga ain't even have no protection on him," he lied. "No gat, not even a fuckin blade." The kid shrugged. "That nigga was a mark. He got caught out there. Plain and simple."

He went in his pocket and came out with an expensive Jacob watch and two platinum chains and three rings.

"I got these back for you too."

Xanbar glanced at the jewels, then frowned.

"Where them fiend muhfuckas at?"

"Popped. Slumped. I did 'em both."

Slowly, Xanbar looked down at the package, then back up again. He picked it up and tossed it around in his hand, feeling the weight. Satisfied, he stared at the kid and said coldly, "Now where's my fuckin money?"

The kid wasn't even pressed. He stared right back. His

voice was quiet and just as cold. "*What* fuckin money?"

Xanbar grilled the boy for long moments, then suddenly a smile cracked his face and he laughed loudly. This
kid had some nuts. Not only had he deaded them fiends, he
coulda took Kraft's stash and tried to hustle it for himself,
or he coulda turned that shit in for some reward money
from the 73rd precinct. Or worse, the lil muhfucka coulda
took it across town and dished it off to Chaos, that come
up nigga who was running shit in Ocean Hill. Either way,
the boy had had options, and he'd chosen the right one.
Damn right "what money." Xanbar believed in eating. The
kid had earned that little bit of bank.

Getting up from the chair, he clapped Lamont on the
back, shaking his head.

"This lil nigga right here is *hood*, goddamn it!" Still
laughing, he grabbed his coat from a hook and pulled his
skully low on his head, then motioned to his entourage
who immediately got up to follow him.

"Yo," he said grinning at his boys. "I likes this lil muhfucka. He what? Ten? Eleven? And already he a fuckin
gangsta *and* a business man. Come'ere, Hood. I tell you
what. You all about business and you got a heart. I'ma put
you to work. You ain't fuckin with that regular corner action, though. Come see me tonight at Baller's Paradise,
aiight? Kraft left behind some territory that needs to be
covered, man, and you just the kinda lil nigga who can
handle that shit."

$ $ $

Minutes later, Fat Daddy had taken Lamont into the back room and the boy was standing in front of him with cold determination in his eyes.

"Here you go," he held out a C-note, offering it to Fat Daddy. "This oughtta cover that sandwich and them haircuts you gave us."

Fat Daddy eyed the money the kid had stolen off Kraft. This lil nigga acted like he was paying taxes or some shit. He waved the kid off.

"Nah. Keep your money. What I gave you was a gift."

"I don't need nobody to give me shit."

Fat Daddy turned and stared. This lil muhfucka was serious. He snatched the hundred dollar bill with his pussy-sticky fingers and pocketed it. "Yeah, okay. This might just be about enough then."

The boy pressed on. "You got anything else around here that's up for sale?"

Fat Daddy shrugged and raised his eyebrow. "Depends on what you lookin for." He nodded toward the room where his fenced goods were stored. "A whole lotta shit out there got some value to it. For the right price you could pretty much have whatever the fuck you want."

"Well, how about the whole room," the boy said with a straight face. "I'll take the room and that little green couch you got back there. Let me and my brother use the bathroom too, and I'll pay you extra."

Fat Daddy looked up in the ceiling like he was calculating and totaling shit up in his head. He didn't even like little street kids and he sure didn't want none around here

fuckin up his action. But the fact that this one was standing before him negotiating like a grown man made him
eligible to be treated like one.

"I could prob'bly let that couch go for about twenty-
five a week. It ain't all that clean but it's somewhere to
crash. Maybe twenty if you wanna sweep up the shop
every night. I can't go no lower than that though."

The kid thought for a minute. "Cool. I'll sweep up.
Throw the kitchen in on the deal too. Just the microwave.
My little brother gotta have some hot food."

It had been a long time since Fat Daddy had seen a
young cat as calculating as this raggedy little kid, and although he didn't show it, he was impressed.

"That's righteous," he said nodding, then looked down
surprised to see that the kid was holding out his hand.

Fat Daddy took the small fingers and ground them
tightly in his fist as he shook the boy's hand. "All right
then. We got a deal and you got yourself someplace to
rest." He nodded. "I call that good sense."

The kid took his knuckle grinding like a man. His
bones rubbed together and he didn't even flinch. When
Fat Daddy finally let go of him the boy looked dead in his
eyes and nodded right back. "I call it good business."

CHAPTER 6

I'ma twist my weed, I'ma get my G's
I'ma G, I can see why niggaz don't want me to win!
Never kneel, I don't care how whoever feels,
I'm forever real and I came here to get mine in!

LATER THAT NIGHT, with Moo sleeping on the sagging couch in Fat Daddy's back room, Lamont sat in a booth at Baller's Paradise surrounded by countless members of Xanbar's click. The owner of the club had a deal going with some Haitians who had some connections in the state liquor authority, and his liquor license was just as phony as his name.

Lamont sat up there with the big willies, his hand wrapped around a glass of St. Ides that Xanbar had put down in front of him. Somebody passed him a dutch and he puffed and coughed so hard tears flooded his eyes. Niggas laughed, but he didn't give up. He hit the blunt with small puffs until his chest could stand it, then he pulled on that shit like he'd been born with a tree in his mouth.

"Check this out young Hood," Xanbar said, leaning toward him with his elbows on the table. Xanbar was the kind of nigga who attracted loyalty, and something in his gut told him that Lamont was gonna be loyal to him for a good long time. "I'm giving you a crew, ya heard? Now normally when I first put cats on they gotta start as lookouts. Niggas gotta prove themselves to me. Show they G and ere'thang all the way through. And tonight you done just that."

The big kid Dreko slammed his glass down on the table and stood up.

"Yo Xan! I thought you said I was gone be moving up! This nigga just came on, man! What about me?"

Xanbar stared at the young cat. He was mental, and unlike young Hood whose senses were keen and in search of an opportunity, this cat could think no further than most kids on the streets.

"Nigga sit ya ass down. You can't even get your dick sucked good without making noise and getting noticed. That shit coulda got real ugly with that white bitch you almost killed up in here. You gotta learn how to hold ya head, homey. That's truth. But dig this. Even though you fucked up a lil bit, Xan still got love for you. So no more lookout duty. You officially a trap boy now. I'm putting you down on Hood's team. Get you exposed to some new territory. Hood gone be my number one over on Chester Street now, and you gone be my number two."

Xanbar pretended not to see the dark look that crossed Dreko's face as he turned his attention back to Lamont.

"Hear that shit? You 'bout to get some real special treatment around here and that shit is all good, but it can turn out to be a burden on you too. Niggas who been out here bucking for their own territory gonna resent your little ass coming in and hopping over they heads like that, but that's exactly why I want you. You young and you hungry and your eyes is wide open. You looking for opportunities and you got a heart. Now you mighta slumped you two fiend niggas tonight, but tomorrow you gotta get out there and prove ya gangsta all over again. And you gone get it tested every single day too. Your name is Hood now, nigga, and you gotta be ruthless to live up to that shit. If any of them cats out there wanna know how you got your job, tell 'em to come see your boss. Anybody fuck with you, just let me know."

"Any of them dudes fuck with me—" young Hood's hand shot out as he refused the dutch Dreko was passing to him. He had a junkie mother and one tree to his lips had been more than enough to last him a lifetime. "I ain't runnin and telling no fuckin body. I'm just gone crack they ass. They'll learn."

Xan nodded. That's exactly what he'd expected to hear. This lil cat was gonna work out just fine. He'd shake shit up amongst Xan's older crew for a minute but the noise wouldn't last long. Them niggas out there was getting lazy on they trap anyway. They needed something to wake they asses up and keep 'em scrambling for them clients.

Wasn't nobody on no crack diet around here, so them boys need to push harder for that doe.

Yep, Xanbar thought, snatching his dutchie outta Dreko's hand and taking a pull. There was a time when old heads ruled the streets and all the youngsters would be on the block shook and salivating as they looked up to these older men and dreamed of becoming kingpins, pimps, and street hustlers. But not no more. Shit had changed drastically in the game, and today's drug dealers, ballers, and come ups were eleven-, twelve-, and thirteen-year-old kids with cold hearts, street cunning, and absolutely no compassion.

He could use more young cats like Hood on his team. Too tender in age to get hit with any real heat from the establishment, but unparented in the world, with no family to keep 'em in check and absolutely no fear. The kind of boys whose cold hearts were invincible and who would count it a miracle if they survived past their twenty-first birthdays. Plus, these cats were economical assets too. With no kids of their own, and too young to drive a whip or rent an apartment, he could pay them far less on the dollar than he had to tear off to some grown nigga who was destined to either get knocked and locked, or leaded and deaded.

Rising from the booth Xan slipped a curvaceous hottie named Destiny a fifty-dollar bill and told her to take young Hood in a back room and turn him out real good. The boy might could turn down a tree, but he damn sure wasn't turning down no pussy.

Xan was pleased with himself for giving Hood his own territory, and saw the move as a slick business decision that would pay out lovely in the future. But Dreko? Xan chuckled and shook his head. Hotheads like him came a dime a dozen and he could find ten of them to fuck up his organization any day. But this crafty lil nigga Hood was just what he needed.

$ $ $

Hood's dick had never been so wet in his life.

It stood straight up as she licked it, jerking like it was plugged into a socket and had sparks of electricity running from its swollen head down to his balls.

"Feel good?" Destiny giggled as she teased him, her tongue gliding along his eleven-year-old shaft with expert precision.

A low groan was all Hood could manage as he lay on his back, pumping his dick up at her and fighting hard not to squirt. He grabbed her head and fucked up at her, not caring if he stuck his dick in her mouth, up her nose, or in her goddamn eye socket. Just as long as he hit something warm and wet.

"Slow down," she whispered, slapping his hand away. She cupped his balls, then opened her mouth wide and slid his whole dick inside, gripping him tight with her lips until his penis pushed against her throat. She slurped up and down, bathing his member in the warm springs of her mouth as she applied a rhythm to her sucking that was out of this world.

Hood could have cried out loud it felt so good. It was his first time getting his dick sucked and the first time he had been up close on a naked female too. He couldn't stop himself. His hands were everywhere. Groping her big round titties, digging into her wet slit, palming her soft, beautiful black ass.

He was almost crazy with it from the moment she got undressed. His young dick leaked pre-cum that coated its head and dripped onto his thigh. He wanted to sample every part of her at once, and she had to slow him down as his lips pulled on her nipples and his teeth bit into the softness of her stomach.

"We got a whole hour," she laughed, trying to control him. She'd had young niggas full of cum before, but not like him. This cat was almost out of his mind for the pussy, and Xanbar was gonna have to pay her another fifty behind all the hickeys and welts and shit he was leaving on her body.

"Here," she grabbed his hand and helped him cup her swollen breast as she took him to school. "Touch it like this. Not so hard. Squeeze it gently, now stroke my nipples."

Hood rubbed her thick nipples until she moaned, then opened his lips as she pulled his head to her breast.

"Suck them softly," she breathed from her knees above him. "Yeah, now add a little tongue to it. Flick them back and forth with the tip of your tongue."

Sweat ran down Hood's face but he was a fast learner. Destiny guided his head with her hands as her bomb titties swelled under his touch and her pussy began to cream.

"Okay," she panted. "Take care of down here now."

She massaged her thick clit, then slipped a finger inside of her hotness, gripping down on it as she swirled her juices. She placed Hood's hand on top of hers, allowing him to understand the rhythm. Breathing hard, he pushed down gently on her hand as she fucked herself, his motion becoming even more stimulating than her own. Destiny didn't protest when he pulled her hand out and replaced her finger with his own. His lips found her nipples again as she fucked up into his hand, her pussy juices spilling out and running onto the bed as his middle finger slid up into her too, filling her up.

There was no stopping him as he grabbed her by the ass and pulled her against him. Destiny yelped as he shoved his hard dick inside of her as deep as it would go. It scraped her walls and banged against the back of her pussy with mad force, and then there was no more student and no more teacher. Hood was through with his lessons and he fucked her deep and fast, like a jack-hammer. Rolling her onto her back, he spread her legs wide, pushing her knees back against her chest. He had a direct aim as he pounded his young pipe into her softness, all kinds of crazy nonsense noises escaping his lips as he got his first taste of pussy and tried to kill it all in one session.

Destiny rode with that shit, his dick slamming one of the best she'd ever had. Not many niggas could make her cum with just their dicks, but this one was special and she found her body convulsing twice, back to back, a record for her.

Destiny was still naked and on her back when Hood dressed and left the room. He'd only been in the game for two minutes and already he was loving this shit. The music was still going strong and he was thirsty. He walked toward Xanbar's booth feeling more like a grown-ass man than an eleven-year-old kid who had just conquered his first piece of ass.

Xanbar looked up and saw him coming, and waved him over. But before he could get there a loud disturbance near the front door caught his attention. Hood strained to see through the sea of bodies, trying to figure out what was going on, and when his eyes finally focused on the cause of the commotion, he bolted toward the door, pushing through the crowd.

He had just reached the door when he was grabbed from behind. All the good feelings he'd just experienced in that back room disappeared as pain struck him in the heart. Struggling against the muscular arms that held him back, Hood watched as the bouncer carried his mother across the sidewalk and out to the curb, then pushed her into a car waiting outside.

"Be easy," Xanbar cautioned, whispering in his ear as Marjay tried to fight her way back inside the club.

"I said let me the fuck in! I just wanna make some money in the back," she screamed and pleaded, arms outstretched. "How the fuck I'm supposed to get my shit if y'all won't let me make no motherfuckin money?!?"

Hood had seen his mother on the streets and out of control before, but never like this. It had been bad enough when she was mute and wouldn't speak, but hearing her talk like a tramp was even worse. Marjay's coat was open and she flailed her legs, pushing her skirt up to her waist and showing her torn black panties. She was mental for real. She'd started collecting buttons around the same time she picked up the pipe, and the millions of buttons pinned to her coat rattled in the night as she screamed and cursed, fighting the bouncer and demanding to be let back inside the club.

"You out, Marjay," the bouncer said gently as he folded her up and placed her inside of a car driven by the guy she'd come with. The bouncer was an older cat who had grown up in Brownsville. He had known Marjay when she was looking fine and doing good for herself, and had secretly had a big hard-on for her during those good years.

"Please don't bring your ass back here, baby," he told her gently, "'cause I don't wanna hurt you. There ain't no more work for you here no more. Not tonight, not ever."

A black feeling hit Hood as he visualized his mother grinding in one of those same rooms he had just come out of. Looking at her now it was hard to detect a trace of the woman she used to be back when his father was alive and they lived up in Mount Vernon. In a way, the dirty cops who killed his father had deaded his mother's life as well, and they had almost succeeded in taking him and Moo down too.

"C'mon," Xanbar said, pulling him back inside. "You got an audience, man. Don't play into this shit. Fuck around and ya street career will be over before it even gets started."

Hood strained angrily against the veteran hustler, the frigid night air blowing through the door doing nothing to calm the ball of heat burning in his heart.

"Relax, nigga!" Xan whispered in his ear. "You remember what I told you, right? There's more than one way to get ya gangsta tested out here, young Hood. That ho might be your mother, but don't you never let these niggas know you got a sweet spot. Never. Now turn your back on that junkie bitch and slide back in that booth like a man so we can finish handling this business."

CHAPTER 7

We the spokesmen! For the niggas who popped toast in!
For mothers who lost sons
And got stuck with their hearts broken!

"DON'T TOUCH NOTHING in here that don't belong to you," Portia snapped as she frowned at her son, Andreko. She watched him like a hawk as he moved around the small, tidy bedroom he used to share with his eight-year-old brother, wondering how in the hell she had managed to give birth to such a monstrosity and why she couldn't find the courage or the strength to destroy it.

Dreko and her younger son, Drew, had different fathers, which was one reason Portia felt they were so different in their personalities. Drew's father had been a star college athlete who collapsed and died on the basketball court of a sudden heart attack when Drew was three. He'd been two days away from signing a pro contract, but they'd never married so either way Portia was out of luck in getting any financial benefits for herself or her son. She was struggling to raise her two boys in one of the most dangerous ghettos in the nation. For the past five years she'd held down a stressful nine-to-five as a bank teller as she tried to save enough money to move them down to Alabama where the last of her family members lived.

Dreko's father was the exact opposite of Drew's. Boss Dawson was a fine-ass street hustler who had intimidated her into giving up the pussy when she was fifteen. His jealous temper and controlling rages had terrified her on a daily basis and had directly contributed to the fatal asthma attack her father suffered when he jumped in to protect her during one of Boss's countless beating tirades.

Boss had been locked up in Coxsackie for the last ten years on an unrelated murder charge, and it wouldn't surprise Portia if one day his son followed right along in his criminal footsteps. That was, unless somebody put Dreko's ass in the ground first for fuckin with their child, which was a real possibility considering all the dirty shit he did out on those streets. Especially to little kids.

Portia stared into the face of her firstborn son, seeing his father's handsome chisled features and her own brown eyes and smooth skin. He was more good-looking than he had a right to be, considering the fact that he was little more than a twisted demon on the inside. Lately, he'd been staying away from the apartment for days at a time, which was just fine by her. On the nights he did come straggling home drunk or high, she would use her dresser to barricade her bedroom door, then put Drew in the bed with her, against the wall, and sleep fitfully with her fingers curled around the handle of the butcher knife she kept hidden beneath her pillow.

"Where's baby boy?" Dreko asked, digging through the small closet they shared. He pulled out a heavy sweater and sniffed the armpits.

Portia shrugged. "Don't worry about where Drew is. He's straight. Just get whatever you came for and go back wherever it is you been."

Dreko turned and stared at his mother. She was pretty and petite, a hard working black woman who had suffered quite a few knocks in life. Something dangerous glinted in Dreko's eyes, and even though he was only twelve Portia shrank back against the wall under his eerie glare.

"Why you always trippin on me like that, Ma?" he asked quietly. There was a hint of innocence and pain in his voice, and for a second Dreko sounded almost like the lovable little man she used to adore before his true colors started showing. "You know me and Drew is tight. He's my little brother, damn. You crazy with your shit."

"Humph," Portia chuckled bitterly. "I ain't the one crazy, mister nasty. You was sitting right there when Miss Newman knocked on the door and told me what you be doing to all them little boys on the back staircase. That shit is plain nasty, Dreko. How could you do something so low to them kids when you got a little brother yourself?"

"I already fuckin told you"— Dreko exploded—"I ain't touched none of them little faggots! They just lying 'cause their moms is crackheads who wanna get vials off me for free all the time! Ask Drew did I ever do anything to him, Ma! I love my little brother! You gone take some heroin-head's word over your own fuckin son?"

"But where could you have picked up that kind of nasty shit, Andreko?" Portia asked, ignoring his denial as her heart began to soften. The boy was just like his father: a liar and a thief. He was mean and spiteful and had a jealous, evil streak a mile long. No matter how long she stayed in church praying over him, the child lacked a conscience and could do anything to anybody without feeling a moment's regret behind it. He had a demon living in his heart, that was for sure. But . . . he was still her child. Her first born son, and despite his perversions she couldn't just toss him out of her heart. Not all the way out.

"Tell me, baby. Was it in that group home they had you in? Did some of them big boys do something bad to you and get your mind all twisted around the way it is?"

"Miss Newman is lying, Ma. How many times I gotta tell you that old bitch is lying?!?"

"See there!" Portia bristled, furious with him all over again. "I can't believe shit you say! The truth just ain't in you! Miss Newman didn't tell me about something she heard. She actually *saw* you! She caught you with your dick in that boy's mouth, Andreko! She said the child was just a crying and a shaking trying to satisfy you. Ain't no telling how you done ruined that boy's life. He's gone be all fucked up in the head behind what you did to him! So hell no, you can't get nowhere near my baby. You just like your twisted up daddy and I'm waiting for the day when you get the fuck outta my house for good!"

Dreko stood near the closet staring at his mother as she breathed deeply. Her face was twisted in a scowl, like he was something foul, and her brown eyes flashed in disgust.

He could hurt this bitch. Really do some damage to her little ass up in here. For a brief second he actually saw his hand gripping her neck. Squeezing the fuck outta that shit, making her eat back all them grimy words she'd been tossing at him. He felt like banging her grill up against something hard. The walls, the floor, the windowsill, the sharp edge of a counter. Anything. Bang her up until she bled like a stomped rat.

He could do it too. Yeah, he could.

Portia read her son's thoughts and moved fast. Seconds later she had ran her ass into her bedroom and slammed the door, locking it behind her as his cruel, mocking laughter filled her ears.

The boy was crazy. Dangerous. Twisted right outta his nasty skull. Andreko was a predator and a killer. Damn right he was. Portia was his momma, and no matter what he did or how bad he was, part of her would always love him. So if she could admit to this horrible twisted side of him, then the rest of the world had better watch out. Because if Mama said it, then it was damn sure the truth.

CHAPTER 8

Do you think they hate me, 'cause they ain't me?
Or they just B-A-D D-O-P-E?

HOOD LOVED HIS new job and worked a maximum grind for Xanbar's organization on the streets of Brooklyn. He put his total efforts and concentration into learning how to manage his street workers and their cash-clientele, and above all into gaining Xanbar's trust and confidence.

"You runnin shit from the corner of Livonia and Rockaway over to Newport, then up to Bristol and back," Xanbar ordered. It was Hood's twelfth birthday and Xan had called a special meeting at Baller's Paradise to mark off territory and introduce Hood to the rest of his team.

"I'ma put you out there with five soldiers for now, dig?" He motioned over his left shoulder, and Dreko stepped up. "This ya number two man right here. Your problem solver. Work ya people correct and he'll become your right hand. Anybody act up, you and Dreko handle that shit together."

Xan smirked at Dreko. The boy was still swole behind wearing that number two tag, but he'd get over it. "Both of y'all some skull splitters, for sure," he told Dreko. "But you one of them young niggas who can't be taught shit. Just 'cause you 7:30 crazy don't mean you fit to be no capo in my organization, ya know. You ain't shown the proper respect and obedience yet, youngster. Around here you gotta be able to take orders before I can think about letting you give some."

The next cat up was Lil Jay. At eighteen he wasn't no kid compared to the rest of them, and that could be a potential problem. In the back of his mind Hood questioned why the fuck Xanbar was putting him in charge of a grown ass man.

"Lil Jay is gone be your driver," Xan said, squashing Hood's doubts. "The Brownsville police are way up on this shit and will impound a g-ride in a minute. I don't want y'all young boys even touching the keys to none of my whips. You gotta get somewhere like your re-up spot or back here to fuck with me? Lil Jay is ya pony. Ride that nigga. He's all yours."

Lil Jay came over and dapped Hood out, grinning. "I'm ya ride or die, my nig," he said, breaking the ice and letting Hood know that despite their age difference he respected the g-code and would happily maintain his lane. "We gone do this shit."

A dude they called Sackie was introduced next. He

looked about fifteen. He was tall and built and had some ice-cold blue eyes. Hood just stared as Xanbar introduced him.

"Don't let the blond hair fool ya. Sackie a gangsta down to the bone. One day we gone be able to dress this cat up in a suit and tie and send him into places the rest of us just can't go. White boys got that kinda privilege in this world. And this one's got a heart. Plus he got a head for numbers and that's gonna work for us too."

Xan introduced Bones and Riff next, and with the addition of these two young lookouts Hood's five-man team was set.

"Remember," Xanbar pulled him aside and warned him again. "Don't let none of these muhfuckas think they can run you. If they even try to step outta line you got my permission to fuck 'em up and put 'em back in pocket."

Hood shrugged. "Oh yeah, I'm for that. Matter of fact I hope one of them niggas do go bananas and try to fuck with me."

"That right?"

"Yep. I'll cut his ass so deep the cat standing next to him gonna need some stitches."

Xan laughed. "Yeah, lil nigga. You got the right attitude. Hit 'em hard in a brutal fashion, my man. They'll get the message. Who you think gone try to yank your dick first?"

Hood grinned. "Man, you already know."

"Yeah I do. It's Dreko. That cat is ambitious but he psycho. The kinda wild-head nigga you gotta keep ya eye on. He the type a' goon you send to guard a schoolhouse and he end up slaughtering all the fuckin little kids. Just crazy like that without putting no thought behind the shit he do."

Hood shrugged, then shook his head in disagreement. "Nah, Dreko gone be easy. He only thinks like a predator when he know he fuckin with some prey. Dreko is cool. I'm already feeling him. It's Riff who I gotta fuck with. He ain't smart, he just wanna come up real fast."

"What?" Xan chuckled. "You smell that kinda drive on a bitch like Riff?" He glanced at the tall, light-skinned kid, then squirted spit through his teeth and pushed his hands into his pockets. "I can't see it, but cool. Fuck that nigga too. Do what you gotta do, lil man. Just watch your back."

It didn't take Riff long to step outta line and when he did, Hood was ready.

Less than a month after assuming command of his territory, Hood watched the streets from the window of an abandoned apartment across from Jerri's Liquor Shop. Earlier in the day he'd peeped Riff talking on the low to a cat from Ocean Hill who rolled heavy with that rival nigga Chaos. The two had gotten into a dark blue sports car and headed up toward Pitken Avenue. After some long thought, Hood found a spot where he had a good vantage point and made his way into an abandoned building. He sat in the busted-out window for over two hours until he saw the little sports car come rolling back down the avenue again.

Hood scrambled downstairs and waited as Riff stepped outta the enemy's car looking warm and happy, then he went straight to that ass right up on the avenue. Right where every nigga in town could see. He banged Riff in the forehead with the butt of his Sig, then beat him down just like he was a pimp cracking a ho for coming up short on her bank.

"That's right, boss," Dreko yelled out loud as Hood gun-cracked Riff all over his head. Riff had people in the game and his family name rang bells on the streets, but just like Hood, Dreko had no fear of their get back. His gat was comfortable in his hand as he stared down a couple of Riff's boys with menace and murder in his eyes.

"Gone and put that bitch-ass nigga in check, Hood. We can take this shit to war with an army of two right here, right now. Any one of these boys feel like battling and I'll grab him and gun-beat his ass down too."

After that bloody incident Hood's leadership and Dreko's loyalty was never challenged again. Not up close, anyway. Hood was a hard-body soldier and ran his small crew with such authority that even grown-ass dealers had to give it up to him because the nigga was street buff to his core. He was principled, though, despite the harshness of his young life. He forbid his crew to conduct transactions if there was a kid in sight, and demanded they respect the elderly at all times. It was nothing to see him strolling down the block pushing a shopping cart full of food for somebody's moms in the projects, and when the work was done and it was time to play, the child in him came out and he flexed his thumbs and reigned surpreme on every action-packed video game on the market.

But when it came to moving his product and collecting his doe, Hood didn't give up shit. Niggas on his block couldn't get no credit, no sympathy, no nothing. And as they found out from his dealings with Riff, who ended up in a brief coma for riding with the enemy, they couldn't even get no second chances.

But while Riff was a minor annoyance, much more than Hood's coldhearted reputation had been tested on that day. His soft spot had got mashed up too, and in the worst way possible for a gangsta. Hood had been so furious behind Riff bringing one of Chaos's boys on the block that he probably would have ended it all and beaten Riff to death right there on the street if somebody hadn't called out his name and frozen his hand.

"Monty! Stop that fighting, Monty! You got any money, Monty?"

Hood was on one knee, his fists slick with Riff's blood, his sleeves soaked red up to his elbows. Niggas was standing with their backs up against the building giving him room to put in work, and when the bony, light-skinned lady wearing a million fuckin buttons on her jacket ran across the street begging for money, Hood had stood up breathing hard, shook.

"Hey baby you got something for me, huh?"

Whenever he bumped into his moms it was painful, and this was the third time their paths had intersected in the last few weeks. One night he had run into her as she stumbled high out of a club, and it had hurt his heart when he'd had to remind her that he was her son. The next two times he'd seen her in the daytime and bought her some Chinese food, then taken her over to Fat Daddy's place. Fat Daddy had let her come in and take a shower and tried to talk to her about rehab a little bit, but Marjay couldn't sit still for more than a minute. Not even long enough to spend any time with Moo, who just sat there with his mouth open, holding tight to her hand and staring at her like she was God or somebody.

But not even the sight of her baby boy was enough to cure the crack demon that was crawling around raising hell inside Marjay. In what seemed like seconds Moo was sitting on the lumpy green couch alone and crying, and Marjay was gone again. Needing a high more than she needed her children, she ran clanging out the shop's door and back onto the city streets.

Remembering this, Hood stared at his mother and tried not to hate her for allowing drugs to reduce her to the wasted, devastated sight standing before him.

"C'mon on now," she said, hopping over Riff's bloody body as she tried to get closer to him. "I'm needy right now, baby. Tell me what you got in your pocket that's good?"

He appeared cold on the outside, but deep inside Hood was crushed. His mother had that classic crackhead-on-a-mission look. Her eyes darted around and she licked her lips, then she grabbed hold of his arm like he was her trick nigga instead of her young son.

But he held his ground. He didn't have to glance around to know he was being observed. Niggas wanted to see how he was gone handle this part of the job. Riff was still moaning on the ground with his forehead and his grill busted up. Hood's crackhead moms had on a mangy-looking rabbit jacket, a short black skirt, and some run-over space boots. She curled up her tongue, then pressed her shriveled breast against his arm and winked at him, flirting for that yay.

Hood hardened his heart, and shook her loose.

"Moo up the street," he answered her coldly. "At Fat Daddy's place. Take ya ass up there and check on your baby."

Marjay smiled and reached for him again.

"Why don't you check on *me*, huh?" she laughed like a silly little girl and switched her bony ass around, her buttons making crazy noises as she lunged for his arm again. "You wanna check on me for a minute? Huh? You wanna check on some of me?"

"Ma, stop," he muttered under his breath. She was so dirty he could smell her stank body through her clothes. Just looking into her deranged eyes was enough to make him wanna break down and question his own sanity for selling the drugs that had taken hold of his mother's life and turned her into one of the walking dead. But how else was he gonna feed Moo?

"Gone back to Gramma's house and wait there with Aunt Pat. I'll come over there later and check you out."

"Oooh! What you gonna bring me?" she squealed hopping up and down, her hundreds of buttons jingling as her crazy eyes grew hopeful. "You gone bring me something good?"

Hood bristled as some stupid nigga snickered behind him. Then Dreko's voice boomed as he went ballistic on the whole row of cats who were lined up listening and watching intently.

"Yo! What the fuck y'all muhfuckas gawkin at? Man, all y'all fake niggas turn around and face the fuckin wall! Y'all heard me! Turn around and put ya grill to the muhfuckin wall!"

Hood grabbed his mother's shoulders. Dirty rabbit hair stuck to his hands as his boys faced the wall like Dreko had ordered, giving him his space. He steered Marjay gently in the other direction, toward the projects. "Gone back down the block, Ma. I'll get with you later."

CHAPTER 9

I'm doin grown man thangs . . .
I'm trying to stay outta trouble,
I'm doin grown man thangs . . .
But it's a day-to-day struggle . . .

RATS SQUEAKED AND gnawed the walls in the back room
that Hood and Moo shared in Fat Daddy's shop, but neither noticed or cared, because for the first time ever they
were a part of a real family. Dreko, Sackie, and Lil Jay
were the siblings Hood and Moo never had, and whether
he liked it or not, Fat Daddy was looked up to in a fatherly
way.

But a father to those boys Fat Daddy was not. He pur-
posely steeled his heart away from all that paternal shit
because caring for a couple of street kids could be more
than dangerous. He gave a damn about them being "just
kids" too. Them lil fuckers paid rent and bought their own

food, and Fat Daddy made it a habit to show them his cold side as often as possible. Just to let them know he wasn't fuckin with them on that level. He wasn't no parent to them and he was no role model either, and he wasn't trying to be. But he did make Hood and Moo go back to school, though. Not because he gave a fuck about educating them or expanding their young minds, but because he knew it would keep the heat off his neck that way.

"You ain't gone have nobody from the city coming up in here fuckin with me, baby. Uh-uh. No way. Both of y'all gotta at least show up at the school house door. What you do when you get up in that mug is up to you. But when Egypt leaves outta here in the mornings, both of y'all gone be stepping out right along with her."

Hood was all for that. He jumped at the chance to be around chocolate Egypt as much as possible. There was a bond between them, something secret and special, and he would have followed her anywhere, even without Fat Daddy telling him to. They'd gone from shy smiles, furtive looks, and holding hands, to sharing their first tongue-kiss weeks earlier. And when Hood held her close in the tiny kitchen behind the shop and told her that she was his only girl, he meant that shit from his heart.

So while Moo started classes in kindergarten, Hood went to junior high school every day and came back home and chilled with Egypt and ruled his sector every afternoon. He hung out at Baller's Paradise learning from Xan and his crew every night, so at first all he did was spit mental lyrics all day to keep from dozing off in class. He was too exhausted to concentrate on the lessons they gave him until Egypt busted hard on him about not doing his homework.

"What's up with that, Lamont?" she asked him with her round eyes flashing and her long earrings jiggling. They had just gotten their report cards and even though Hood was still considered a new student, his report card was full of F's solely from nonparticipation. "You ain't ashamed of all them damn F's on your report card? What? You plan on hustling drugs all your life?"

"Hell yeah. Hustling and spittin my song until me and Reem cut us an album. Why not?"

"'Cause that's some stupid shit, that's why. Ain't no future in drug dealing, Lamont. Unless you count Rikers or getting locked up someplace upstate." They walked along the trashed streets passing gutted-out buildings, salvage yards, and a couple of stray, mangy dogs. "You always talking about how you might lose the words out your head. Don't that scare you enough to make you have dreams about other stuff? Stuff besides what you got right here. You know, places you wanna see outside of dirty-ass Brooklyn?"

Hood shrugged as he walked beside her. He was oblivious to the grime and didn't even notice it. All he could see was beauty. Egypt's beauty, and the beauty of what he felt for her deep in his soul. She was tall and pretty and kept herself looking real neat and fresh at all times. She liked nice shit, and since her father was the neighborhood 'ence, she had plenty of it. They passed a corner game of cee-low and two winos sleeping in a stripped down car balanced on four milk crates. Egypt grabbed one of Moo's hands while Hood grabbed the other. They walked with him between them and Moo grinned up at them as they swung his arms back and forth.

Hood spoke again, hoping he was saying something Egypt would want to hear. "I'ma prolly check out Harlem one day. I got a cousin up there I wouldn't mind getting with."

"Harlem?" Egypt smirked over Moo's head. "That's as far as you wanna go?" She peered at him over her glasses and gave him a crazy look like he needed to reconsider his response. His little dun duns on the corner worked hard to keep his head on swole, but Lamont knew Egypt was always gonna give it to him straight and keep it real.

"Man, Harlem is far. You gotta take the number 3 train to the number 4. That'll take you over an hour."

Egypt cut her eyes at him.

Hood felt a rock growing in his pants. He ignored the look of disapproval on her face and eyeballed her long legs and high, bouncy ass.

"Well that's some stupid-sounding shit too, Lamont. What about Las Vegas? Or California? Or even Africa or the Bahamas? Brooklyn ain't everything, I want you to know. You need to open your mind up a lot wider and let some real-world shit in."

He gazed around at the borough sights. "LA is cool for the music industry and all that. But what's wrong with Brooklyn? Ain't shit happening in them other spots that

ain't going down even better right here. I'm with Brooklyn, girl. You with it too."

"Whatever. When I grow up my daddy's sending me
away to medical school. I'ma be a doctor and get with
a man who wants something out of life. Somebody who
wanna do more than just grind on the corner trading
goods with crackheads and hoes. A paid nigga with a real
profession, ya know? Somebody with some education
about himself."

Hood let go of Moo and grabbed Egypt's arm, his voice
a deadly whisper.

"Your daddy ain't sending you nowhere. You ain't
never gone have nobody else but *me*. You got that girl?
You mine, E. Mine forever. Believe that shit girl."

Egypt pulled away from him laughing sarcastically,
even though she liked it. "You always talking that 'I'm
yours' shit, Lamont. How you gone tell me who I'ma be
with or where I can't go? Boy, you just don't even know.
My daddy got money and he's gonna make sure I get the
word 'doctor' in front of my name. You must gonna gradu-
ate from college and marry me if you want me to be yours
forever, boy. That must be what you're gonna do."

Hood had kissed her full lips and laughed too, but just
those few admonishing words were enough to make him
start looking for beats and writing down his lyrics in a
notebook so he could eventually get up enough tracks for
a mixtape. Reem was already working on his and a lot of
cats got deals that way. He even considered taking his
schoolwork seriously too. He actually started paying at-

tention in class and turning in his assignments. Since he was naturally smart, he caught up fast, making up for all the time he had missed while him and Moo were living on the streets.

Egypt saw the effort he was putting forth and she liked it. She liked him. Truly, on both their parts it was love. Yeah, they were young but already they knew. And like a lot of kids in the hood their lives moved at a faster pace than most. They snuck around and found a way to get what they wanted. And despite their tender age, what they wanted was each other.

Hood made love to Egypt for the first time on a rainy Wednesday afternoon. They had the day off from school for some dead president's birthday. Fat Daddy had taken a three-day trip to Vegas, and Uncle Chop had been left to watch the shop and the kids. Moo had complained about a sore throat and had sucked a Sucrets before falling asleep on the back room sofa. Hood and Egypt were upstairs in Fat Daddy's plush living room watching a movie on his wide-screened plasma. Hood brushed the bare skin of her arm as he kissed her and held her close. Egypt shuddered pressing her taut young body against him.

It was chilly in the room and the pittering sound of windswept water hitting the windows was seductive. Egypt kissed him hard, urging him on. For a fleeting moment she thought of her father, knowing he would kill her if he could see her now. But what she was doing felt more than good. It felt right.

She lifted her shirt so Hood could see her young breasts, nipples hard and pointed. Hood gasped and finished undressing her. And when they were naked he covered her cool skin with kisses as their whispers of love filled the air.

They rocked the couch, exploring and experimenting. Hood knew more, so he took the lead. He touched her in places no one had ever been, and in return she held him and stroked him with a love he'd been yearning for. They were tender with each other. Patient and easy. But they were careful too. They used protection, laughing as they tore holes in two condoms before they got it right.

What they shared was intense and deep. Their emotions were as real as any under the sun. When it was over they clung to each other. Weakened physically, but each much stronger emotionally. Hood knew that he had found his salvation. The one solid thing in his life that would never leave him and never change. And Egypt knew the claims Lamont had made were without a doubt true and correct: She was his. He was hers. And that's all there was to it.

$ $ $

Life was falling into place for Hood and the streets were treating him grand. While Xan still had his doubts about Hood's right hand man, Dreko was making the best out of his second-string status and was showing up on point for Hood in every possible way. He squashed niggas down at the slightest sign of beef, and wherever Hood rolled Dreko was always strapped and on guard, never far behind him.

The pair became tighter than tight. Their bond was forged through trials and trust as they earned their stripes on the corners. They were known to roll up as one and compliment each other's fearless style of street management. Their youthful faces belied their inherent brutality when crossed. Even older and more experienced hustlers were awed by their heart and their loyalty, and started calling their brutal roll ups the one-two punch. Their motto became D.W.I.T. or "Do Whatever It Takes," and they lived by that shit on their hustle every day. Game recognized game, and Hood and Dreko parlayed their individual strengths into the ultimate enforcement team. Hood was typically the planner and Dreko was the pain inflicter, but both would dead a nigga in an instant behind some doe or some yay. Their business creed was simply nonnegotiable, and on count day they never feared Xan's wrath because their cash was always legit.

Over time Hood and Dreko made a deadly name for themselves on the streets of Central Brooklyn, and from weed to crack to heroin, loyal drug users flocked to their corner to hand over the doe. On the few occasions where some old head tried to muscle in on them and try their metal, Hood and Dreko made heating a nigga look real easy. Xan was never worried about his goods when Hood's street team re-upped on a run. Some of the cats he'd been running with for years spoke of the two with pride in their voices and a big measure of respect for the lil young niggas too.

There was a big difference between the two young boys, though, and it was obvious to almost everyone. Dreko was reckless and wild. What you saw with him was exactly what was there. Grime. But Hood could get real quiet sometimes and go inside of himself to think and rhyme. On the grind he was a straight shooter who lived by the street code, but he was guided by his own set of principles too.

All in all, shit seemed like it was lining up for Hood, except for one thing.

Monroe.

"Take this," he told his little brother one Saturday night. The school nurse had called Fat Daddy every single day that week telling him to come and pick up Moo. The boy stayed sick. It seemed like he always had a fever and he was always coughing.

"It's nasty," Moo complained swallowing the cherry-flavored cough syrup. "I don't like it, Lamont."

Hood pressed his ear to his brother's chest, listening to wet rattling noises as the boy wheezed. He made him take another teaspoon and then covered him up and wrapped a blanket tightly around his thin shoulders.

By the next morning Moo was even worse. Fat Daddy, Felton, Lil Jay, and a bunch of other old heads had gone to Atlantic City to the casinos, and once again old Uncle Chop was the only one home. Moo was real bad off. He coughed so hard he peed on the sagging green couch and his whole body shook. He had a fever and his blanket was soaked through with sweat. Hood was mad worried but he tried not to show it.

"I'm sick, right, Lamont?" Moo wheezed. Dreko had just swung by to see what was happening and Hood told him to stay in the room and watch Moo while he went to call Fat Daddy on his cell phone. He didn't know what else to do.

"I know I'm sick," Moo declared. His eyes were runny and he didn't even complain when Uncle Chop came in the back room and gave him some liquid Tylenol and some more cough syrup. "I must be sick 'cause even my fingernails is hurting me, Mont," he said with his eyes wide. "That's what Moo know."

Hood lay down on the damp couch with his brother and put his arm around him. He felt Moo struggling to suck air in, then struggle just as hard to push it out again. By later on that day Moo's skin was half-gray and he was out of his mind as he desperately tried to breathe. Egypt came downstairs and stood in the doorway watching them. When Lamont looked up and nodded her over, she crossed the room and pressed her lips to Moo's hot, shrunken face.

"Moo," she said softly. "You okay, little man?"

Moo tried to smile at her but he was too weak to even open his eyes.

"I'm scared, Lamont," Egypt whispered, her own eyes wide. She didn't want to say it out loud, but there was a reason she had stopped in the doorway and just stood there instead of coming in. Moo had looked dead laying there like that. She'd thought he *was* dead.

"Fat Daddy said he'll be back first thing in the morning."

"Mont, I don't think we can't wait for Daddy to get back. I think Moo needs to get to a hospital right now."

Seeing the tears forming in her eyes, Hood agreed.

Egypt ran and told Uncle Chop to call an ambulance. But them muthafuckas hated coming in the hood without a police escort, and after what seemed like forever and a day they still hadn't shown up.

Dreko and Egypt paced while they waited, sticking their heads out the door and looking up and down the street for the flashing lights of a phantom ambulance.

Hood sat on the couch holding his little brother in his arms, talking to him softly as he rocked back and forth and counted each second that went by.

"Oh shit," Dreko said suddenly. He had been watching Moo closely and now he put his hand on Hood's shoulder, stilling him. "Man, hold still. Quit rocking him. Shit." He stared at Moo for several long seconds. The boy's chest only moved every so often and it didn't seem like he was taking in no air at all. "He ain't even breathing, yo. I think he dying, man."

At that, Hood jumped up and hoisted Moo and the blanket over his shoulder. "Get out the way!" he said, running. He was through the shop and out the front door before he could be stopped, and he had carried Moo halfway down the block before Dreko and Egypt caught up with him.

"Man what you doing?" Dreko blurted, jogging beside his boy.

Hood kept moving fast as he headed toward the hospital with his sick brother in his arms.

"Hold up," Dreko said, taking long strides until he was jogging in front of them. Hood could prolly get Moo to the emergency room all right, but Dreko was bigger and he was stronger. He could get him there faster. He lifted Moo off his brother's shoulder and cradled him. Then both boys took off running through the streets of Brownsville, rushing little Monroe toward the nearest city hospital.

CHAPTER 10

Life just ain't worth it at all without you . . .
I don't wanna do it at all without you . . .

"IT DON'T MATTER how much this shit cost," Hood bargained with the old white nurse at the desk. Moo was so sick they had put an oxygen mask over his face and taken him to intensive care where the doctors were now working on him. "I got plenty of cash so everybody gone get paid, cool? Just tell them doctors to do everything they gotta do 'cause I'm straight. Don't worry 'bout how much it's gone cost or none of that stupid shit 'cause I been stackin my shit. Just let my brother be okay, cool? Go in the back and tell all of them I said to take care of my little brother for me, aiight?"

The nurse looked sympathetic and assured him the doctors would do their best.

Hood and Dreko both walked the hall nervously. Hood

kept his eyes on the checkered floor as he tried to remember how to pray. His mother had taught him a long time ago, but none of the words would come to him now and his heart was beating so fast it made his mouth dry. Panic had his mind going cloudy, and the only thing he could do was spit himself a mental rap to keep his thoughts sharp and his fear at bay.

My lil brother in this 'spital,
I feel like clutchin' on my pistol
Black Glock! The military issue!
Chest full of stress, what better way to get it off
One by one, I gotta pick these feelings off!

Uncle Chop and Egypt had somehow managed to flag down a cab and were now waiting with them. Somebody musta called Sackie 'cause him and his sister Zena were there too. Every few seconds Hood came out of his zone and looked toward the door real quick, hoping that a miracle would transpire and his moms would come walking in. He wasn't supposed to be doing no life-or-death shit like this by himself. Moo was his little brother, not his son. Something inside Marjay's heart shoulda pulled her here straight off the streets. Her mother-instincts should have told her that her baby was real sick and needed her bad. They should have sent her running outta whatever crack house she was holed up in and straight into the emergency room.

But in the end it didn't matter where Marjay was getting high at, or what mental lyrics Hood spit, or how much bank he had stacked. Money didn't fix everything, and it sure couldn't save Monroe.

"We tried," the doctor said, shrugging as he came through the door. He was a turban-wearing Pakistani in an inner-city hospital besieged with gunshot victims, AIDS patients, and other casualties of the violent crime that encapsulated the cold Brooklyn streets. His eyes were tired but emotionless, and he looked straight through Hood as he spoke. "But the boy is dead. He should have been seen in the hospital weeks ago. The child had one of the worst cases of pneumonia I've ever seen. He did not survive."

Hood stood there in shock. The doctor walked right past him and approached Uncle Chop.

"Are you the grandfather? You'll need to select a funeral home so the nurse can tell the morgue who will be collecting the body." And with that he walked off, sighing as he grabbed a chart off the wall so he could attend to his next patient.

The nurses drew the privacy curtains in Moo's room as Hood shed hot tears over the body of his little brother. Moo looked even smaller in death, especially with all them tubes going in him and the big machines he had been hooked up to. Hood cried. He might have been living a grown man's life, but in reality he was still just a child. Sniffing, he climbed up on the hospital bed and joined Moo whose tiny body remained warm, and snuggled his little brother in his arms for the last time. He closed his eyes, his tears dampening his brother's face as he pretended that Monroe was just sleeping and would wake up any minute with big trusting eyes and a long list of crazy questions coming outta his mouth.

It was Fat Daddy who had Moo buried a week later. He had sent a crew out looking for Marjay, but she must have been locked up because nobody had seen her on the streets and she ended up missing the boy's funeral, just like she had missed almost every other event in his life.

Hood's heart was crushed. Reem and his mother came by the shop and cried with him. Dreko was there for him too, night and day, and so was Sackie. His boys didn't crowd him or nothing, but they definitely let him know that their hearts was paining for him and Moo and that they had love for him like a brother. Moo had been their baby boy too.

But something deep inside of Hood seemed to be permanently damaged after Moo's death, and for the first time Fat Daddy allowed himself to feel for the boy. His grief was strong, almost overwhelming. But there was something else mixed in with it too, and Fat Daddy saw that shit real clear. It was rage. Aimed at life on these streets and at his mother, Marjay, too. Complete rage and utter helplessness. The kind of dangerous emotions that if not countered, can drive a man to commit an act he could wind up in jail for.

Fat Daddy walked up on Hood in the small kitchen behind the shop late one night three days after Moo had been buried. He had eased downstairs and into the back room, lured by a sound that he had never heard before. The boy stood next to the microwave with his back to the door. His head was bent and his small shoulders shook as he cried from his natural soul.

Fat Daddy never said a word. Instead he walked up behind Hood and put his arms around him, comforting him. To his surprise, Hood accepted his touch and didn't pull away. Fat Daddy wasn't father-figure material and wasn't even trying to be. But he was the only man alive who could show Hood any real concern or affection. He held the boy and let him grieve.

Regardless of the distance Fat Daddy had tried to keep between them, from that day forward Hood saw himself as Fat Daddy's son. As much as it hurt him he'd had no choice but to say good-bye to his little brother, and while searching for a connection to fill up the emptiness left by Moo's death, Hood rebuilt himself a family out of the people who were there for him in a major way every single day. Egypt became his soul mate and lover, Sackie became his closest confidant, and Dreko became his brother.

CHAPTER 11

I can tell watchin her walk, what she workin with,
Frame-fitted cat suit like Eartha Kitt . . .

SACKIE HAD A sister named Zena. She was a blondie who liked to fuck. The two of them had been sent to Brownsville to live with their elderly grandfather when he was four and she was two years old, after their parents were killed in a boating accident. They were two blond-haired, blue-eyed white kids in a tough neighborhood overflowing with brown bodies. Quite often they stood out in a crowd, but they were just kids and Brownsville was the only home the pair had ever known.

Sackie and Zena attended the mostly black and Hispanic schools in their neighborhood, and by the time they were in the third and fifth grades the fact that they were geographical minorities was no longer easy to ignore.

While Sackie was big for his age and had been quick to join up with the dominant click and earn himself a rep as a white boy who had mad fist skills, Zena had always been shy and hesitant and very insecure. Her timid demeanor made her an easy target for the chicks in the hood who felt superior to her, and whose impressions of white people in general were already mostly negative and contemptuous.

But it didn't take long for Zena to figure out something that the black girls in the hood didn't like and definitely didn't care to admit: Zena had a nice plump ass and brothers wanted to fuck her. Yeah, she knew the guys weren't all up in her face because she was brilliant and popular or anything, because she really wasn't. She had gotten the looks in the family, while Sackie had gotten most of the brains. But when the black boys crept upstairs to the apartment she shared with her brother and grandfather and closed the door to her bedroom, Zena became the sole focus of their attention and she loved every minute of it.

Zena might have been lonely and love-starved, but she wasn't street dumb. She didn't give the pussy up to every dude who wanted it, only to those young ballers who could either provide her with something she wanted in return, or those who could advance her standing in the hood in some kinda way. Lately she'd been fuckin with a trap boy named Roller, who worked for Xanbar up on Sutter Avenue, but there were a couple of guys much closer to home who were clocking her too.

"Don't let these broke niggas use you," Egypt had warned her. They were good friends and Zena was trying hard to pay attention and take her advice. Egypt was one of the few black girls in the hood who actually talked to her like she was a real person and wasn't pressed out about the shit other people talked when they ate lunch together in school or were seen hanging out together in the hood.

"You see that shit?" Egypt had said one afternoon as they walked home at the end of the school day. She grabbed Zena's arm and pointed her toward the corner where a patrol car was double parked and two officers were patting down a group of young thugs they had hemmed up against a fence. "They might be going to juvie today, but most of them gonna be in somebody's state prison by the time they turn twenty-one. Ain't no future in what these idiots is doing, girl. Don't get all blinded just because one of them brings you some slum earrings or buys you a slice of pizza and Chinese food two nights in a row. That shit ain't nothing. Fuck around and you'll be looking like one of them stroller chicks on the porches in the projects. Dummies walking around here fifteen years old and already got three kids. You see 'em pulling, pushing, and kicking all them babies down the street. You're real pretty, Zena, so be real smart too. You need to hold out for somebody who got a future out in front of him. A cat who's going somewhere far and wants to take you along too."

"Somebody like Hood?" Zena asked, although she was secretly thinking of Dreko. Hood's man had been pushing up on her hard, letting her know how much he wanted some of what she was holding.

Egypt nodded. She'd been Lamont's woman for a minute now, and she knew him like a book. His flaws, his weaknesses, all of his shortcomings, and yet she still loved everything about him.

"Yeah, somebody just like my Lamont. He might be down with Xanbar's operation in a major way, but he ain't stupid. I can't say I like all the shit the D.W.I.T. boys is out here doing, but if it wasn't them it would be somebody else. But on the real, though, Lamont gonna be somebody big one day. You just watch," she said, secretly wishing Lamont would show interest in something other than spittin rap music and making money. "My man is ambitious. He got dreams and big plans. Goals and intentions. Don't sleep on him baby because one day Mont's name is gonna be ringing big bells up on all of Brooklyn's boulevards. He's gonna be well known in this hood."

$ $ $

Egypt mighta been speaking the truth when she described the kind of guy Zena should be looking for, but Zena's lot in life was a whole lot harder than hers. Things just didn't flow for Zena the way they did for her friend. For one thing, Egypt commanded acceptance on the streets just because of who she was. Fitting in wasn't a problem for her. She had a paid father, a capo boyfriend, and she looked just like everybody else looked in their hood so she dripped with confidence and never worried about whether or not she was doing or saying the right things.

But Zena's reality was way different and so was her mind set. Sackie mighta been brilliant with numbers, but Zena's talents lay in other areas. She liked to floss. To be seen and to be admired. To fit in. She had learned to boost at an early age, and between that grind and Sackie's hustle, they were pretty good on money and Zena used most of hers to keep herself popping tags and looking good.

While Egypt was running back and forth to dance class and piano recitals and talking non-stop about college and medical school and what she was gonna do as soon as she got out of Brooklyn, Zena's mind had never been stretched that wide. She'd grown up without a mother figure anywhere within reach. She'd had no one to school her on the ways of womanhood, or to tell her about her period, or even to show her how to take proper care of herself down there, let alone how young girls were supposed to navigate the waters of life to become a success. She was a tentative girl searching for a spotlight. Low on confidence and wanting badly to be a part of something big.

So the first time Dreko stepped to her she was on receive mode. Wide open and delighted that a ruff-riding willie like him was showing her so much attention.

He was real sweet at first too. And real possessive.

"Bring that phat ass over here," he would laugh and snatch her up in front of all his friends. "Girl you gone need an armed escort, rolling down this block looking that fine!

Hey, yo!" he'd warn all the cats on the corner, "This me, ya dig? I know this shit looks good, but don't get no ideas because all this fluffy angel cake is about to be mine."

Zena would blush and squeal like she was embarrassed, but the whole time she would be clinging to his strong brown arms, loving the way they felt wrapped around her, and enjoying the spotlight and the way the other guys gazed at her with hunger and envy in their eyes.

To have a cat like Dreko wanting her also gave Zena mad credibility with other bitches and made her legit on the streets. Even some of the chicks who used to flex on her knew better now. Once word got out that white girl Zena was rolling with Big Dreko, it seemed like her whole life changed. No more was she on the outside looking in. She was the shit now, and the D.W.I. T. crew treated her like a queen. Zena basked in that glow, feeling glorious and goddess-like. She hung at the right spots, drank, smoked weed, popped X, and even hit the pipe every now and then. Anything to fit in with the crowd and stay on par with the crew who rolled with her new man.

But Sackie was dead-set against her getting with Dreko from the beginning and he let her know it too. He'd run into them at a party and yanked Zena out of Dreko's lap and taken her outside to scream on her while Dreko laughed behind them and reached for the next bitch.

"You don't wanna fuck with him, Zena. I mean it. You might think you know the streets but you don't. That cat is a fool. A straight-up fool. The only thing he can do for you is bring you down."

Zena was high and feeling large. "Damn! Every fuckin body has somebody, except me. Don't you want me to be happy for once?!?"

"Not with Dreko. Ain't he fuckin with that girl Fatima from Riverdale? You don't wanna go up against her, Z. She carries a razor and she's wild as hell."

Zena put her hands on her hips. Sackie just didn't know. She had already beat Fatima's ass into the concrete for wagging her bubble ass around in front of Dreko.

"Nobody tells you who you can be with! You fuck that grimy bitch Tina on our couch almost every night and I never try to stop you. She was the one who got those girls over on Dumont to jump me that time. But I didn't shit on her name or tell you you couldn't be with her, did I?"

Sackie glanced around the streets, then shook his head, concern shining in his eyes. "This ain't the same, Zena. That girl is just a piece of ass. Dreko is something different. He's off, Z. Mental. No chick is safe around him, if you ask me. Especially a chick like you."

Zena moved closer to her brother. She put her hand on his arm and pleaded with him. "But I like Dreko. And he's feeling me too. He treats me right, Sackie. He makes me feel good. He might be wild and crazy out on the streets, but when he's with me he's all the way straight. I'm serious."

"You don't even know that dude, Zena. Trust me. He leaves shitty footprints wherever he goes. Find somebody else. Sip is in there, right? He's a cool guy and he's always liked you. Go back inside and hang out with him tonight."

"I don't like Sip."

"I'm telling you, stay away from Dreko or come home with me, Zena. That's it. Those are your only choices."

Zena had gotten pissed off then. Sackie was probably jealous. He'd never approved of none of the guys she liked. It had always been just the two of them against the rest of the world, and while Zena loved her brother from the heart, he wasn't her damn father and he couldn't tell her what to do.

"Too late," she said defiantly. Dreko had already fucked her so good she'd lost all sense of herself. She would have cut some damn body if they tried to come between her and all that good black dick he was laying on her. She backed toward the club entrance, about to dip back inside and leave her brother standing alone on the streets. "Me and Dreko are already together. All the way together. We gonna stay that way too."

Sackie swallowed hard. He knew what that shit meant and it scared him. He glanced around, then lowered his voice. He didn't wanna say it, but he had to. "Be careful, Zena. I heard some real foul shit about Dreko back in the day from Miss Newman. I used to go to the store for her all the time, remember? Well she told me something so grimy I never repeated it. Not even to Hood. So watch yourself, you hear? Dreko might have some unnatural tendencies about him, nah'm saying? He's a hard body soldier right now, but he ain't always been no straight shooter."

"You just don't wanna see me with nobody. Especially nobody who's riding harder than you."

Sackie sighed. "Make him wrap it up real tight, Zena. Make him double-bag that shit, ya hear?"

Zena smirked. "You don't rule me. Just let me do me, okay?"

Sackie's heart fell. Zena was right when she said it was too late. He could have muscled her down and forced her home, but then what? Lock her up in the crib forever? His sister had never been slick or street savvy, and Sackie knew if she was defying his word, then Dreko already had her by the brain.

Tears of anger and frustration were in his eyes as he turned away from his little sister so she couldn't see his pain. He started to call out over his shoulder, but then he said fuck it and turned around again. If seeing the hurt on his face would help wake her up, then let her see it.

"You've got a hard head and you're making a mistake, Zena. A big one. That fool is gonna dog you. Fuck up your whole life. He'll turn you out, then drag you down in the sewer with him and toss you off when you start stinking. You gonna end up just like these other bitches out here who fuck with these crazy ballers. Strung out and on the streets. Just remember, I love you and I tried to warn you."

CHAPTER 12

Bacardi and a O.J.!
Got me in my zone, eh!
Ready to touch something,
Mami please gimme the okay!

IT WAS LATE night in Brownsville and the streets were just going quiet. They would stay that way for less than three hours, then the cycle of work and play, hustle and grind, would start all over again.

Egypt lay in her bed waiting. Xan's crew had hung out in the shop later than usual so Hood was probably still down there. With her eyes wide open Egypt thought about all the things she wanted to do in life, and all the places she wanted to see. She thought about the boy she loved too, and tingled inside as she anticipated what the rest of the night held in store for them.

About thirty minutes passed, and after Fat Daddy's

snores had been rocking the apartment for a good minute, Egypt heard a faint tapping sound. She answered the
door for Hood and let him inside. They tiptoed back into
her bedroom quietly, then Egypt giggled as she opened
her closet door and pulled him deep inside.

"I luh this pussy," Hood panted in the darkness as he
slobbered and kissed all over her collarbone. He helped
her pull her shirt over her head, then threw it to the floor.
She wasn't wearing a bra and her fourteen-year-old titties
was still small, but very firm.

His fingers found her zipper and lowered it. She
moved like a snake as she wiggled out of her jeans. The
muscles in her stomach curled under his hand, and he had
the urge to stick his tongue inside her navel. She hooked
her thumbs in the waistband of her panties and slid them
down until they were halfway off her hips. Hood pulled
them the rest of the way down, his fingers touching the
wet fabric of her crotch that was soaked through with her
early juices.

Bending over to help her step out of her panties, his
nose picked up the scent of her heated sticky and he
couldn't wait to get into it. Fuck Fat Daddy snoring in
the room next door. Hood was about to give his baby girl
some real good dick up in this closet. Already he could feel
his nut rising and he pressed himself against her body
grinding slowly, his wood hard enough to poke a hole in
her leg.

He nibbled up her neck and she parted her lips, sucking
his tongue. Hood gripped her long chocolate thighs, spread-

ing them as wide as he could. He moved his hardness between her damp thighs without inserting it. Just playing with the pussy as her clit dripped with liquid sugar.

"Oooh, yeah." His hands cupped the high, round muscles of her ass cheeks and he pushed his rock against her. Hard. Harder.

"Suck my nipples," she demanded, and he did. Licked them two chocolate buds like there was honey running out of them.

"Now put it in," Egypt whispered after helping him slide into a condom. She threw her head back, knocking clothes down and clanging hangers against the wall as Hood guided his dick deep inside her wet gushy.

Holding tight to her ass, he beat that thing up real good. She moaned on his tongue as they both whispered words of love. He stroked it proper, and pounded it up into her as she screamed and her young juices wet up his pubic hair and ran down his balls.

"I love you, Egypt," he told her from the heart, then backed off as she reached for the bottom of his shirt and yanked it up over his head.

"Yeah," he whispered as she held him to her, the sensation of her naked breasts pressed against his heart the best damn feeling in the world. "I love you, baby." He started stroking again. Gentle. Slow pull outward, then nice deep thrust inward. "You know that right? I'ma always take good care of you, baby. You ain't gotta worry 'bout a damn thing."

Egypt responded by clamping her pussy muscles down on him and sighing. She wrapped her long legs around his back as he hoisted her in his arms, then held onto him like he was the only damn thing keeping her on the face of the earth.

With his dick in her up to the hilt, Hood lost it. He bounced her ass up a few times, and her breasts jiggled. Heat and the scent of sex rose between their bodies and her nipples glided across his sweat-coated chest, sending his nut rushing up out of his balls.

His dick jerked and spit, and Egypt screamed out her love, coming hard as her pussy muscles spasmed uncontrollably. Hood waited until she was through and then lowered her until she was standing again.

He kissed her forehead and laughed. "I bet you wasn't worrying about Fat Daddy hearing you just now, was you?"

"Hell no! Besides, if he had heard us fuckin in his house he woulda snatched both of us out this closet by now."

Hood smirked in the darkness. "I keep telling you I ain't scared of your daddy. This my pussy all sticky between your legs, girl. Mine. Not even your father can tell me shit about that. It's mine."

Egypt smiled. She liked the way Hood claimed her body and her heart. If it ever came down to it she knew he would walk straight through a wall of fire over her and she would do the same for him. She loved Lamont. With every bit of her young, tender heart, she loved him.

So what she had lied to Zena and Lamont didn't plan to see any more of the world than what was right before his eyes? There was nothing he seemed to be passionate about at all, other than moving those lips and composing mad rap lines, or his far-out dreams of joining forces with his man Reem Raw and owning a record company, a mansion, and an NBA franchise one day. It was his his strength that she admired. The way he handled the curves life threw at him with a straight back and squared shoulders, like a real man should. All that other street shit she had learned to accept about him, and she was confident that once he saw her in college and pursuing a real career, he'd hop on it and get busy too. But in the meantime she was cool with things the way they were. It was kinda nice knowing she had a street baller with a powerful reputation who would eat out the palm of her hand just as quickly as he'd lick out the center of her pussy.

But a few minutes later Lamont surprised her as they sat together on the warm radiator and looked out of her bedroom window. The streetlight was bright outside and the cool air felt good on her face even as the iron radiator grooves dug into the back of her legs. They gazed down at the street below as the el train roared overhead, zooming down its shiny silver tracks.

A just-fucked peace had settled down over both of them and Egypt was startled when Lamont jumped up and stuck his whole head out the window, then cursed loudly.

"What?" Egypt asked. She followed his gaze, then looked up at him and froze. A wall of stone had slid down over Lamont's face. The only sign of emotion she could detect was the deep pain that shone in his eyes. Moo had been dead for over two years, and this was one of the sporadic sightings they'd had of Marjay. She was an all-out fiend now who stayed in and out of jail, and Egypt wasn't sure if the woman even knew her baby was gone.

Egypt looked back down at the street below and sighed as they watched Marjay come around the corner, running from a cop. The man caught her easily and twisted her arm behind her, then forced her to the ground. The faint sound of clanking buttons rose to their ears as Marjay tussled with all her might, and Egypt couldn't bear to watch as the cop's partner pulled up in a patrol car and got out to help him. The first cop picked Marjay up by the back of her jacket and flung her inside the car as soon as his partner opened the door. Seconds later they drove off toward the precinct with her wilding out and kicking on the back window.

"C'mon," Egypt urged Lamont, pulling him back inside. She closed the window then shifted her position until she was sitting on his lap. "It's okay," she whispered, stroking his rigid face. "It's okay, baby. They gone let her sleep it off and then they gone let her go like they usually do. Really, everything is gonna be all right."

The glow from the streetlight spilled into the room casting radiance over his features, and the tears she saw him trying hard to fight were heartbreaking.

"Nah, it ain't all right," Lamont finally said, wiping his eyes with his arm. Egypt pulled him down to the floor and cradled his stiff body. Yeah, her man was a stone-cold street thug, but it touched her soul that he still had a tender place in his heart for his mother.

"They need to keep her ass in jail because as long as she on that shit ain't nothing never gonna be all right."

"Baby, don't say that," she urged, taking his hand. She'd never known her own mother but that didn't stop her from missing her and feeling Mont's pain.

He snatched away from her. "I lost Moo behind her craziness, Egypt. Because of her suckin on a pipe, me and my brother stayed out there on them streets! Cold. Walking. Scrambling. I lost my baby brother, but she lost her fuckin son. And what makes it so bad is that she didn't even notice."

Egypt took his hand again and held it tightly, but she had to agree. "In a game like this, *everybody* loses, Mont. There ain't no winners on these streets. Just losers, baby."

"I know," he said, sounding almost like a little boy again. "But I just wish she could get clean, ya dig. I want her clean. I just want her clean! What kinda chick puts a fuckin crack pipe in her mouth anyway, E? Tell me what it takes to make a woman do that kinda shit because I just don't fuckin get it."

Egypt shrugged. "It's this street life, Mont," she said. She kept her voice low and gentle, but that didn't stop the truth from ringing out clearly in her words. "I guess anybody can fall victim to it. I mean, we gotta keep it real, baby. You out there slinging the same shit your mother craves. You even selling it to other people's moms. You think the pipe can only get hold of strangers, and the people you love and care about gone be immune to that shit? This is real-world poison we talking about, Lamont. It produces mass casualties, baby. And what you're doing out on these streets is a big part of all that."

"I know," Hood said. Yeah, he had a big hand in the drug game and the guilt was definitely there. He took a deep breath and the set of his jaw looked harder than concrete. "But I'd give up everything, the slanging, the clothes, the jewels, the fuckin status and the long papers just to have her off the pipe and Moo back in my life. 'Cause this shit didn't have to happen, E. My fam was rolling before she picked up that glass dick. Even with my pops gone, we was still rolling."

He raised his head and looked Egypt full in the face. "I ain't gone never forgive her for being so fuckin stupid and so fuckin weak. For loving that shit more than she loved Moo. More than she loved me. Never! No bitch should let herself rot so low in the gutter that she jumps totally out of pocket just to worship a little piece of rock! I'm telling you, E, no matter how much piff I pass, or how much yay I sling, I'll never understand a bitch who puts her lips on a pipe. Never!"

CHAPTER 13

Before death grabs me,
God please hold me,
I'm done with the days of saying my soul's lonely . . .

TIME FLIES IN the hood when you're making money, and six years after coming on board with Xanbar, Hood and everybody else associated with Xanbar's crew was yanking in plenty of doe. The drug business was booming and Xan was looking to diversify his holdings, eyeing other areas where he could make his money work for him. He'd had a long run holding down the streets of Brownsville, and like most good gangstas he knew that the sweet shit wasn't gonna last forever. The way Xan saw it, he could either get knocked and sent upstate or get caught out there by some hungry young come up who felt his time on the throne had passed. Or, and this was his favorite scenario, he could score one more big win and retire somewhere down south like a fat muhfucka living in a house made of cake.

His mind was in business attack mode when he called Hood down to Baller's Paradise to have a little chat.

"Dig," he said, nodding to the barmaid who had just brought two shots over to his private booth. "You been with me for a long minute now," Xan said swirling his finger around in his shotglass. "You was what? Twelve when I put you on? You about eighteen now. I practically raised you up on these streets. Put you in a prime position and taught you everything you know about the game, right?"

Sensing some real gutta shit coming, Hood just listened without responding. Yeah, they'd been doing business together for a long time now. Xan had put him on and set him up lovely, no doubt. But raised him? Nah, the streets had done that all by themselves.

"Check this shit out. And the only reason I decided to put you down on all this, to give you this big opportunity really, is because I know how tight you is with Fat Daddy. But that nigga been fuckin up in the worst of ways, so I also know you'll appreciate the seriousness of what I have to say."

"Aiight."

"Dig man. Fat Daddy gone fuck around and get hit. The nigga got his head on the chopping block, ya heard?"

Hood gazed at Xan evenly, giving nothing away. He'd grown into a hard-body man over the years and was nobody's fool. He knew a lot of shit about street life today that had escaped him years ago, and the truth of the matter was, Fat Daddy was a gambling junkie. He would turn a fuckin trick just to place a bet, and over the past couple of years his craving for the game of chance had gotten him in the red with gamblers and gangstas and grandmothers too.

But what the fuck was Hood supposed to do about that? Xanbar had already taken over Fat Daddy's shop and exiled the man up into his apartment while he raked in his profits. What the fuck else did he want?

"Man, that nigga's dick is in the hole way past his fuckin nuts," Xan said. "Deep in that shit. Real deep. We had a little business venture going, you know. He signed over the deed to his apartment and the shop, and I spotted him some cash so he could go down to Atlantic City and make a payoff." Xan shook his head in disgust, then downed his drink in one swallow. "That old fool shit on me *and* them Italians. Gambled my entire investment up in less than an hour. Now cats is getting cranky. They want their money and I want mines too. Difference is, them cats don't feel for him the way I do. They ready to take they doe straight outta his ass, nah mean?"

Hood felt his stomach sink although not a single thing about him changed on the outside. He'd seen Fat Daddy in action and knew his gambling habit had an addictive pull that was just as strong as crack. The nigga would bet on two raindrops hitting the ground if he could. Over the past couple of years he had overstated so many bets that he had some big willies gunning for him in Vegas, and was completely barred from two casinos down in Connecticut.

Fat Daddy had lost almost all of his fenced inventory in a single poker game, and his cash flow had gotten so raggedy that niggas who used to pay big dollars to get into one of his cee-low games were now acting as bankers and could walk through the door for free.

"What all that shit got to do with me?"

Xan sat up straight. "You his boy, right? He been daddying ya ass all these years in the back of his shop, correct?"

Hood remained silent, giving up no leverage.

"I tell you what," Xanbar said. His whole demeanor had gone from easy to deadly in about three seconds. "Fat Daddy in the hole so deep he'd have to hit the number ten times straight to pay me *and* them Italians off. I ain't taking no heat for that fat fuck and I ain't taking no loss on my investment neither. That old fool either gone pay his fuckin debts or pay the fuckin cost. Now since we all know he ain't got no change, then that means he eligible to get crushed. Nah'm sayin?"

Hood shook his head. "That man been real legit with you over the years, Xan. You can do that kinda shit to him?"

Xan didn't even blink. "That and a whole lot more, my nig. You the one love that old baldhead muhfucka, not me. Fat Daddy came and asked me for help, then he tampered with my doe. That means he gots to go down hard. But you know," he shrugged, "it ain't just Fat Daddy who I'm worried about. You know how these gambling cats is. Ruthless. They ain't got no love for nobody. I'm thinking

Egypt could fuck around and get in the way and then they might look at her like she eligible for some get back too." He swigged back his second shot of yak and grilled Hood with deadly eyes. "That is, unless you and Dreko gangsta up and give the old guy a little help. I got a small job over in Ocean Hill with that pussy nigga Chaos that needs handling. The proceeds should snag us about a cool half-mil. Five G's go to you, and five to Dreko. The rest will be just enough to pull Fat Daddy through and square him with me *and* them Italian cats. I bet it'll keep Egypt safe too. So you ready to talk some business, or what?"

CHAPTER 14

You my sister and my soul at the same time
One of the reasons I'm going so hard when it's game time . . .

ZENA BLOW-DRIED HER just-shampooed hair and admired its thickness in the mirror. It felt clean and healthy as it bounced around her shoulders like a golden halo. She fluffed it from the roots with her fingers making sure it was completely dry, then unplugged the dryer and picked up a comb. Her hand shook as she leaned close to the mirror and pressed the tip to her scalp. She slid a straight part along the left side of her head and combed her hair downward around her face. With that done, she straightened up and put on a pair of gold clip-on earrings, then carefully picked up her false eyelashes from their case. Her fingers were sweaty and she dropped the spidery-looking things three times before she was able to get them on.

She'd been Dreko's bitch for over three years and the whole experience had been brutal and destructive. Sackie had tried to warn her but she'd been blinded to her man's true nature, and every single thing her brother had predicted had ended up coming true. With Dreko ruling and ruining her life, Zena had gone from a pretty white chick with a cute smile and a banging ass, to a washed out pipe fiend who got her grill smashed on the regular. Her slide downhill had been painful to watch, especially for her brother. Fucking with Dreko had put a wedge in their sibling relationship that left Zena feeling guilty and ashamed, but unable to find a way out.

"Aiight, you the one whose gotta live with your choices," Sackie had told her after rolling up on her high for what seemed like the two-hundredth time. Him and Dreko had beefed and almost come to blows over Zena on more occasions than she could count. Sackie was furious because Zena had let Dreko talk her into giving him a key to their apartment, and then the fool came up in there with his boys and did any damn thing he felt like doing.

But if she thought the beatings were bad, sex with Dreko was the ultimate punishment. It may have started out hot and fabulous, but these days it was just full of depravities. Zena knew her man was wrong to be filling her up with liquor and drugs, but she had to get high just to force herself to do the sadistic shit he demanded. One time Sackie had come home and found her naked and high and fucked so bad she lay bleeding on their kitchen floor. He'd flown into a rage and gone looking for Dreko with his gun.

Luckily, Hood was able to step in and shut shit down before it got ugly, but the bad blood between her brother and her man was almost always on boil.

Eventually Sackie had grown fed up. At a certain point he gave up and didn't even try to keep her away from Dreko anymore. In fact, he told Zena she was a lost cause and said she should go for what she wanted with gusto.

"I'm out here deep in this game slinging rock to take care of us every day, and you out there smoking that yay just like you one of my customers? Fuck it. Do you, Z. Do you to death, baby sis."

Yeah, the years of drugs, beatings, and torment with Dreko had just about sucked the life out of Zena and turned her into a shell of her former self. But things had changed for the better when she told Sackie she was pregnant. Sackie had offered to help her take care of the baby, and Zena was happy to have her brother back on her team. Sackie was showing affection and concern for her again, and she had promised herself that she wouldn't let him down.

But today was a bad day, and that promise was feeling like a hard one to keep. It had been months since Zena had touched the pipe, and right now she felt so nervous and scared that she needed a hit and she needed one bad. Crack memories swelled inside her brain, giving her get-high flashbacks so vivid they made her shiver with desire.

Sackie had the music turned up loud in the living room, and Zena sang along to a Thug-A-Licious song being spit as she tried to distract herself and take her mind off both the pipe and the letter sitting on her dresser.

> *I got the haze, a whole batch to puff out*
> *Goons in the back waitin for cats to stunt out*
> *Ladies in the dugout,*
> *Big breasts and butt out,*
> *No names needed*
> *That takes the fun out!*

With the fake eyelashes secured, Zena pencil-darkened the arch in her eyebrows and then drew a faint line around her lips. She was bullshitting and wasting time and she knew it. Makeup wasn't even her thing. She was just stalling and trying to find a way to convince herself not to do what she knew definitely had to be done. She covered the two steps between the bathroom and her bedroom and stood facing the dresser. The folded sheet of paper she had been trying so hard to ignore sat harmlessly beside her radio.

Zena touched her thick stomach and lost every ounce of her false bravado. For the third or fourth time she fought the urge to show the letter to Sackie. She was too pregnant and too scared to go through something like this by herself with no drugs or drink to help her. Zena wished there was someone she could depend on for comfort and help. Anyone. She'd wanted so badly to confide in Egypt, but shame had kept her lips locked. Besides, Egypt was busy all the time. She was hardly ever around. It was her last year of high school and she was taking pre-college night courses at a school downtown. The two of them were still really close, but Egypt's life seemed to be going somewhere while Zena's had stalled and felt like it was about to fizzle out.

Deep inside Zena hated that she'd ever gone to the clinic in the first damn place. Most girls she knew never bothered to get any prenatal care at all. They just showed up at the emergency room when they went into labor and it was time to have their baby.

And hell yeah, she'd seen all them stupid commercials on BET talking about wrap it up and know your status, but that shit wasn't for real. Those was just paid actors up there on a screen who weren't even facing what she was facing, and Dreko wasn't the kind of guy who would ever agree to use a condom anyway. The truth was, she felt better not knowing her status. She could have lived the rest of her life not knowing, and been cool with that.

But it wasn't just about her no more. At the risk of pissing off Dreko, Zena had put the brakes on all that partying and getting high and drinking and unnatural fucking stuff. For the past seven months she'd had something other than herself to think about, and unlike some girls, she had wanted the best for her baby and that meant putting down the crack pipe and seeing a doctor and getting a checkup and some vitamins. She'd gone to her first prenatal appointment when she was four months along, and had submitted to all of the necessary blood tests and stuff with no problem.

Ignorance had been a good thing at the time, and even though she had her suspicions about Dreko, she had no idea they'd be giving her that particular test. But the nurse at the clinic had filled up quite a few of those glass vials for blood, and when they'd called her a couple of weeks later she'd sat there dumbfounded as the doctor patted her hand and told her that one of her important test results had come back abnormal.

"Don't start worrying yet," he had reassured her. "There are a lot of factors that can cause a false positive response. We'll take another blood sample in a few weeks and go from there."

Zena had forced herself to go back and be tested the second time, but now her fear was strangling her and she was too scared to return to the clinic for the final results. She'd been getting out-the-ass phone messages from the nurse instructing her to come in to the clinic immediately, and when she didn't respond they'd sent the certified letter she now held in her hands.

Zena unfolded the letter and a shiver ran through her as she read the words that had been neatly typed in the center of the page. "We have been attempting to contact you regarding the results of your laboratory tests. This could be a health care emergency detrimental to you or your unborn child. Please contact the clinic immediately."

Panic held her in a tight grip. Fear of the unknown. But for her baby's sake she had made herself call the clinic this morning and had quietly agreed when the nurse demanded she come in today. Right away.

All kinds of twisted images were running through her head as Zena left the apartment without confiding in her brother. She walked past the projects slowly, heading toward the health clinic and remembering every horrible thing she had ever heard about people who got caught out there with this particular disease.

She'd taken a couple of sex education and health classes before she dropped out of high school, and there were enough people walking around with it right here in Brownsville for her to know what the future held. It might take a long time, but unless you were Magic Johnson or somebody rich, eventually it showed up on you in unmistakable ways. She'd seen the kind of damage the sickness could do. Stick figures with sunken eyes and skin stretched tight over their skulls. Wasted-looking skeletons walking the streets filled with hopelessness and despair.

Zena raised a hand to the thick, bouncy hair she loved so much. All that shit would be gone. Either on the floor or down the drain, leaving her with nothing but a few scraggly strands floating around on her pink scalp. And what about her baby? Would it be sick too? If something happened to her, who was gonna take care of her child?

She was scared out of her mind, but a part of her was mad as hell too. The moment she got with Dreko she had stopped fucking around with ten and twelve different dudes like a cheap jump-off, so if she had caught some scary shit it wasn't her fault. It had to be Dreko. It could only be him. Him and that grimy shit he did when he didn't think nobody was watching.

Zena had faked confusion the first time he made her wait downstairs as he took a young pipe-head cat up on the roof to get his top done. She had gotten her ass kicked good that night too. The guy she never saw again, but Dreko had come back down fifteen minutes later sweating and looking fucked-out in the face, then started a fight with her over something stupid. By the time the night was over Zena had a split earlobe, a busted lip, and a loose bottom tooth.

Another time he had gotten a set of SUV keys from Lil Jay, then made her stand in the lobby of the building while he put a neighborhood cat named Turtle in the front seat and made dude bob his head to pay off a ten dollar debt.

"Wait ya ass right here," he told her as he pushed Turtle toward the whip. Turtle stumbled over to the Expedition with his head held down, and Zena felt sick as she watched Dreko toss the young man inside the ride and then climb in beside him on the other side.

She was really sick when she saw Turtle lean over as his head disappeared in Dreko's lap. Zena watched wide-eyed as Dreko lounged back in the seat and Turtle's red skully appeared and disappeared, like he was bobbing for apples.

There was no mistaking what was going down. Especially since Dreko had yelled like a girl the moment he nutted, and even though she was standing inside the foyer behind a pane of glass, Zena had heard him hollering loud and clear.

"Mind ya fuckin biz and keep ya gums shut," was what he told her when she got up the nerve to question him later on that night while he lay across her bed waiting for her to toss his salad. "What I do is what the fuck I do."

"But—that guy's head was going up and down. He was in there sucking—"

Bang! Dreko capped her so hard in the nose that she lost her breath and rolled off the bed, collapsing on the hard floor.

"And stay your simple ass down there!" he had growled as she tried to rise up on her knees.

Terrified, Zena dropped back and lay on the cold floor crying and swallowing the hot blood that was running down her throat. It was a good hour before he let her get up to put some ice on her face, and by then not only did she have a broken nose, she had two black eyes to go along with it.

Zena wasn't dumb, but she was stuck. And scared. Dreko wasn't the kind of gangsta who would let something walk away from him. When he was done with something he either destroyed it or killed it. He never left anything laying around for somebody else to use.

Sackie was right. This is what your dumb ass gets for fucking with him in the first place, Zena chastised herself as she thought about the girl Fatima she had beat down over Dreko back in the day. Egypt had warned her to let Fatima have Dreko, but Zena wouldn't listen. Instead, she had stomped the shit out of Fatima and won the right to be Dreko's bitch. But while Zena's looks had fallen off fast, whenever she happened to run across Fatima these days the girl looked better and better. Whipped like butter. Fly and pretty. Happy as hell.

And now Zena was the one walking around pregnant and run down and craving a hit. She crossed Bristol Street and headed toward the clinic wondering what the hell it was that had had her so bent on Dreko from the gate. It was probably because she'd been secretly jealous of the closeness Egypt had with Hood. She had wanted a high-post baller of her own to roll with, but here she was almost three years later, hating the very thing she had begged for, fought for, and had gotten on her knees and sucked a glass dick for.

And look where all that bullshit had gotten her. Zena's feet were heavier than concrete as she trudged down the street filled with dread. Damn. She could sure use a hit right now. It wasn't just her mind that wanted it. Her body seemed to be screaming for it too. She'd taken a shower but still her skin was clammy and coated with stank sweat and her heart pounded so hard it made her back hurt.

Zena made it all the way to the steps of the clinic, but standing outside of the drab, gray building she could force herself to go no further. There were only three steps standing between her and the truth. The clinic doors stood slightly open and she could see a pale yellow wall decorated with baby emblems on the inside, but no matter how hard she tried, she just couldn't move.

Suddenly the door opened as a pregnant girl and a toddler came out, followed by a slender nurse with long hair and light brown skin. The nurse reached down and smiled as she handed the toddler a green lollipop, and Zena panicked and ducked her head so she wouldn't be seen.

Tomorrow, she lied to herself, desperately craving a hit off the pipe. *I'll come back tomorrow.*

She turned around and ran.

CHAPTER 15

Niggas show respect when I enter the building,
My team treatin grown men like they women and children!

"SO YOU DOWN for this shit or what?"

They were sitting on a bench in Brownsville projects watching a bunch of goons banging each other up in a game of full-court street ball. Ten hard-body niggas hustled up and down the concrete court sweating and going for the ball like there was money riding on it. Their natural athleticism was astounding, and getting called on a foul was rare. With their superior agility, strength, and big-time hops, they faked out, crossed over, and dunked the ball with a brutal finesse, like the only thing in the world that mattered was getting that win.

Dreko glanced at his boy and grinned. They were far enough away from the other spectators not to be overheard, but close enough to appreciate the intensity of the game.

"Nigga how you even gone ask me some crazy shit like that. Hitting Chaos's spot? Hell yeah, I'm down."

Hood nodded. "This ain't no group project so we gotta keep it on the low. Not even Sackie. Just me and you. Xanbar got the whole timing thing worked out. We slide in at night and put in our work, then lay low until the next morning. As soon as we get with Xan and turn over the goods, Fat Daddy'll be squared up and he can walk free. Then shit can calm down and get back to regular biz at the shop too."

"Damn. We gone gank Chaos's shit right out from under his fuckin nose. How much product Xan think we gone get in the take?"

"A lot," Hood said. "Enough to pull Fat Daddy out the hole and pay off them cats in A.C."

"And Xan gone get him a big chunk of doe too, right? That nigga wouldn't even be thinking on this shit if there wasn't something sweet in it for him."

Hood shrugged. "Think he ain't? When you ever known Xan to do anything unless there's something big in it for him? It don't shock me that he's gunnin for Chaos. He been wanting Ocean Hill for a good minute now. He's prolly using this shit with Fat Daddy as a smokescreen so he can strip Chaos's boys outta all their product and then make his move on that territory."

Dreko whistled, then stood up and clapped as a giant

cat on the court got packed hard by a little nigga with rockets in his shoes.

"Xan is slick as hell," he said. "That cat's about to get over clean and muscle in on some new ground, man. And he's using me and you to accomplish that shit."

Hood slid his hands in his pockets. "I don't give a fuck what he do. It ain't about us, man. I'm doing this for Egypt. Fat Daddy gotta get his shit together and stop all that fuckin gambling and shit. But my baby ain't did nothing wrong. I can't risk having her getting exposed to no crossfire. If them cats come rolling for Fat Daddy and get a piece of my girl, I'ma have to go on a killing spree man . . ." Just the thought of something happening to Egypt sent fire racing through Hood's blood. "I just can't risk that shit, Dre. I just can't."

Dreko clapped again at the court happenings then looked over at his friend. "That ain't gone happen, man. You ain't even gotta think it. We gone get up in there and hit that mule so hard we break his fuckin back. And when we get back out here we'll take care of Xan and Fat Daddy too. Egypt gone be straight, my nig. Don't even worry about it. Ya girl is gonna be straight."

$ $ $

Egypt's last year of high school was turning out to be her best.

Unlike a lot of young chicks in this hood she had defied the odds and just about made it through four years

of high school without dropping out or getting pregnant, even though her and Lamont fucked like a bunch
of little devils every chance they got. Lamont *had* become a statistic though. One of those black males who
quit school early. While Egypt was disappointed that
her man hadn't hung in there to complete his education,
she had accepted his decision without tearing him down
for making it.

At seventeen and a half she was excited about college
and looking forward to the new challenges awaiting her.
Although going away someplace far for school had always
been her dream, Egypt's priorities had shifted over the
years and she was no longer in such a rush to get to Paris,
or London, or even to Washington, D.C.

The puppy love she had shared with Hood from childhood had never fallen off. If anything, what they had together had deepened and matured, just as they had, and
she couldn't even imagine going somewhere and not being
able to see him every day.

Besides, New York City had some of the best damn
schools in the world and it was definitely full of cultural
events and museums and stuff. Instead of leaving the
circling, protective arms of Fat Daddy and Hood and
traveling all over the planet by herself, Egypt planned
to get into the city more often and take in some Broad-
way shows, visit art galleries, and obtain a student mem-
bership to see the New York Philharmonic symphony
orchestra.

Egypt had applied to several schools, but Columbia University was tops on her list. It was in the Morningside Heights section of Manhattan, and she looked forward to putting on her iPod and riding the train there and back each day and enjoying the pulse of the city for hours in between.

But college tuition could be really expensive, and her guidance counselors in school had encouraged her to ask her father to go online and fill out the free federal application for student aid. Egypt had smiled and told them she would get on it right away, but that was a damn lie. Fat Daddy's cash and carry dealings were so far below the legal radar that it wasn't funny. There was no way in hell the proceeds from his shop were enough to support their hood-fabulous lifestyle, and he had long ago warned her that the IRS was always watching so she should never put his real social security number on anything.

But worrying about money was the furthest thing from Egypt's mind. Her father had all that on lock. She'd never worried about where cash was coming from before, and she wasn't about to start worrying now. Egypt thought about chicks like Zena, or even some of the other less fortunate girls in her graduating class, and while her heart hurt for them, she also thanked God she wasn't walking in their run-down shoes.

She was grateful and realized that she had been double-blessed. She'd grown up with an icon of a father who had given her the world and could hustle his way into anything he wanted. And she had a street nigga who had been loving her since childhood and who would gift wrap the moon and put it in her hands if she wanted him to.

The future loomed bright for Egypt and she was constantly giving thanks. She'd entered this world as the motherless child of a street hustler, and was on her way to graduating from high school and becoming a pre-med student at a prestigious university.

God was smiling down on her and Egypt knew she was exalted and highly favored.

CHAPTER 16

What kinda world you think you bringin babies in?
Another fatherless child around here runnin loose again?

WHILE EGYPT WAS basking in dreams of college and Hood and Dreko were out planning a lick, Zena was in hard labor and screaming as loud as she could.

"Don't scream. *Push*," a middle-aged nurse urged as she squeezed the young girl's hand and used a clean towel to pat perspiration from her flushed face.

Zena gasped against the pain and pushed down hard, grunting.

Her contractions had come on fast and furious, and if it wasn't for the Asian lady who worked in the neighborhood cleaners on Rockaway Avenue, Zena probably would have panicked and wilded out. Her feet and ankles had been swollen the whole day, but she'd had a craving for pancakes that just wouldn't go away. Sackie was out handling some business in the streets, and Dreko wasn't answering his cell, so Zena had pulled on some clothes and trudged up the street to Key Food to buy some pancake mix and a bottle of syrup.

It was on her way back that it happened. A breathtaking pain sliced through her stomach and shot out of her back like a bolt of lightning. Zena had been so surprised at the intensity of the pain that she doubled over and clutched her stomach, her breath snatched away. She stayed in that position until she was able to move, and had just stumbled toward a parked car when the second pain slammed into her and warm liquid gushed from between her thighs. Zena dropped her bag of groceries and screamed out loud.

The woman in the cleaners saw her from the window and came running out to help. She held Zena by her shoulders, and when she saw the big belly and the telltale wetness running down Zena's legs, she sat her gently down on the ground, then pulled out her cell phone and dialed 911.

For the past several hours Zena had been in hard labor, alone and terrified. She'd begged the nurses to call Dreko, but he still wasn't answering his phone. Neither was Sackie. Zena thought briefly of asking someone to call Egypt, but knew her friend was more than likely at school.

There was no one else she could count on, and Zena cried as she tried her best to do what the doctors were telling her to do: push her child out into the bright lights of the cold world.

While the pain was really bad, the fear that gripped her was even worse. Zena had never gone back to the clinic for her test results, despite the repeated letters and phone calls from the health-care nurse.

There was no telling what she might have been carrying and exposing everyone else to without their knowledge, but there was also no way in hell she could speak of it. For almost three months she'd been a big coward who couldn't muster up enough courage to face the truth, and now as her body was stretching and writhing and preparing to give birth to a new life, Zena wondered if her past was about to come back to haunt her.

The contractions were devastating. She grit her teeth and rode the agony, praying hard that her baby would be born healthy. With nurses on either side of her and a doctor between her legs, Zena talked to God and in her pain-induced delirium, she could have sworn He talked to her right back.

Later that night, in the early morning hours of the new day, Zena reached for the last of her strength and gave one final push. Her body submitted and her child entered the world, screaming in displeasure.

"Oh!" one of the nurses exclaimed with joy. "It's a girl! You have a beautiful baby girl!"

Zena's eyes crawled all over the baby when the doctor held her up in the air. Her heart pounded as she searched the tiny infant for some sign of a defect, but she saw none.

"Is she okay?" she asked, searching the doctor's face for a hint of concern. "Do you think something's wrong with her? Does she look okay?"

"She looks just fine," the doctor reassured her. We'll run a few routine tests and know a lot more later, but right now she looks just fine."

Zena sighed with relief then collapsed against the pillows. The child was small, but she looked perfect. She looked like her father, except her skin was pink and she had a full head of curly hair. Just perfect.

"Good job, mother," the other nurse complimented her, beaming. "She's going to be gorgeous. Have you picked out a name for her yet?"

Zena sighed weakly. Strands of hair stuck to her damp face as she grinned at her new baby. "Andreka," she said firmly, and despite everything she wished her baby's daddy could have been here standing right by her side. "I'm gonna name her Andreka. After her father."

CHAPTER 17

Speak no evil, just have your fun . . .

IT WAS DURING her four-week checkup at Brookdale Hospital that Zena finally got the news she had been running away from for months. Sackie was at the crib babysitting Andreka, and Zena was sitting across from the doctor who had delivered her child. She had come expecting them to ask her a few questions about how she was doing "down there" and to probably get examined, but instead the doctor had taken her into his small office where the words he spoke beat into her like a sledgehammer.

"I'm sorry, Miss Woodson," Dr. Beatty said softly, "the HIV test you took while you were in labor came back positive. According to the records kept by the Department of Health this is your third positive test result, which would indicate to us that you've been exposed to the virus that causes HIV and AIDS."

All the color drained out of Zena's face at the sound of those words. Thinking it might be true was one thing, but hearing the truth confirmed out loud was devastating.

Tears slipped from her eyes as Zena asked in a tiny, fearful voice, "W-w-what about my baby?"

The doctor's voice went even softer. "I'm sorry. Your daughter has tested positive for HIV antibodies."

Zena gasped and bit down on her lip as the doctor quickly reached for her hand.

"But that doesn't mean she has the virus or that her test results will stay that way," he added quickly. "Many babies seroconvert from a positive status to a negative one during the first year or so of their lives. We'll have to retest Andreka in a few months, but right now we need to concentrate on you. You'll have to keep yourself healthy if you want to keep your daughter healthy. Let's use this time to discuss a few treatment options."

It was all Zena could do not to jump up and rush out the room. If the doctor hadn't been sitting between her and the door, she would have busted out of there like a wild animal and never looked back.

Instead, she sat there and listened as he gave her a brief medical background on HIV and talked about the risks and benefits of drugs such as AZT and certain antibiotics.

He gave her a follow-up appointment but Zena just folded the paper in a small square and stuck it into her purse. She couldn't bring herself to talk or to ask any questions. She just cried silently as he spoke, and when he was done he took her hand again and looked deeply into her teary eyes.

"I know this is a lot to digest right now, and you don't have to try to understand it all right away. You'll continue to learn more about the disease as time goes on, and I'm sure you'll have a lot of questions then. The important thing to remember right now is that HIV is no longer an automatic death sentence. With the right attitude, counseling, medications, and proper nutrition, many people have learned to live with this virus instead of expecting to die from it. There's someone else who would like to come in and talk to you now, and I believe you'll find her a source of information and a great source of comfort as well."

Moments later Zena found herself staring at a woman who smelled like McDonald's apple pie and whose presence filled the room with soothing compassion. She was an HIV counselor. A sturdy-looking black woman in her fifties who had a big gap between her two front teeth and wore long, silver-dotted cornrows in her hair.

"Hello, darling," the woman said, her words riding on a kindly breath. "I'm Flora Baker, and I'm here to help you."

Instead of taking a seat at the desk Miss Baker came directly over to Zena. Without reservation she put her warm arms around the girl, enveloping her in something Zena had never felt before: a tender, motherly hug.

"It's okay," the woman said gently as Zena cried. She soothed and rocked her until signs of tension began leaving her body. "I know right now you're frightened and you probably feel like you're all alone. But you're not, baby. From now on I'm going to be here for you day or night, whenever you need me, and I promise you, we'll get through this together."

Zena was shocked. Wrapped for the first time in a pair of safe, womanly arms, she just let go. She opened her mouth and cried. Loud and hard. For herself just a little. For her infant daughter, a whole lot.

"M-m-m-my *baby!*" she wept into Miss Baker's breasts. All the fear and guilt she'd been carrying for months, and now the shame of what she may have done to her child came pouring out. "I gave it to my *baby!*"

"Yes," Miss Baker said gently, patting Zena's back. "Yes you did. But little babies are remarkable, sugar. A lot of times they surprise us, and with God's help they do all kinds of miraculous things. Now you'll have to bring her back to be retested, but in the meantime you just wait and pray, sweetheart. Wait and pray. Help is here now, for you and for your baby. Just wait and pray."

There was a strong sense of conviction in the old woman's words, as though she knew of what she spoke. But Zena had no such confidence in time or in God. She left the hospital with tears still in her eyes and headed back to the projects, on a mission. Less than thirty minutes later she had copped five vials and a stem from a trap boy on Newport Street. Back at the crib she marched straight past Sackie without saying a word and went into her bedroom and closed the door. With just a glance at her baby, who was sleeping soundly in her crib, Zena pulled out her stem, then dropped two rocks and sparked them up. She sat back and proceeded to smoke until the pain was no more.

CHAPTER 18

If you could see my face
You'd know not to hit your brakes . . .
We on ya heels nigga!

A FEW WEEKS after his meeting with Xanbar, Hood was moving through the darkness of a tiny project apartment in Ocean Hill, gat in hand. Ignoring the old lady crying on the floor, he stormed into the kitchen and swung his pistol, busting the lip of one of the three crack dealers they'd just tied up and robbed.

Blood splattered. Dude screamed. A click sounded behind him and Hood whirled around.

"Yeah, muhfucka," Dreko said gleefully. His eyes were cold and dark. He held his Sig out away from his body and a sickening grin spread across his handsome face. "I got one in the head now, nigga," he shouted to Hood. "Which one of these pussies you think I should blast first?"

Hood held his hand up, checking his boy. These niggas ain't mean shit to him. Xanbar had sent them out on a mission to hit Chaos's spot, and the only reason he was out here ganking the joint at all was to pay off Fat Daddy's debt.

Hood kept searching, looking for the package that would save Fat Daddy's life, and probably Egypt's too. He turned over furniture and pulled out drawers, tossing the crib up trying to find the goods. Behind him he could hear Dreko still in the kitchen pistol-whipping niggas left and right. He laughed the whole time like he was getting off on that shit too.

Hood checked behind the shower curtain in a small bathroom, and then went inside a dirty bedroom. He pulled a pissy mattress off the bed, then swept all kinds of musty shit off the top shelf of the closet. Frustrated, he kicked over a dresser and yanked out the drawers, throwing clothes in the air as he ran his fingers over the rough wood making sure there were no secret compartments.

A funny sound put him on alert, and he turned his head in the direction of the kitchen. Dreko wasn't laughing no more. That nigga was cursing now.

Hood crept out of the room with his arms outstretched and his gat trained. He kept his back to the wall, and as he approached the living room the picture became crystal clear. The front door was open a crack. Glass hit the floor in the kitchen and shattered, and the sounds of a brutal fight could be heard. He crossed the living room in five long steps and swung his arms left, aiming into the kitchen.

Dreko was scuffling. A big nigga wearing a leather coat had rushed into the spot. He had a thick bull head and he was going at Dreko's ass. They struggled over Dreko's Sig, punching, grunting, and kneeing. Flinging each other from the stove, to the window, they crashed into the small table as they both tried to stay out of barrel-range. Hood was a skull-splitter to his heart but he didn't wanna shoot his boy by mistake. He cracked Chaos's mule in the back of the head with his piece and drew bright red blood. Dude turned and glared at him, but kept right on fighting like it wasn't nothing but a mosquito bite. Hood cracked him again, and went in for one more, but the nigga swung Dreko around to get his dome smashed instead.

The three of them tussled some more, everybody trying to gain control of Dreko's gat. Hood was dead on him, jumping up to nail the cat in the forehead this time. But a hard left got swung and down his boy went. Now Dreko's Sig was in dude's hands, with a round already in the head, ready to fly.

There was nothing to think about. Hood fired at close range, striking the cat in his neck. The force of the bullet spun the guy halfway around and he dropped the gun. Blood gushed and his feet got twisted beneath him as he crumbled to the floor clutching his neck and moaning.

Them niggas tied up against the wall was really scared now. Screaming, "Umph! Eeehh! Omghf!" around their gags, they tried to duck their heads and ball up in knots, scared the next hot one would be sinking into their own flesh.

"M-m-uhfuçka!" Dreko stuttered. He'd caught a killer blow to the temple that had damn near knocked him out. Reaching for his Sig, he steadied himself on his hands and knees, shaking his head to clear it. Hood kept his gun trained on the dude who lay writhing on the floor.

"Get the fuck up, man," he told Dreko. Already he could hear nosy people poking their heads outta their apartments asking what was that. "We gotta roll, my nigga. Five-o gonna be crawling all over this bitch in a minute."

Dreko grabbed hold of the counter and pulled himself to his feet. Swaying, he stuck his gun down his pants then rocked backward and fell against the refrigerator, still drunk from that killer punch. Hood grabbed his boy by the shoulder and steadied him. Nigga was gone hafta get his feet under him real quick because it was jet time.

The thought that Xanbar mighta been wrong about this being the drop spot ran across Hood's mind for a second, but as dizzy as Dreko was, his G senses was still working. Hood glanced toward the apartment door. Voices were right outside. When he looked back, Dreko had the situation in hand. There was a small black duffel bag leaning against the refrigerator. The hammer-head nigga moaning and rolling on the floor musta brought it in with him because it hadn't been there before. Relief came down on Hood as Dreko grabbed the bag and staggered toward him. Together, they ran toward the back of the apartment where a second door served as an emergency fire exit. There was one like it in every apartment, and each one led to a back staircase that would bring them out in the rear of the building.

It was dark on the windowless stairs, and most people used the area to store bicycles and boxes full of old shit. Hood and Dreko tripped and slipped, jumped over rusty shopping carts and broken TVs, until they burst through the exit-only doorway and out onto the busy streets.

The moment they hit the pavement they took off in opposite directions, traveling different paths to a pre-arranged location.

Hood had gone little more than half a block when he heard the sirens blaring. Forcing himself to slow down and be easy, he stopped to dap a couple of come ups hanging on the corner, then sauntered into a Spanish grocery store and bought a bottle of water and an apple.

He walked the rest of the way munching slowly on his apple like he didn't have a care in the world. An ambulance sped past him followed by a police van, but they didn't fuck with him and he sure didn't fuck with them. He made it back to their prearranged rally spot—an abandoned building on Hopkinson Avenue—with no problem, and after crawling through a back window he went up on the second floor and stepped into a back room to wait for Dreko.

$ $ $

The take was grand. They didn't get no cake, but the yay was lovely.

"Yeah!" Dreko was excited as fuck as they stared at the endless rows of packaged powder stuffed in the bag. There was an easy half mil in street value cocaine staring up at them, and Hood was more than satisfied. There were two things in his life that nobody better not fuck with. Egypt and his mother. While he couldn't make his moms act right and stop getting high, pulling this lick to save Fat Daddy and Egypt was well worth the risks he'd taken and the nigga he'd had to pop.

"All right," he told Dreko. He was ready to get down to business but his boy was fuckin fascinated. Dreko stared at the dope and ran his fingers over the baggies like he was standing in front of a duffle bag full of big tittie bitches.

"Man, pay attention," Hood told him. "We still got moves to make. Xan gone meet us up on Lott Avenue in the morning and we need to sit on this shit until then. Chaos might come gunnin but fuck that grimy nigga. His shit was weak and we got the drop on him. That's how it goes."

"Nah," Deko waved his hand, his eyes never leaving the goods. "Don't worry about Chaos. That nigga ain't gone be on the streets much longer. His reign is almost over. I can feel it." He grinned and shook his head. "Man, we got that shit, didn't we?!? Aww, man!" He held out his hand for some dap, and Hood let him have it. "Yo nigga, you smart as hell. How much you think we got here? I mean, cut up, cooked, and packaged right and ere'thang? What you think that'll bring us?"

Hood shrugged. "It don't matter 'cause it ain't bringing us nothing but five G's a piece, Dreko. This is Xan's fuckin product, remember? This dope got Fat Daddy's head riding on it. And maybe Egypt's too."

Dreko nodded real quick. "Yeah, nigga! I know all that shit. I'm just sayin . . . how fuckin much you think *Xan* gone pocket off this shit?"

"Shit," Hood laughed bitterly. He zipped the bag closed and a light seemed to shut off in Dreko's eyes when the dope disappeared from view. "Like he said, it gotta be at least half a mil. Minimum. Prolly more. Depends on the cut."

"That's a lot of fuckin paper," Dreko said. "A nigga could build an empire off some loose change like that. Xan a lucky muhfucka."

"Nah, Fat Daddy the lucky one. Nigga squared up now and he betta keep it that way."

All night long they nursed that bag full of drugs like it was an egg that needed to hatch. By now word was sure to be all over the streets about the robbery, and definitely about the shooting. Hood and Dreko took turns standing guard over their take in shifts, sleeping very little. They switched up every two hours. While one was in the front window watching the street, the other was in the back room guarding the dope.

By the time the sun came up both men were anxious.

Hood stuck his head out as far as he could, peering down the street. He'd wanted to move out early, but Dreko cautioned him to wait.

"You need to chill, nigga," Dreko warned, shaking his head. "Let's stick to the plan, baby. Nine-thirty, and not a second before that. We're going up on Lott Avenue. There's a school right there, remember? The last thing we want is to be waiting out there too early. Little kids be out there holding hands crossing the street and shit, and two hood niggas standing around holding a fuckin duffel bag. Full of dope. We might as well walk on into the precinct and give it up."

"Yeah. You right. Nine thirty."

But at nine fifteen shit popped off from an unexpected direction.

Bam! Bam! Bam!

Hood was sitting on a cold radiator when the sounds of drama arose from the side of the empty house.

"Shit!" Hood was on his feet in a flash and looking around for someplace to stash his burner. The cops had teams coming in from all directions. The closest one had busted through a side window after hopping the ledge from an occupied apartment building next door. Other sounds of smashing wood and glass filled the air as Dreko's voice rang out above the noise.

"Right here! Slide that shit right here!"

Hood slid the gat all the way across the dirty linoleum and Dreko scooped it up and ducked back into the rear of the apartment.

"The roof!" Hood called at his back, and he saw his boy nod as he jumped on top of an overturned box and pushed out a ceiling tile, disappearing from sight.

Hood never even turned around when he heard the running footsteps barreling toward him. He just raised his hands in the air as he was tackled from behind, his mind cold, but his heart warm. Dreko had the product and Xanbar would get paid. Fat Daddy's life would be spared and Egypt's life would be saved. Sometimes it be like this on the streets. It was all part of the game. Hood nodded to himself as they put the cuffs on him, satisfied. His bank was stacked and his team was straight. What more could a G nigga ask for?

CHAPTER 19

Now it seems so funny when they see you getting money . . .
How the jiggas all smile and pretend to be friendly,
Now the haters getting loud but we see it's all envy,
We was down, we was out, but we couldn't get a penny . . .

DREKO MOVED FAST.

Crouching down, he watched from the roof as three detectives broke down the front door of the building and tossed Hood out like a bag of dirty laundry. One of the DTs, a fat cat with bright red hair swung his revolver across Hood's face, busting him up. Then the other two picked him up and slammed him against the squad car and punched him down to the ground. His boy was handcuffed and defenseless, and Dreko's breathing was heavy with excitement. Even from where he crouched he could tell that despite the ass-stomping they were putting on Hood, the shit didn't seem to bother him one bit. He took the punches and the club-blows with nothing more than a grunt or two in response, and when Hood was viciously cracked across his face with a backhand billy-club blow that sent blood spraying across the hood of the police car, Dreko grinned.

He was down off the roof and back on the streets moments after the police cars cleared the area, and even though he had a tight plan he was really relying on his street senses to get him through. He stashed the drugs in one of his old spots, pulled his hoody over his head, and took off walking down the back alleys toward Ocean Hill.

He stayed off the main streets and away from the projects as much as possible. With a million apartments and ten million windows, you could never tell who was watching you or from where. Moving around in daylight was dangerous as fuck, especially since the element of time was no longer on his side. It had taken them fuckin cops forever to show up, and that meant precious minutes had been wasted. He took a longer path than he wanted to, but it gave him the least amount of exposure to anybody in his old crew so he figured it was worth it.

By now Chaos was well aware of what he'd lost the night before. No doubt some of his most loyal niggas was already out there gunning for some get back. But in the weeks since Dreko had agreed to Xan's proposition to hit Chaos's mule, Dreko had been scheming and planning harder than a muthafucka. Night and day he had been gaming and setting shit up for a big showdown. In just a short period of time he had managed to assemble himself a loyal cast of come up gunners, and catching both Chaos and Xanbar out there was gonna be one sweet party that Dreko couldn't wait to attend.

Forty minutes after coming down off that roof, Dreko slipped into the foyer of an Ocean Hill building next to a pizza shop. There were two doors facing him, and before he could knock the one on the left opened.

"Whattup, Riff."

"Time to roll?" asked a tall light-skinned cat dressed in the latest fly gear. Jewels dripped from his neck and a large scar ran across his forehead from the brutal denting he'd taken from Hood's gun.

Riff's eyes glinted with excitement. He was about to undergo a serious career change. Chaos was about to be out and Ocean Hill would be his. In exchange for his co-operation Dreko was gonna slide him half a duffel bag of dope, and in return Riff would supply the manpower and the clips full of lead.

He dapped Dreko out and nodded. It was his time, and his dun dun status was about to be elevated to boss don. Riff gestured inside the room where there were about twenty other rollers. Chaos's disgruntled best. Strapped and ready to lock it up with their former boss and any of his loyal goons who wanted to go down with him.

Dreko dapped Riff back and grinned. His boy didn't hold no hard feelings behind that shit with Hood all them years ago. It was business back then, and it was still business now. Besides, Dreko's plan was tight and his dick was hard. Hit the head, then watch the body fall. He'd smash 'em with a vicious combination. Chaos first, then that boastful nigga Xan right after. Yeah. Them muhfuckas might didn't know, but they was about to find out.

$ $ $

"I got some bad news."

Egypt pressed her cell phone closer to her ear. She'd heard what he'd said, but didn't understand why Dreko was on the other end of her line with those words coming out of his mouth.

She glanced toward the door. She was at the Washington Heights medical school campus of Columbia Univerisity interviewing with a panel of four doctors who would determine if she was worthy of participating in a full mentorship program. She thought the question and answer session had gone extremely well, and not only the panelists seemed to be impressed by her grades and her ambition, they'd complimented her on having such a vivacious personality and the drive to pursue her personal goals.

"Would you please excuse us for a few minutes, Egypt?" the lead panelist had asked as all four doctors rose from their seats. "We're going to step into the conference room and give your application one last review. It shouldn't take long, so please help yourself to some coffee and cookies on the back table. There's juice and bottled water available as well. We'll be back very shortly."

The door closed behind them and Egypt listened to their retreating footsteps as she mentally analyzed every amazing detail of the interview. She had smiled brightly and answered all their questions with passion and intelligence. They seemed highly impressed when they learned that she'd been raised by a single father in one of the worst neighborhoods in Brooklyn, yet she still managed to emerge as a well-rounded A student who was also a skilled dancer and had trained as a pianist.

Egypt walked to the back of the room and nibbled on a cookie as she tried to maintain her confidence. College was going to be tough, but she'd been preparing for this day her whole life. It was the financing part of her dreams that was starting to make her wonder.

"Don't you worry about nothing, baby," Fat Daddy had repeatedly reassured her over the years. "You just do your part by making them grades, baby. Work hard to get into a good school 'cause the money ain't gonna be a problem. I'll handle that."

But Egypt was starting to wonder if all the dreams her father had sold her were anything other than just pipe dreams. These days he walked around worried and nervous all the time, and Egypt had overheard him telling Felton that he'd fucked up on some business dealings and was just about broke.

While Fat Daddy had made it a rule to keep Egypt busy with her activities and away from the shop and his business as much as possible, she had picked up on some of the recent drama going down between Xanbar and her father, and that shit had pissed her off.

Fat Daddy had always been a well-respected big willie, but something must have happened to cause him to lose his status, and now Xan was out to humiliate him. It hurt Egypt's heart to see them young street niggas bossing her father around like he wasn't shit. Ordering both of them to stay cooped upstairs in the apartment while they tore shit up downstairs in the shop like it was theirs.

But what was worse was what Egypt saw in her father's eyes. Fear. Big time fear. And shame too. In almost no time Fat Daddy had gone from a street icon whose barber shop was a central spot for niggas in the know, to a low-level sniveler who had to beg cats half his age just to walk outta his own front door.

Egypt's stomach tightened with worry. She had just put a mint chocolate chip cookie back on the sterling tray when her cell phone vibrated and startled her.

"What bad news?" she said, walking back to her chair and sitting down.

"It's about Hood," Dreko said softly. "He got in a little trouble. We was trying to help your pops outta a bad spot, and Hood got knocked."

For a moment Egypt lost her breath. Her stomach clenched hard and her bowels turned to water. "Knocked? Mont's locked up? What did y'all do? What the fuck happened, Dreko? He tried to help my father out of *what*?"

Egypt could hear the footsteps coming down the hall but the only thing real to her was Dreko's voice.

"Not on the phone," he said gently. "Meet me at Zena's crib and I'll fill you in later."

Egypt's mouth hung open as Dreko hung up and the line went dead in her hands. There was nothing in her world except Lamont. Nothing in her vision, nothing she could hear, nothing in her heart. Nothing in her universe. Only Lamont.

And when the door swung open and the smiling doctors walked back into the room, they were all shocked as the pretty young black girl who seemed so full of promise rushed past them with tears streaming down her face. The look of torture and pain in her eyes was so shocking that all they could do was watch in silence as she fled from the room, the sound of her footsteps echoing miserably down the hall.

CHAPTER 20

How you gone come at your father?
That's like a character in a book tryna come at the author!

THE GAME DIDN'T change for Sackie when Hood got snatched off the streets. If anything, it had gotten even grimier. Hood hadn't even been in cuffs for more than a few hours when the hood alarm sounded, signifying that trouble was on the streets and that Dreko had bounced and was absent from the game.

Sackie's gutta instincts were really on fire a week or so later when Xan called him down to Fat Daddy's shop to tell him about a little organizational restructuring.

"You next, baby!" Xan told Sackie. Business was booming in barbershop-land and Xanbar was now raking in all of Fat Daddy's profits. Every chair in the shop had a street hustler sitting in it, and even more cats was congregating around waiting their turn to get trimmed up. "So congratulations. Unless them motherfuckers get soft and turn Hood loose, you the number one man on your strip now. You runnin your sector."

Sackie kept his mouth closed. Word on the street spread fast. It didn't take no mathematician to figure out that shit wasn't adding up. Chaos's night crew had been tied up and gun-beat. His mule had taken one to the throat, then lost possession of his product. Hood got knocked, and Dreko got ghost. And now Sackie was supposed to get out there and play front-man in one of Xan's largest sectors? He felt like a white-ass sheep getting set up for slaughter.

Xan turned and nodded to Lil Jay. "Nigga, that means you number two now. Live up to that shit."

Lil Jay got swole. "Man, you gone elevate this cat on top of me? What? I followed behind Hood, now I'm supposed to follow behind his pale ass too?" He shook his head and frowned, defiant. "Hell nah. Why I gotta roll second to a fuckin white boy?"

"White boy?" Xan looked around. "What white boy?" He glanced over his left shoulder, then over his right. "You talkin 'bout Sackie?" He laughed. "Nah, you got it wrong, Jay, Sackie ain't no white boy. This cat here is a down-ass *nigga*. This dude been ya man since the sandbox and just 'cause he a light-skinned G you got problems with him?" Xan laughed again. "Sackie's my number one nigga in your sector." Xan's eyes suddenly became cold and dangerous. "You got that?"

"So whattup with Dreko then?" Lil Jay pressed. "All of a sudden that dude's whereabouts are a big mystery. I thought he was next up?"

At the mention of Dreko's name razors stopped buzzing, all talk ceased, and every ear in the joint went on high alert.

"Dreko . . ." Xan said, twirling his thumbs. Sackie could feel the danger in the air and sensed he was about to get caught up in it. "Oh, don't worry about that nigga. He gone get set straight."

Later that night Sackie found himself sitting in on a death council in the back of Fat Daddy's shop, right in the same room where Hood and Moo used to sleep. Fat Daddy had been barred from his own establishment, and right now he was huddled upstairs in his apartment, guarded by four goons. For months Xan had had his ass on a total debt repayment plan. Not only wasn't Fat Daddy making a dime off the shop's register, all the hot shit he hadn't gambled away had been dished off, the proceeds going straight into Xan's pocket.

Sackie wasn't feeling the shit that was about to jump off. Hood hadn't been able to save Fat Daddy from Xan's deadly wrath, but with Dreko and a stolen half mil in tan goods missing, somebody had to pay. For the hundredth time he hated what Dreko was about. He hated that his sister had gotten so deeply involved with him even more.

"So that's how it's gone be," Xan said, finalizing things. "Dreko gotta pay. Easy, you and Gardner, I want your crews out there sniffing for that muhfucka," he ordered. "Fif, y'all niggas go get Fat Daddy. Tell him he better get on the phone and say good-bye to his fuckin daughter 'cause his clock just ran out."

Ten minutes later Sackie and Lil Jay stood by as Fat Daddy was muscled down the stairs and into the back room. His mouth had been gagged and his hands were taped behind his back, but that didn't stop him from struggling.

"Omhueee! Eeeeuh! Ohh!" His muffled cries were pitiful as he let his weight fall back against the goonies while he tried to kick out with his feet. Two niggas went down under all that glob, pulling Fat Daddy down on top of them. His legs flailed in the air as he screamed and tears fell from his eyes. "Eeeee-uh! Eeeee-uh!"

Sackie looked away when he realized that Fat Daddy was calling out his last words to Egypt. Fif stepped around the bodies struggling on the floor and gun-smashed Fat Daddy across his mouth, cutting off his cries. Blood soaked the rag that had been stuffed halfway down his throat, and Fat Daddy went limp.

A true product of the hood, Sackie had seen many cats get theirs. A couple of times he had been the one giving it to them too. That's how shit went on the streets. Anybody could get took down at anytime. But still, it was hard for him to watch Fat Daddy get worked over. Yeah, the dude had fucked up and lost his spine, but c'mon . . . Sackie couldn't help curse that slimy fool Dreko. All this shit woulda been squared up if Hood hadn't gotten knocked. If the drugs had been delivered to Xan as planned.

Xanbar's boys worked quickly on Fat Daddy. In minutes he was hog-tied to his barber chair and the rags removed from his mouth.

Xanbar taunted him. "What's that you tryna say, nigga? Huh? Oh, you got my money? Where it at then, big man. Where it at?"

Fat Daddy babbled. "Please man! C'mon, Xan. Hood gone get you the money! My boy gone come through. I swear to God!"

"Hood knocked, nigga! Got himself a piece of that big stank rock!"

Terror shone in Fat Daddy's eyes. "This me, Xan! This ya Fat Daddy! We been through a lotta good shit over the years, man! I been down for you your whole fuckin life!"

Sackie turned his head. He couldn't stand to watch Fat Daddy beg.

"Fuck all that. You know the rules, muhfucka. You trampled on my doe," Xan said. "And that shit is unpardonable."

"I was your *man*," Fat Daddy pleaded. "And you can do some shit like this to me? Huh? My little girl *loves* you, and you know I'm all she got, Xan! Man you can do this kinda shit to *me?*"

Xanbar frowned, and moved in closer. "Now you graspin, nigga. You desperate, and you graspin. This ain't about Egypt, fool. You knew you had a daughter when you was out there overstating ya fuckin bets."

"FUCK YOU!!" Fat Daddy screamed. It was his time to die and the cruelty in Xanbar's eyes told him there was no hope left. Sweat dripped from his face and his eyes bulged. He strained against his binds, his flesh jiggling as blind rage consumed him.

Lil Jay stepped out the way as Xan cursed and lunged. He grabbed one of Felton's electric clippers from his station and rammed it straight into Fat Daddy's mouth. The big man yelped, then gurgled, choking as Xan drove the clipper home, stuffing it as far down his victim's throat as he could.

Fat Daddy thrashed against his ropes. With wild eyes, he whipped his head back and forth desperately trying to dislodge the clippers from his bloody mouth.

Sackie couldn't watch anymore, but he didn't really have to. Listening to the hitching sounds Fat Daddy made as he tried to suck air around the clippers was just as bad as watching him choke to death with the razor cord hanging out of his mouth.

And if he thought that shit was bad, it was nothing compared to the painful, deep-throated squeals Fat Daddy let out when two of Fif's sons bent his fingers back and used one of his own barber tools to peel off his fingernails, one by one.

Sackie was sickened as blood ran from Fat Daddy's torn nail beds and dripped onto the floor. Tears rolled down his fat face and he was still gasping for small breaths, but he was no longer struggling. Only suffering.

"Hey son," Xanbar called out, pointing his chin at Sackie. "Its time to get'cha gangsta tested. Grab your burner and blast this fat piece of shit into next week."

There was no hesitation in Sackie whatsoever. He was white, not fuckin stupid. If he bucked Xan's order he'd find himself tied up in a chair right next to Fat Daddy with who-the-fuck-knew-what stuffed in his mouth. He pulled his tool out of his jacket and proceeded to aim at Fat Daddy's top.

"Wait!" Xan hollered, halting him. "Crazy muhfucka what you doing? You can't cap this nigga in the head! How the fuck he gone look laying up in his casket with half a face? You want Egypt to flip the fuck out?"

Sackie lowered the piece until his barrel was at the level of Fat Daddy's chest. *This is a mercy killing*, he told himself then squeezed the trigger twice. Fast. Fat Daddy's body jerked, and then he was still. That horrible sound coming from his throat was gone, and Sackie was relieved. *You put him outta his misery*, he told himself, trying to ease his feelings of guilt. It was no different than putting down a horse or a wounded dog. Egypt oughta thank him for doing what he did to her father, but deep inside Sackie knew she wouldn't.

$ $ $

While Dreko's life had suddenly changed for the better, Egypt's life had fallen completely apart. Nothing about her world was right anymore, and she couldn't believe how fast she'd fallen into the gutter. She had visited Lamont on Rikers two days after he got knocked, and she'd cried so hard that she had probably embarrassed him.

"It's cool, baby," Lamont had whispered as he tried to comfort her. "I'm straight, E. Don't worry about me, baby. Please stop. Don't do this to yourself. The only thing in here that I can't handle is your tears, baby. So please. *Please* don't cry."

But Egypt just couldn't stop. The tears ran from her eyes like water. She was weak and worried and her emotions were totally out of control. She wept at the thought of her man sleeping in a cold cell at night, and at the sight of him wearing those prison clothes, and even at the jailhouse sounds that assaulted her ears. She wept at the situation she'd been facing at home too, as her father tried hard to pretend everything was all right and that with Xan holding him prisoner in their apartment and Lamont being in jail, all her dreams hadn't suddenly dissolved into nightmares as her life was ripped from its foundation and turned upside down.

Almost overnight Egypt's world had begun to lose its balance. She'd been dragging herself to school each day but found it almost impossible to concentrate as her final exams neared. Her advanced classes at night seemed pretty pointless too. It had become real clear to her that there wasn't no damn college fund waiting for her after graduation. Medical school was out the window too. A few days earlier she and her father had cried together as he held her in his arms and confessed that the reason they were broke and Lamont was in jail was because Fat Daddy had gambled on their future and lost it all big time.

Of course Egypt had been angry, but sadness and despair had quickly replaced her anger. She loved her father with all her heart. No matter what he'd done. He had raised her to be the best and to have the best, and he'd done it alone and the only way he knew how. Fat Daddy's pain was Egypt's pain too, and she could see how embarrassed and ashamed he was of fucking things up for both of them.

"Just stay in school," Fat Daddy had told her. "I'll figure something out, baby. I swear. On your mother's *grave*. I'll figure something out."

So Egypt had trudged onward each day although her focus was completely gone. She had trouble sleeping at night and staying awake during the day. Tonight she'd fallen asleep in her class and on the way home she'd almost slept past her stop on the train too.

And now, standing in front of the shop, Egypt was preparing to unlock the door that led up to their apartment when she realized something was wrong. For the first time since she could remember the shop was dark and quiet way before midnight. No Xan, no henchmen, no hustlers, nothing. Just quiet.

Craning her neck, Egypt looked up at her second floor window. The multicolored lights coming from the background of the living room window told her the television was on upstairs and her father was there.

She stepped toward the shop entrance and stuck her key in the lock. The moment the door swung open and she clicked on the light, Egypt began screaming, and over a week later it didn't seem like she had ever really stopped.

The sight that greeted her would haunt her to her grave.

A slumped figure faced her in the barber's chair. It was Fat Daddy. Her *father*.

His dead eyes were wide with pain and horror. An electric clipper was crammed halfway down his throat. Most of his fingernails were torn off, and the black and white tiled floor was splattered red with his blood.

Egypt's screams were more like death wails. She squeezed her eyes closed and sank to her knees, nearly blacking out from grief. Big Monk ran over from the hero shop next door, and several customers followed him. He lifted Egypt to her feet and she passed out in his arms.

The police were called for Fat Daddy and the ambulance came for Egypt. They medicated her at the hospital, and at some point Sackie had shown up and taken her home with him.

For days Egypt cried a constant stream of anguished tears. Her heart was swollen with grief and she was far from being the tough, strong sistah she'd always thought she was. She didn't eat, she didn't wash her ass, and she definitely did not close her eyes. Because when she did, all she could see was the horrible nightmare image of her father's bloody, tortured corpse. No matter how hard she tried, she could not erase the grisly death scene from her mind. She couldn't erase it from her heart either.

CHAPTER 21

Dead prez niggas'll be bootin you down,
If he move, I'ma Uz him, I ain't foolin around!
Niggas fuckin wit' a hooligan now!

LESS THAN A week later Lil Jay was standing on his corner like a good little trap boy. Sackie was his man and all, but he was still pissed about having to take orders from the cat. It just didn't look right.

Jay pulled hard on his Newport and wished he had a beer or something. A lot of shit had gone down in a short period of time, and with Hood off the streets the whole neighborhood felt shook.

He leaned against a stoop and watched the traffic. Whips and hoopties swished up and down the avenue and winos stumbled in and out of the liquor store on the corner. The owner of the store was in Xan's pocket, and that's where the corner boys warmed up in the winter or ducked inside to take a piss during the summer.

A tiny sister with a blond weave and a fierce booty walked past teetering on high heels. Lil Jay gazed at the definition in her thighs as her emerald green skirt flapped out and back, stopping right beneath her bold ass.

His eyes were deep in that split between her legs when a beemer sedan rolled up and the passenger window went down. The first face he saw was real familiar, but his mind couldn't compute it when he glanced at the driver. What the fuck was these two niggas doing together? And then it hit him. Dreko was on the move, and had run straight to Chaos's crew.

"Whassup?" Lil Jay nodded. Why the fuck was this crazy nigga still rollin for one, and rollin up in Xanbar's territory with that banned nigga Riff and a car full of Chaos's boys for two? That's not how the game was played and Lil Jay smelled that nasty rat. Him and the rest of the dope boys had been hoping Xan's gorillas would straight smoke Dreko's ass for dippin with that product, thus making the strip safer for them all.

But the cat was very much alive. In the flesh, and holding his gat.

"I heard Fat Daddy got popped. That your body?"

Lil Jay shook his head. "Nah. Sackie's. Fucked up, though. Fat Daddy was legit. Shit ain't have to go down that way. So whassup?"

"You tell me." Dreko smirked, then nodded his head like yeah nigga, what?

Lil Jay shrugged, his eye on Dreko's gun. "Same shit, man. On this grind. I heard you ran into a little static yourself. You cool?"

"Nah, no static. I'm straight. I want this corner though."

Lil Jay stood up straight. His eyebrows went up.

"*This* corner?"

Dreko nodded. His tool looked like ebony evil in his hands.

"*Xan's* corner?"

"Ain't none of this shit gone be Xan's in a minute. So you got a choice, Lil Jay. You wanna go down defending ya block, or you wanna switch teams?"

The decision was a no-brainer. Dreko's piece would spit hot death before Lil Jay could make a move.

"You offering me a new job, Dre?"

Again, Dreko nodded.

"Sheeit," Lil Jay laughed and stepped down off the curb. "Man . . . when a nigga start?"

$ $ $

Taking Chaos down was easy.

He went peacefully too, without a single shot being fired.

It was almost comical to watch as the feds rolled up on him coming out of a pizza joint and slapped him in cuffs. Dreko stood across the street in a darkened doorway and laughed at the look of surprise and bewilderment on Chaos's face when he realized that he'd gotten knocked without warning.

Chaos had got caught out there all alone on the strip without a single soldier left guarding his perimeter to send out a street alarm. Riff had choked his former boss's goonies so tight that not one little birdie had managed to fly in and whisper a heads-up in his ear.

Riff had wanted to just take the nigga out and be done with him. Pop one off in the back of his dome, but Dreko had checked him. "Nah. That nigga got mad enemies. Putting him out on that Rock's gone be a punishment worse than death."

With his son Riff in charge and Ocean Hill under his thumb, Dreko and his crew crept into Brownsville. One by one they rolled up on Easy, Fif, Gardner, Sip, and Georgie, and popped them all. They ran up on a lot of other dudes too. Those cats who wanted to live, like Vandy, Kels, and Monk, switched sides with a quickness. Those whose loyalty to Xanbar ran bone-deep . . . died.

By the end of the night they had enough flipped niggas in the cut to straight catch Xan with his pants down. They slid up to his crib about twenty deep.

Kels's brother Calvin was on the front door and the moment he heard Dreko's prearranged knock, he eased that shit open.

He waved Dreko and his crew toward a back bedroom where the sounds of good fucking could be heard. Inside, they peeped Xanbar banging a local freak. With his pants around his ankles, Xan had her bent at the waist dog fucking the shit outta her. Wearing only a wifebeater, his naked ass swirled and pounded, digging that gushy out as the chick moaned and panted.

"Freeze, muhfucka!" Dreko laughed, pointing his Glock.

Xan's ass kept pumping as he turned his head slowly to the side.

His shooter was strapped to his calf, too far away to reach, and besides, he had two hands full of titties anyway.

Xan's eyes met Dreko's over his shoulder. Fear wasn't in them. Danger was.

"Go head," Dreko told him, nodding at the burner strapped to Xan's leg. "Let go a' one of them titties and reach for that burner nigga. I'll wait."

Xanbar's dick slid out of the broad with a wet slish. He pushed her down to the floor, then slowly dragged his feet around until he was facing Dreko, Kels, Falcon, and Lil Jay.

Kels chuckled. Xan stood there with his wifebeater pulled up above his navel, and his fat dick semisoft and glistening with pussy juice.

He looked at Lil Jay with cold contempt in his eyes. "You lil bitch," he said, spitting toward his former cat. "I always knew Dreko had some street game, but I shoulda known your bitch ass couldn't hold. Why you think I put a smart white boy in charge of your stupid black ass?"

Lil Jay popped one from his gat before he even realized it was in his hand. Fire flew from the barrel and Xanbar screamed.

"Oh shit!" Kels hollered. "You shot that nigga's dick off!"

Xanbar went down to his knees clutching his groin and screaming in agony. Lil Jay glanced at Dreko and shrugged.

"Ooops. My bad."

Dreko walked over to Xanbar and watched him writhe and scream on the floor. The trick he had been banging had crawled underneath the bed and was down there screaming too.

Dreko dragged her out by one ankle.

"C'mon, baby. Get out from there." He helped her stand up, then put his arm around her as he let his fingers brush her naked breast. "Was that nigga's dick any good? It's laying over there on the floor now, in case you still want it."

The girl didn't know what to do. She cried and babbled, "No! No! I mean yes it was! Oh, no! I mean it wasn't!"

Dreko laughed, then picked up a bright orange dress from the bed and tossed it to her. "Get dressed. We got some biz to see about in here, and you don't wanna be around for this."

"Th-th-thank you!" she stammered, nodding her head and making her titties and her fake curls bounce. "I'm leaving," she whispered, pulling the dress over her head. "I'm leav—"

Pop! Pop!

She hit the floor and the dress fluttered down with her, her head and shoulders encased in the material, the rest of her naked body on display for all to see. Bright red blood pooled on the floor beneath her, spreading out in a circle around her body.

Still clutching the stump of his torn-off dick, Xanbar chuckled, grimacing in pain.

"I knew you was a fuckin bitch!" he laughed. "Taking out a chick! Suck my nuts, Dreko, you mental mother-fuckah!"

Dreko didn't bother to answer. Instead he fired twice. The first round caught Xan in the shoulder and he grunted. The second one was lower and it shattered his shin. Dreko's third shot hit Xan in the crook of his arm in front of his elbow, and his final shot was supposed to strike him in the throat, but Xan jerked and the bullet tore into his mouth instead.

Mission complete, Dreko thought as his team strolled from the apartment and hit their whips, pulling off slowly into traffic. Dreko's sweep plan had been sweet. Now the corners belonged to him, and his army was on guard. He was a fuckin general who had finally taken his place at the top. Dreko laughed, then checked his watch. Time was money. He had an empire to run.

CHAPTER 22

This ain't love, but I would love it to be . . .

EGYPT WAS COMPLETELY torn down.

If it wasn't for Zena she wouldn't have had the will to get out of the bed. Not even to use the bathroom. The pain was just that bad.

"I wanna die, Zena," Egypt had moaned over and over as she tore at her own clothes and rocked herself in grief. "Oh, God . . . I just wanna die."

Zena shook her head firmly and fought back her own tears. She felt for her friend, and while she was battling her own demons too, there wasn't gonna be no damn dying going on. Not for either of them. Lying down and dying just wasn't an option for bitches in the hood.

Zena sighed and tugged on the ends of the robe Egypt was wearing until it covered her friend's legs. The girl been left with nothing to her name except the clothes on her back.

Zena eyed her girl with pity. She'd never seen Egypt knocked so low. And to top off everything else that had gone down, Fat Daddy's shop had mysteriously caught fire a couple of nights after his murder. The apartment upstairs, and even Big Monk's hero shop next door had been burned almost to the ground. Gutted and filled with nothing but ash.

That in itself had sent Egypt spiraling even further downhill, but Zena believed the biggest part of Egypt's problem was that she had lived too much of a protected life over there with Fat Daddy and Hood. She'd lived with too much security. A big willie with money and status had taken care of her every need, day in and day out. Egypt had never been forced to find out what she was really made of. She talked a good game about what she was and wasn't gonna do all the time, but really, the girl had been living a life untested.

Nothing had ever crushed her or knocked down on her ass real good, so Egypt really had no idea if she was the type of chick who could pull herself back to her feet and stay up standing strong.

But Zena and Sackie had grown up fending for themselves. Their grandfather had died years earlier and they were all alone. With no mother and no father to guide her, Zena's whole life had been about survival and she was used to doing whatever it took to keep her head above water. Her life had gotten even harder after having An-dreka and finding out she was HIV positive, but even as Zena struggled to deal with her guilt and her crack addiction while caring for a new baby at the same time, giving up and dying had never even entered her mind.

She put her arm around Egypt and shivered. "Stop talking that dying shit. Please."

Egypt's whole face was swollen as she sniffed deeply and wiped tears from her red eyes. "Zena my daddy is *dead*! I just can't believe it even though I can't stop seeing it!" she wept.

"How the fuck could anybody do something like that to my father? He had love for all these niggas around here! What kind of grimy fool could do something like that to him, Zena?"

Zena just closed her mouth and let the question ride. Fat Daddy had been stupid with his game. Plus, he'd kept his daughter too blind to see the kind of drill that had been going on right under her nose. In truth, Egypt was even greener than Zena had been. That's what happened when you had people carrying you through life. You never learned how to really stand up and walk on your own. Zena started to say something slick, but she cared for Egypt so she shook her head and said instead, "You just gotta hold on, E. No matter what, don't give up on yourself. Your father wouldn't want that and neither would Hood."

Just a mention of Lamont was enough to start Egypt crying deeply again. His absence cut her so sharply that some nights she prayed God would be merciful enough to take the breath from her body and leave her cold and dead. Her daddy was gone, and her man was locked up for attempted murder and could be getting crazy jail time. There was no sanity to be found in her life anymore, and despite Zena's comforting hand stroking her back, Egypt knew she was truly alone in the world and it terrified her.

Eight days after Fat Daddy's funeral, Dreko came by the apartment. With Hood knocked and Xanbar smoked, Dreko was now ruling supreme on the block.

Egypt had been laying in the king-sized bed next to Zena and baby Andreka, crying softly into her damp pillow with her eyes squeezed closed. When she opened them and found Dreko standing over her, she was startled.

He looked tall and fine standing there dressed in fresh gear from top to bottom. A diamond earring twinkled from his ear and his middle finger was encased in a hot platinum ring. He held his finger up to his lips to quiet her, then motioned for her to get up and meet him out in the living room.

"I'm sorry about what happened to your pops," Dreko said, wiping tears from her red, swollen eyes. Sincerity creased his forehead and shone in his big brown eyes. "Fat Daddy was like a father to me too. To have him get took down like that almost deaded me inside. It was Xanbar who did him, E. And trust, I took care of that nigga for you, ya heard? I just wanted you to know that. I hope you satisfied with how we sent Fat Daddy off, though. I put a lot of money into giving him the same funeral he would have given me, if he could have."

Egypt nodded, her tears falling once more. Just hearing her father's name sent the pain of a blade stabbing through her heart. Dreko made a sympathetic noise in his throat and his pretty brown eyes went soft. Then he opened his strong, muscular arms, and an exhausted, needy, and grieving Egypt walked right into them.

"It's okay," he said, rubbing her back and soothing her sobs. He rested his chin on top of her head and comforted her as she wallowed in her grief. "Just let it out, baby. You can cry on me, Egypt. I'm right here for you and I can help you feel better too. If you trust me."

"Trust you?" Every single thing she had ever trusted in her life was gone. Snatched away from her. Wiped out.

"Yeah," he nodded. "Trust me, baby. I can make it stop hurting. For real. I can take the pain away."

Egypt didn't want to be so weak, but her loss was excruciating and it felt like her heart would never stop aching. All she wanted was for it to stop hurting so bad. She wished she could go to the dentist and get a shot of something that would numb the pain. Not in her mouth, but in her heart and in her soul.

She longed to close her eyes and not see her murdered father. She was desperate to turn off the horror movie that played nonstop in her head. And she needed to quiet the soul-ache that came from the gaping space left by Lamont's absence in her world. Egypt wept deep, exhausted tears.

She didn't want to be numb forever. Only for a little while. Just long enough to turn the pain down on simmer until she could catch her breath and figure out how to cope with the harsh realities of her new life.

She watched trancelike as Dreko slipped a stem from his pocket and packed it with the tan substances that were the tools of his booming trade.

He took her in his arms again, then squeezed her gently before offering her a painkiller. "No . . ." Egypt turned her head as he urged it toward her lips.

"It's okay," Dreko said softly, squeezing her closer and stroking her arm. "I'ma take real good care of you, baby . . . it's only a little bit. Just enough to make you feel good."

His voice was like a song. Mesmerizing. Persuasive. Promising.

"Just a little bit," he whispered, holding her close. "I got you, baby. I got you . . ."

Egypt was dizzy with confusion and weak with need. His body was hard and strong, propping her up. She leaned heavily against him, grateful for the emotional crutch.

And as Dreko stroked her arms and whispered to all the ailing places in her heart, Egypt closed her eyes and accepted the glass god he pressed to her lips.

Yesss . . . she sighed, going to jelly inside.

He numbed her up for over an hour.

He was sympathetic and unselfish as he took away the pain and confusion, the heartache and the fear, and replaced them with relief and euphoria. She found herself connecting to Dreko on a very special level, and he kept right on numbing her up until all the pain was gone and there was nothing left except pleasure and gratification in her heart.

But Egypt came to understand something crucial long before her night of emotional ecstasy with Dreko ended. Whoever said you couldn't get strung out on the pipe after only one mission must have never tried no good rock like this. Because after taking only one long hit Egypt was well aware that she'd been run over. And as she sucked that glass dick and watched the white cloud swirl and rush toward her lips like a toxic tornado, Egypt knew she was sunk.

CHAPTER 23

Them cowards gone pay dearly for what they did,
I'm focused and I can see shit clearly for what it is!

SACKIE WAS DAMN good with numbers, but no matter how he added shit up Hood getting knocked and the assassination of Xanbar just didn't compute. The streets were in a state of turmoil and news of Chaos's arrest had gone out on the wire as well.

Pulling a fitted cap down on his head, Sackie pushed his hands in the pockets of his hoody and continued his walk down Rockaway Avenue. He'd been working the streets moving vials all night, and even though the sun was up going back to the crib didn't appeal to him. Because Egypt was up there, and his guilt made it hard for him to be in the same space with her.

Sackie walked on, tossing shit around in his head. Cats were acting flaky, choosing teams, and trying to

save their own asses. Lil Jay had abandoned their corner
for a minute, but when he came back he walked up on the
block with a whole different game plan.

"Xan is out the picture and from now on Dreko is
the man. I'm running shit in this sector and now you *my*
boy." He looked at Sackie with beef in his hooded eyes.
"Problem?"

Sackie had grinned and shook his head. Lil Jay was
walking around like he was blind to the shit that was going
down. Dreko had pulled a coup on Xan, and yeah that shit
was real smelly. But who was next? Besides Sackie and
Lil Jay, every other cat who had sat on Fat Daddy's death
council and heard Xan say Dreko dipped with his product
had already been smoked. There was nobody else left who
could have verified Dreko's treachery but them. Even Riff
had taken a round. Less than a month had gone by after
Chaos's arrest when Riff was found executed, his body
propped up in an abandoned car.

Dreko had killed off anybody else who might tie him
to that robbery, and surrounded himself with a whole
new crew of come ups. Sackie wasn't sure why him and
Lil Jay had been left standing, but he kept his guard up
and his strap on. He wasn't taking no chances.

And now Lil Jay was beefing in his face.

"I said do you got a problem?"

"Nah," Sackie told him, dapping his partner with fake
love. There was a time when Jay wouldn't have spoken
to Sackie with nothing but adoration, but he was feeling
large these days. Real large. Sackie shrugged. He could

have stomped Jay's fragile ass four feet into the ground, but Dreko had left them both alive for a reason so he checked himself. "I ain't got no problems with you, Lil Jay. It's all love."

Late on the night of Xan's murder Dreko had held a meeting with his new crew up in Baller's Paradise.

"Xanbar got deaded. His niggas and his old way of doing shit is now deaded too. Anybody got some beef with me driving this train, speak out on that shit right now. Let the most vocal man in here go head-up with my gat and stand up and be heard."

Nobody had moved.

"Good. Now if this shit is just too juicy for y'all niggas, here's ya chance to bounce with no problems following you out the door. Get up right now and scat, because this gone be your one and only chance to step outside of my circle, ya dig?"

Again, nobody moved. Nobody wanted to get shot in the back.

"Aiight. Cool. If you still here, then you in it with me and I mean all the way in it. We about to make this shit grand and high post. Ten times bigger than that flimsy operation that small-minded, small-dicked Xanbar was running. Stick with me, my niggas. Ya man Dreko is both a sinner and a winner."

$ $ $

Zena had never gone head-up against Dreko and she wasn't about to start now. Ever since he had taken over the Brownsville drug trade six months earlier, he'd been coming by the apartment almost every day, and not because he gave a damn about her or his daughter neither.

"Where's Egypt?" he demanded one morning entering the apartment with a key. Sackie had changed the locks, but Dreko had taken Zena's key away from her. She didn't want no static between them, so she was reluctant to tell her brother about the key or to ask him to make her another one.

Zena was in the kitchen frying bacon and her first thought was of grabbing the pan of meat and hot grease and just throwing it at him.

But if the grease didn't kill him, he would damn sure kill her.

She nodded toward a closed door off the living room. "I guess she's back there in the room."

Dreko reached into his pocket and tossed her a vial, then walked into the bedroom and closed the door behind him.

Zena turned off the frying pan real quick and moved it to a cold eye. She'd gone right back to drugging after having Andreka, and once Egypt moved in and started getting high too, there had been no holding back. They both hit the pipe with mad intensity every chance they got.

The vial of crack seemed to be throbbing in her hand, and she wished Dreko would have passed her at least two. With Egypt around he was being real generous with his product, tearing them off as much as they wanted whenever they wanted it. Zena knew his charity wouldn't last long so she took advantage of that shit and made sure she smoked as much rock as she could, even if it meant passing out with the pipe in her hand.

But even as she searched the kitchen drawer for a fresh stem Zena's guilt crept up on her. She'd stayed clean for almost her entire pregnancy and now she was right back in the same predicament. The only difference was that she'd had some real good company ever since Dreko had turned Egypt out on the rock too.

The tragic transformation that her friend was going through was all too familiar to Zena. After all, Dreko had done her almost exactly the same way. First the sweet talk, then the comfort, and then he went in for the kill. Before she knew it, she was dreaming about crack in her sleep and begging him for even more when she was awake.

And that's just the way Dreko had wanted her. He was even willing to keep passing her off vials while she was pregnant, just as long as she kept doing all the nasty shit he wanted her to do.

That part bothered Zena most of all. Dreko's heart seemed to be totally cold when it came to their child, and not even the ass-whippings he put on Zena hurt her that bad. Really, a beating was the kind of shit you expected out of a gangsta in these parts, and every now and then a bitch had to take a beat-down just to keep her man feeling like a man. Zena wasn't mad about that. But a daddy was supposed to love his little girl to death, and Zena had a big problem with the way Dreko seemed to be emotionless when it came to their daughter.

While everybody else always had mad compliments about Andreka's sweet nature, curly hair, and pretty eyes, her own father could give less than a damn about her, and couldn't stand being around her at all when she cried or got cranky the way most babies did.

Zena scraped the screen on her stem and sparked it up. The first hit killed all of her anxiety and quieted the misgivings in her head. By the time the vial was empty she was way up there, giddy and free.

Setting the hot pipe on the counter to cool off, Zena gazed down the short hall and eyed the doorway that Dreko had entered. It was quiet in the room and she wondered whether Dreko had the girl in there sucking a pipe, or sucking a piper.

Listening close, she could have sworn she heard moans coming from her bedroom. She knew that motherfucka wasn't crazy enough to be trying nothing right there in her bed.

Stomping past the couch where her young daughter slept, Zena twisted the knob and pushed the door open wide.

Dreko was in a position she had never seen him in before.

On his hands and knees.

Egypt lay naked on her back in Zena's bed. Her long, elegant legs were open in a wide *V* as Dreko licked her pussy out with deep hungry strokes. Zena watched as her man's hands dug into Egypt's toned thighs, her shapely brown ass quivering on the sheets. She had never seen a black pussy before, and the way Dreko ate that shit out told her it must have tasted good.

Egypt moaned, tossing her head back and forth. Her pubic hair was dark and curly, and her clit looked like a baked bean as Dreko slobbered on it, sucking it between his juicy lips. Egypt's insides were a pretty pink silk, her cum off-white and thick as it slipped from her folds only to be quickly lapped up by Zena's man.

Zena pouted, her mind racing. She could smell Egypt's pussy from where she stood. Dreko had never eaten her out like that. He'd never tasted her at all, which was why it was so hard for her to watch him devouring another chick's yummy.

Zena made a noise and Dreko turned around. His goatee was wet with cum, his lips glossed and sticky looking.

"C'mere," he told her, and even though his tone was calm she knew he was dead serious. At the sound of his voice Egypt's eyes flew open. Zena could tell she was smoked up too as she tried to close her legs and cover her naked titties.

Dreko shook his head. "Uh-uh," he told Egypt, pushing her back down into Zena's pillows. Then he motioned to his woman and when she was standing by the bed he nodded his head, urging her on.

"Taste this," he told her. "This the best pussy I ever tasted, yo. Come get you some."

The look in his eyes was enough to make Zena do anything he said, even if it meant jumping off a roof. She glanced at Egypt, who shook her head no, and tried to twist from Dreko's grasp.

"Bitch hold still," he told her, prying her legs open again. He swiped her pussy with two long fingers, then held them out to Zena. "Taste," he demanded.

Zena lowered her head and touched her tongue to his fingers. Dreko laughed, then snatched her by the hair and shoved his fingers deep into her mouth. "Taste," he demanded again, and this time she did.

Egypt's pussy tasted like nothing Zena had ever known. It wasn't bad and it wasn't good. She just didn't have anything to compare it to.

But minutes later it was no longer just a snack. It was a full course meal.

"Yeah," Dreko told her as he watched Zena lick Egypt's pretty brown pussy meat. Zena held her breath at first, refusing to let herself think about what she was doing. Instead of feeling nasty or clammy, Egypt's pussy was hot and sweet, and the harder Zena licked her knob, the more creamy juice squirted from between her swollen lips.

On the bed, Egypt moaned, trying not to like it. She'd never had the slightest sexual attraction to Zena or to any bitch, but right now her pussy didn't care if there was a woman down there licking it into a foamy frenzy. She raised her hips off the bed, arching her back to get closer to that probing, licking, and flicking tongue.

"Y'all done partied before?" Dreko asked with a laugh. Egypt twirled her dark fingers in Zena's hair, and Zena had reached up to fondle Egypt's full breasts and rigid nipples. Dreko got behind Zena and cupped her small titties, then touched her clit and dragged his fingers along her sopping pussy.

"You don't get this fuckin wet for me," he muttered, but Zena never heard him.

Using her thumb and forefinger, she spread Egypt's lips wide and inserted her tongue as deeply inside her gaping pussy as she could get it. Keeping her tongue stiff, she fucked Egypt with it as Egypt whimpered and ground her hips up to meet her. Pussy juice was flowing like water. From Egypt and from Zena. And when Dreko plunged his hard dick into Zena from behind, her juices were so plentiful that they dripped from his balls.

"Oh shit," Egypt began to whisper sweetly. Her eyes were squeezed tight and the sheets were in her grip. "I'm about to come. Yes . . . oh damn, I'm gonna cum."

Zena licked that pussy out deeper and faster, sucking on the clit with gentle pulls. She was getting that good dick from behind, but what she really wanted to do was rub her pussy on Egypt's and get her own clit as wet as her lips were. Instead, she slid her hands under Egypt's curved ass and gulped. If she'd known pussy was this good she would have been licking this shit for years. She inserted one finger into Egypt's hole and felt her muscles contract as she nutted, grabbing Zena's hair and moaning from deep in her chest.

To Zena's surprise, the minute Egypt came Dreko snatched his dick out of her and pushed her aside. He positioned himself over Egypt and plunged into her gaping wet pussy, driving that dick home with long hard strokes until Egypt screamed out another climax and Dreko grunted, plunged, shuddered, withdrew, plunged, and then banged that pussy five times real hard until he spurted too, withdrawing his wet black dick and letting it jerk and spit on Egypt's flat stomach.

Suddenly Zena felt like the odd chick out in their little threesome.

It wouldn't be the last time.

CHAPTER 24

I hear that loud talk
I hear that whisperin
I hear that bullshit,
Think I ain't listenin?

IF LIFE WASN'T fuckin grand, then Dreko didn't know what it was.

Time was flying and he was damn sure having fun.

Six months had passed since he took over the Brownsville drug trade, and he'd done more crazy shit than a little bit. Dreko was a shrewd nigga, constantly in scheme-mode, and he commanded loyalty from his team by striking cold fear in their hearts. One by one he cut down any nigga whose complete and total allegiance to his regime was questionable. If he even thought he smelled anything fishy on they lips, he busted one on 'em right where they stood.

Same shit went for them cats in Ocean Hill. It was nothing for Dreko to jump out of a whip and walk up on a nigga
and press a barrel to his forehead. *Bak! Bak! Bak!* He
cracked plenty of grills and he delivered his heat rounds
personally and did that shit in public too. He wanted niggas to know, not to wonder. It had been easy to flip Xan's
men and Chaos's too, so Dreko knew all it took was one
hungry come-up nigga just like him to start eyeballing
his own lil slice of the pie and determining that it wasn't
enough. If Dreko could figure out how to grab that whole
fuckin pie, so could somebody else. The difference was, he
was ten times more ruthless than Xan and them niggas had
been and he would stick his metal dick in a nigga's mouth
and blow his brains out the back of his head in public, no
questions asked.

Image was a big part of the package in this game, and
Dreko made sure his was impeccable. Whips, jewels, a
hundred pairs of sneakers, he got all that. He took over
twin apartment buildings called Cypress Arms and set up
shop inside both. He found a Puerto Rican connect who
had ties to some come-up Colombians and cut a sweet new
deal for both Brownsville and Ocean Hill that amped up
his profits. And in the middle of all this, Dreko also found
time to pay a little visit to that mule who had caught a
hot one in the neck the night him and Hood pulled that
lick too. He actually sat down at the table with dude and
his moms, and explained to her why her son wasn't gone
remember shit that happened that night when them DA's
put him up on that witness stand.

"So you see, Miss Barnes," Dreko said as he rubbed his pistol along the side of her terrified face, "Your son got a role to play when he get in that courthouse, ya dig? You real pretty for an old lady too. I bet he's gonna make sure don't nothing happen to you. He a real good son, ain't he?"

After eating the last two pieces of chicken from Miss Barnes's stove and calmly strolling out of her house licking his fingers, Dreko was damn sure his boy would be walking free after his court date.

He grinned. That nigga Xanbar had been dead wrong about him. He didn't roll second behind no fuckin body. Dreko had mad discipline and had proven that shit in a large way. He couldn't wait to show his boy Hood what kinda empire he had built on his own, with nothing but his metal and his mind. He'd shown the world that he was the number one gangsta on these streets, and he had all of Brownsville under his command to prove it.

Yeah. It was almost time for the Hoodsta to get back out on the streets of Brooklyn so Dreko could show that nigga how his right-hand man had played leap frog with a couple of big-time ballers and landed his ass square on the number one spot.

$ $ $

Time passes quickly when you're on a mission.

Six months after her father died Egypt was no longer the same tender young girl she had once been. She'd done a lot of dirt in a short period of time and it was beginning to show on her.

For the first month of Hood's lockdown she had made a couple of visits to see him on Rikers Island. After the first time she didn't cry anymore, but she did sit across from him wanting a hit and feeling guilty as hell as she tried not to let him peek inside her soul and see how foul and dirty it had become.

"If you need anything just get with Dreko," Hood told her time and time again. "I stacked my chips real proper, baby, and there's enough in the safe to see you clear."

Egypt would nod and lower her head and wonder how hard he would hit her if he knew his best friend was a snake and that she'd already smoked up almost every dime he'd left behind.

She'd stopped going up on visits altogether after a minute because the grime on her soul had started showing on the outside of her too. It was magnified even more each time she ran into Mont's mother, Marjay, on the streets. They were looking a whole lot alike these days, and when Egypt wasn't high that thought depressed the hell out of her. What Marjay had done to her son was unforgiveable, and he carried her scars deep in his heart. But what made Egypt any better? Mont loved her too. He would die for her too. And here she was shitting on him the exact same way his mother had. Dumping dirt in his game like the world hadn't done enough of that already.

But not even the pipe was dirtier than the depraved shit Dreko had been putting her through.

"Hold ya fuckin hair back so I can see what you doing," he would demand when Egypt tried to fake the funk when she was in bed with Zena. Yeah, Egypt got off when Zena licked *her* down there, but she felt absolutely no attraction to her friend's clammy pink pussy. The only way she was able to get through the act was by concentrating on the prize waiting for her at the end: that first heavenly cocaine smoke blast that would fill her chest and ignite an explosive orgasm in her mind.

Dreko was sexually sadistic and made her go places that no woman in her right mind would willingly go. But Egypt was beginning to realize that she *wasn't* in her right mind. She was a crackhead, straight up. No different than Mont's mother, or a chaser on the avenue who stopped cars and sucked strange dicks for a hit. The only thing different was, she was getting her crack in-house, but even still she had to perform for it. She had to do some shit for Dreko that he didn't want none of his boys to know about.

Like that asshole thing he had going. No real man could even think up the shit Dreko forced her to do. The first time he made her do it she almost couldn't take it and her skin damn near crawled.

"Show her how I like my back done," he'd told Zena. He was standing naked and wide legged in Zena's bedroom. His hand was covered in a thick coat of Vaseline and making squishy noises as he slid it up and down his shaft, pumping his erect dick.

Zena slid behind him and got down on her knees. She placed her small white fingers on his muscular brown ass cheeks, then spread them wide open. Dreko moaned and jerked his dick harder. Egypt almost threw up as Zena stuck her tongue out, stiffening it, then bent her head and inserted her tongue straight up Dreko's ass, moving her whole head back and forth as she tongue-fucked him in his hole.

Egypt had gagged and almost thrown up in her hand.

Dreko groaned and his whole body shuddered.

"Yeah, get deeper baby," he growled, his head flung back and his hand moving faster. He bent his knees and pushed his ass backward. "Fuck me deeper."

Zena kept the motion going as Egypt pulled her knees to her chest and hugged herself, beyond disgusted. But moments later Dreko had another demand.

"Let E take your spot," he instructed Zena. "And you come around in front and suck my dick."

"I'll suck your dick!" Egypt blurted, jumping from the bed before Zena could move. She positioned herself between Dreko and the wall, sliding down to her knees in front of him as she reached for his greasy dick.

But he shook his head and held that shit to the side, away from her.

"I don't want you to suck my dick. I want that bitch back there to suck it. You got a problem taking over her spot?"

Egypt trembled. Her eyes slid over to the dresser where her reward waited. Three vials worth. She looked at Zena, whose reddening face was filled with resignation. Then she looked up at Dreko, whose dark eyes dared her to refuse him.

Egypt crawled behind him, switching place with Zena.

"It's not that bad," Zena whispered as Egypt went past.

She swallowed hard, then gripped Dreko's sweaty ass and parted it the way she'd seen Zena do it. His asshole was puckered wide open and she wanted so bad to stick her whole damn foot up in it. Instead, with one last glance toward the fish scales waiting for her on the dresser, Egypt held her breath and delved inside of him with a stiff tongue, the sweat that was beading on his ass mingling with the tears falling from her eyes.

She plunged deeply inside of him, then eased out. It was worse than anything she had ever imagined. His ass muscles gripped down tightly on her tongue each time she withdrew, like he was squeezing it and trying to suck it back in. Egypt had heard of tossing a damn salad but this was a disgusting oral ass-fuck, which was ten times more depraved.

"Oh shit . . ." Dreko shrieked, fucking back toward her face. His hole was soft and wet. "Ummmmm, yeah baby. That tongue is so damn good!"

Egypt figured she must have been doing it right because it wasn't long before Dreko lost his head. He grabbed his own ass cheeks and bent over at the waist and almost knocked her down as he bucked his sweaty behind backward.

"Get up in there," he yelled. "Get up in that shit!"

And she did. Egypt fucked him until her tongue was sore, and moments later Zena caught his spillage in her mouth as he busted a hard one, gripping his own ass and slobbering as he came.

The fact that she participated in these sexual nightmares disgusted Egypt. She dogged herself half to death in her lucid moments. She hated everything about her life and needed to stay high just to keep from killing herself.

But no matter how bad Egypt felt about what she was doing with Dreko or doing to Lamont, she couldn't stop smoking. The crack jones was on her and she needed those rocks like she needed water and air.

Sackie had been shocked to find her rolling around in bed with Dreko and his sister. When he found out they were getting high together he was furious and disgusted with both her and Zena. He was the one who stayed in closest contact with Mont, and Egypt had been beyond embarrassed when she broke down and got on her knees and begged Sackie not to bust her out. "What purpose could it serve?" she had asked him. The only thing telling on her would do was weaken Mont and hurt him real bad. How much shit did he think one man could take?

"Sackie said Hood is going to court in about two weeks," Zena said one morning. "You gone be there for the trial?"

They had been up trading favors with Dreko all night long, and Egypt still had the aftertaste of his sex-slick body coating her tongue. She hunched her shoulders and frowned. "I don't know. Maybe. He might not even want me there. I ain't wrote a letter or been on a visit in like five months, Zena. Mont probably so mad he don't even wanna see me right now."

"He wants to see you, girl. He loves you. It could be five years and he would still wanna see you."

Egypt gave her a doubtful look. "I don't know about all that. What inmate you know ain't gone be crazy mad after not hearing from his chick in five months? Damn! I can't even believe it's been that long! It seems like I was just up there with him yesterday . . ." She rubbed her nose and sniffed. Mont wouldn't even recognize her if he walked through the door right now. She'd done a whole lot of crack-head shit while he was gone. She'd hit a desperate phase when Dreko first started withholding vials from her, and one night Egypt found herself feening so hard that she'd gotten in the car with an old white man looking for a trick. She had been out on the street getting blasted for three days straight, and when she realized the white man didn't wanna fuck her, she was happy to climb in the backseat and let him eat her stank, cheesy pussy until he was satisfied.

It was amazing, even to her, the kind of twisted spin that drugs had put on her life. A life that had once held so much promise. Just thinking about the possibility of Mont finding out had her shook and craving another high.

"Well whatever you do," Zena told her, "just be on your game if he gets out. Don't let this pipe fuck up what y'all got."

Egypt sat back on the bed and crossed her legs. The sheets they had just tumbled in were so filthy it was hard to make out the original color.

"I don't even know what we got no more, Zena. Maybe all them years we were loving each other were just a kiddie lie. Mont wouldn't even want me like this, and I know it. I gotta get straight for me and for him too. I can stop smoking, no problem. I just need a little more time."

Zena looked at her friend with a load of guilt in her heart. She felt so bad about what her and Dreko had done to this girl. Both of them with their greed and their lies . . . all the unprotected sex and the drugs, the whole disease thing that had never been spoken about . . . they were killing her.

But no matter how much guilt Zena felt, her denial was far stronger. To confess that she had something so foul crawling through her body was more than she could do for anyone. She just couldn't admit to that thing she carried in her blood and had passed on to her little girl. She'd taken Andreka back to the hospital to be retested like they told her to, but she'd never gone back to get the results. It just wasn't something she was ready to claim or even to speak on. Not to Sackie, not to Dreko, not to Egypt . . . not even to herself.

CHAPTER 25

Niggas better let me be!
I'm tryna live it to the fullest till they let me free
I know they comin with the bullets,
God bless me please,
Hope you can oversee my greed, true indeed, true indeed . . .

THE TIER WAS still dark when Hood rose from his bunk. The typical sounds of a jailhouse in the predawn were in the air. His cellie snored, farted, then rolled over in the top bunk. A broom-fucked new jack cried softly in the cage next door. The pleasure groans of a dick-jacking wet dream came from a sleeping inmate who'd been locked down without a woman for far too long.

Down on the cold floor, Hood rose up on his arms and began his daily regimen of push-ups. Today he would do one hundred and eighty reps. Ten push-ups for each day that he'd been confined on the Rock awaiting trial for attempted murder.

His arms, shoulders, and legs had grown thick with muscle. Perspiration covered his skin as he raised and lowered his own weight. The exercise was for his body, but the gangsta lyrics he silently spit were strictly for his mind. For the past six months he'd fought hard to keep both in tip-top condition.

Hood rapped softly as he psyched himself up for the drama he was about to face in court that day.

I'm from the ghetto I'm so hood!
I keep metal in my hood!
What's good? What's good?
Cuz my name is HOOD!
Is you keeping it hood? We will creep thru your hood!
Carry heat if we should
I would cuz I'm Hood!

This nigga right here is so damn hood,
I pull the trigga for the figures if you sell tan goods!
I ride like I'm Suge, big nigga with no help!
The only thing big is the sig by the belt nigga!
I let 'em burn like a cig when I pop the guy . . .
Let 'em fry, plus I got a buzz like I'm kinda high!
I'm that kinda guy you don't wanna mess wit,
I roll with the best click, before I fold I'm letting the text spit,
In the same place till his face split!

Face it, I spray, then I cock again . . . squeeze . . .
Till I see him bleed, stiff with no oxygen
Left in his body!

After the first hundred push-ups he grunted with exertion. His arms burned like fuck and his body begged him to quit, but he pressed on. This was the best part. Pushing with his mind regardless of what his body told him to do.

He heard his cellie stirring on the top bunk. They'd come to an understanding early on, but niggas in jail would still test you if they could. Hood could hear him moving around above him, but he kept his mind focused on completing the next push-up.

His cellie was down with Razor, one of the baddest niggas on the tier. They were the type of inmates who went around bragging about all the cats they had buck-fiffed or caught in the kitchen or the shower and put to sleep.

But Hood wasn't impressed. Some dudes came in the joint and immediately set out trying to earn a rep for themselves. But G's like Hood walked through the doors with their stripes. Hood didn't have shit to prove to nobody. There were plenty of dudes in here from around his block. Nigs who thought just because they had rolled together under Xanbar out on the streets that they was automatically supposed to click up in the joint.

Hood wasn't for it. The quickest way to get ten years in the joint was to come in for ten months and start fuckin around with ya boys. Yeah, when you rolled alone without the protection of a crew you were sure to get tested. But Hood was cool with that. It usually took him less than five minutes to change a nigga's mind, no matter how big the cat was.

And even though his reputation had gotten to the Rock before he did, Hood reinforced that shit his first day on the yard by walking up to the baddest cat he could find and going hard to his ass. Hood fought dirty and he fought with extreme cruelty. He'd swing a blade, a tray, a chain, a shank, or even another nigga. Didn't fuckin matter. He was an animal behind these bars. He had the mind of a beast and went all out at the first hint of static.

Taking a quick break from his push-ups, Hood glanced up toward his cellie. The cat was a stick-up kid from the Bronx who couldn't stop talking about who his team took down and which niggas they punked out. That was some real good shit to work with on the outside of the tier, but the rules for Hood's cell dictated that the nigga had to stay up on his bunk in the mornings until Hood gave him the nod.

Hood chuckled to himself as his cellie swung his legs over the top bed. If that bitch got down off that bunk he'd ring his fuckin neck like he was a bird. *C'mon, baby,* he begged silently. *Get down so I can lock my fuckin hands on you. You'll never get your ass back up.*

I'm on now, niggas can't ignore me!
Still holding the block down
Hand around my forty!

Really though,
Fuck who you punched and slammed
Who you slumped or jammed
Just as long as they don't touch ya man!

His cellie had stayed on the bunk, showing him the proper respect, and two hours later Hood had eaten breakfast and was riding the prison bus and being transported to King's County criminal court to stand trial. Every bit of anger he'd bottled up over the past six months had come down to this moment. A lot had gone down on the streets since he'd gotten knocked, and all kinds of shit had filtered through the prison walls. Reem had stopped through on his way home after touring for his latest album. His boy had signed with a major label and his shit had blown up sky high. He couldn't stay on the visit long, but before he left he stacked Hood's commissary and then kept it topped off for months.

Sackie had kept up the letters and had visited him a few times too. But everybody else had fell the fuck off. Dreko, Lil Jay. Even Egypt. During Sackie's last visit Hood had wanted to know why.

"She's aiight," Sackie lied to him with a shrug. He'd promised Egypt he wouldn't tell on her. But he wanted to tell his boy. He really did. His guilt just wouldn't let him. "I see her sometimes. She's doing aiight."

"She ain't been out here in five months, yo. That don't sound aiight to me."

"Man," Sackie shook his head and changed the subject. "Dreko is large as fuck these days. He's ruling supreme in Brownsville and in Ocean Hill now," Sackie had told Hood during his last visit.

"But the cat is still wild, Hood. He got a real brutal army working for him. A bunch of young boys, and they been pushing up on some good dudes. Stepping on all kinds of toes. They took over Cypress Arms, you know. The whole shit too. Put entire families out on the street. Shit, with Chaos upstate and Xan took down, it's Dreko's world. You only get to live in that shit if he say so."

Hood had thought hard on Sackie's words. He could see Dreko riding hard and living large. He'd had big dreams of flamboyance and that nigga had always craved a throne. But still. They were brothers and that meant Dreko was supposed to hold shit down until Hood got back on the streets.

"Don't worry about nothing," Dreko had told him during his first and only visit five months earlier. "You just make it to court and I'll have a chauffeur waiting outside to bring you home, baby."

He spent three hours waiting in the bullpen. Beside him sat a cat who was praying softly under his breath. Moving his lips and begging God to guide the course of his trial. Hood almost laughed. The details of his case didn't press him out at all. Shit was simple and it would go down the way it went down.

But when he entered the courtroom and looked around, it took him a second to take it all in. The place was packed.

The red-headed cop who had beaten and arrested him was sitting right up front, waiting to be called. The dude Hood had popped was sitting at the prosecution's table, face shining and suited up. Bald head gleaming and dressed like a fuckin banker. Sackie was there, and so was Lil Jay. Egypt was missing, but way in the back row was a real familiar face. Dreko. Sitting there with a bold grin and G'd the fuck out. Shine and floss. Nigga was prepped. Giving Hood a confident look that said, don't sweat shit, homey. I got you.

That one look wiped any beef Hood might been feeling about the last six months clean. Hood sat there chilling as the big-headed nigga he'd popped got up on the stand and caught a case of amnesia. He could smell the fear coming off the cat as he swore on a stack of bibles that he didn't say half the shit them prosecutors claimed he'd said. Then he lied like a muhfucka when the prosecutor asked him in an exasperated voice if his attacker was present in the courtroom and sitting at the defendant's table.

"Nah," the big dude said, shaking his head. "That ain't him. That is definitely not the dude who shot me. I woulda remembered if it had' a been him."

With no other witnesses, the state's carefully constructed case was reduced to mere crumbs and Hood walked free, just like Dreko had promised he would.

They hugged and dapped outside the courtroom and then Hood stood back so he could get a good look at his homey. The nigga had changed gears, that was for sure.

"Look at you, son!" Hood nodded at Dreko's sharp attire and his platinum jewels. "Walkin round here styling like Jigga or somebody!" He noted the fresh teardrop tattoos in the corner of Dreko's eye and the shiny grill affixed to his teeth. "Nigga got tats *and* a goddamn grill. C'mere, homes. Lemmee see what that mouth jewelry be talking about."

Dreko grinned wide and Hood's blood ran cold. The nigga had a gold project scene on his damn teeth. High buildings on either side of two tenements. And a big number one smack on his right front tooth. In platinum.

"Aiight," Hood said still smiling. He was in transition mode so he forced himself to chill. For now. "So you the number one nigga on the streets these days, huh?" he said smoothly. His grin never wavered. "Damn, son. You musta been grinding triple time while I was on lock."

Dreko laughed and clapped Hood on the shoulder. "Yeah, I been holding shit down, baby. But not just for me. For *us*. Me *and* you, ya heard? That's why I couldn't make it out on the Rock to check you out the way I wanted to. Just like you was prolly stompin niggas out and running shit on the tier, I was out here on the streets lookin out for both our interests. We brothers, yo, and I been busy building us an empire."

Dreko laughed again, a heartless laugh. He was glad his boy had finally hit the bricks. What good was having all the riches of the world if he couldn't floss them shits right up in Hood's face?

"Just wait till you see what ya boy been up to. I made some moves and instituted some changes while you was gone, my nigga. Fuck all that living in the back of Fat Daddy's shop. It got burnt down anyway. I got a real crib waiting on your ass. Entire buildings. We got bitches, shine, whips, cheese, the whole nine. It's about us, nigga. *Us*."

They rode back to Brownsville in Dreko's rimmed-out white Range Rover and Hood felt good to be back home. He was amazed at how much the game had changed in just six short months, though. And Dreko hadn't been lying when he told him he had amassed a goldmine. The boy had mad holdings. Just the sound of his name had niggas on the streets shook.

"This ain't no *me* thing," Dreko kept reminding him. "It's an *us* thing, nigga. Just like it's always been."

Yeah, his boy was big, and his crib proved it. Dreko had told the truth. He *had* taken over the two tenement buildings called Cypress Arms. The one he had moved them into had eight apartments in the joint, and he'd run all eight families out into the street too. He'd stuck his lil army of younghead thugs like Buddah, Flip, Barry, Waffle, and Donnie up in seven of the apartments, with his own crib sandwiched right in the middle and protected from penetration. The other building was where he ran his drug operation. It had a count room with a steel safe twice the size of Xanbar's, and it was more heavily guarded than Fort Knox.

"Man, who the fuck you think coming after you?" Hood asked incredulously when he saw the security measures Dreko had employed. Dun duns at the door, sentries on the fuckin roof, double steel doors, triple deadbolt locks, and bullet-proof glass in all the windows. "You been out there fuckin around with the goddamn marines?"

"Pretty close," Dreko admitted. He walked through the crib with his gat out, going from room to room clearing that shit. "Niggas is snakes out there, man. It's a war going on out on those streets. A muhfuckin *war*, homey. This is where you rest, baby. I hope you satisfied with it."

Hood's suite had been hooked up with a big screen, high definition, plasma television and a phat water bed. A real bearskin rug was on the floor and satin sheets and a cashmere spread was on the bed.

"Hey man, where my baby at?" Hood asked. He'd finished looking around the apartment and there was no doubt his friend had changed their lifestyle for the better. Dreko had been living in the lap of luxury, and almost every damn thing they'd ever dreamed about having as kids, he had either bought, stolen, or built it up in the crib.

"Where's E staying at, man? I need to check her out."

"At Sackie's," Dreko said. "She moved in with Zena after her crib burned down. I hear she's doing pretty good over there too. Yeah man, them two chicks done got *real* tight."

CHAPTER 26

I led a sinister past,
But y'all fag niggas livin a laugh,
And I went straight to war, never been in a draft!

HOOD RAN INTO a couple of his old partners on the way to Sackie's house. He could have hopped in the fresh g-ride Dreko had waiting for him, but it was nice outside and he wanted to walk. His mind was full of Egypt, but he forced himself to pause for a few minutes to show his boys on the street some love. For some reason these cats seemed extra happy to see him. Yeah, most of them was glad he'd beat his charge and was back on the outside, but it seemed like there was more to it than that.

"Hood!" Vandy ran up on him near Dumont Avenue. Vandy was a down nigga who had spent a lot of time spittin bars with Hood and Dreko in Fat Daddy's place and Hood had real affection for him.

"Damn, man," Vandy said, showing him love. "When they let your ass out? You's a sight for street eyes, baby! Let me guess. Dreko rolled up on that nigga you popped, huh? I bet that cat got up in that courtroom and couldn't remember shit about shit."

"I don't know how it went down, but it's all good. That nigga shoulda took that heat round like a G instead of snitching like a little bitch. If he didn't like what I put on him then he shoulda strapped on his tool and come gunnin instead of conspiring with them blue boys. I woulda respected that."

Vandy walked along beside him as he moved through the projects and headed toward a row of tenements on the other side. "Yeah. You always been that kinda guy. Everybody know you a cold nigga, but you righteous too. Got some street honor in you, man. But the game done changed. Niggas ain't standing up like that no more. These days you can't trust no fuckin body. Nobody. Everybody is scared. Cats who used to be down from the sandbox is now sliding knives in each other's backs and killing women and kids. Shit is crazy out here. There's a underground war going on in Central Brooklyn. You remember Miss Baker, right?"

Hood thought back to those cold days of his youth. "Hell yeah. I got crazy love for that old lady. How she doin?"

A look of disgust crossed Vandy's face and he shook his head. "Not too good. She got burned out of her crib, man. One of her granddaughters used to be in my class, man. Diamond. The fine one who used to fuck with that guy Bop from the Plaza. Diamond had just stopped smoking when she got killed, man. Her *and* her three kids are gone. Miss Baker was in the hospital, but Diamond and her kids got trapped on the top floor and she tried to throw 'em out the window to save 'em but they still died. Diamond got burned up real bad and she died too. It was all messed up, man."

The good vibe Hood had been riding was suddenly gone.

"Damn," he said as they crossed the street together. "Miss Baker is good people. That lady used to feed me and Moo when nobody else would even open the door and take us in. I remember Diamond too. She was real cool. That's some fucked up shit."

"Yeah it is. They got burned for calling the cops, ya know. Miss Baker was just trying to keep her apartment. You know she's always been real involved in the community and shit. She started telling people they didn't have to move out just so the drug dealers could move in. They got some neighborhood watch shit going and started calling the cops whenever they saw a trap boy. The cats who did it got popped robbing some narcs, but that shit still cost Miss Baker, though. Her whole fuckin family."

"So where she staying at now?"

Vandy lifted his chin, pointing up toward Mother Gaston. "I heard she's over in Seth Low, man. I don't know exactly what building, but I think she got a sister or some-body who lives over there."

Hood veered left, slightly changing directions. He couldn't wait to see his girl, but he needed to make a quick stop first.

"Aiight, later Vandy. Get at me, son."

Vandy nodded, then called out at Hood's back. "You watch yourself out here, man. Shit ain't like it usta be! Especially on the borders. Dreko fucked up and stepped on Reem Raw's toes, homey, and some major beef is about to spark off."

Hearing Reem's name froze Hood in his tracks. Dreko was playing with some dangerous shit. Reem was a powerful capo on the borders of East New York, and had been Hood's loyal friend for a lot of years. He had grown into a hard-body G with a street team twice as large as Dreko's. Not only was he popular and well known all over the map for his music, he was also promoting shows and bringing in other big-name rappers to his club. He rolled heavy with Freedom Moore, and was in on all the hot sets. He'd bounced over to Jersey for a quick minute and put in some work but had returned to Brooklyn with a vengeance, and he definitely wasn't the kind of guy Dreko wanted to be fuckin with.

Later, Hood told himself, thrusting his hands in his pockets and cutting across the pathways between the project buildings. He'd deal with Reem and his boys later. Right now he was gonna check on Miss Baker, then pay a little visit to a fine-ass chocolate honey that he had missed like hell.

$ $ $

One of the cardinal rules of project living was to keep ya damn mouth closed. It didn't matter what you witnessed or what you knew. If somebody came around asking questions the answer was always the same. "I don't know shit," or "I didn't see shit."

Hood approached building 320 from the left side, looking around. There were a crew of thick-booty young girls in tight jeans, fly earrings, and colored contact lenses standing around in front of the building. They were listening to music, gyrating their hips, and licking big red lollipops. Hood knew better than to roll up on them with a bunch of questions. Instead, he skirted around them and headed for the small playground where several kids sped around on Big Wheels and scooters.

"Hey little man." He stood in front of a young rider, blocking his path. "You know Miss Baker who stay in 320, right?"

The little boy nodded, his eyes big and his nose crusty.

Hood went in his pocket. "Can you take this dollar up to 4F and give it to her for me? The other dollar is for you."

The kid shook his head, no. "She don't stay in 4F. She stay in 11B."

"Yeah," Hood said, holding out both bills. "That's right, I forgot. She sure do." He squatted down and put the bills in the boy's hand. He was about seven, older than Moo had been, but he still tugged Hood's heart anyway. "Tell you what. You ain't gotta give Miss Baker nothing. You keep both of these dollars, okay?"

Minutes later he was standing outside of apartment 11B and knocking on the door. When it opened he stood there facing an old woman whose eyes took him in with a quick glance and judged him even quicker.

"What do you want?"

"I'm Lamont. Miss Baker here?"

She looked Hood up and down and her lips turned down in a frown. Hood had been surprised when she opened the door without even asking who it was, but now gazing down the nose of the .32 that had appeared in the hand she'd been hiding behind her back, he could see why.

"Let me tell you something, motherfucker," she said, leaning partway out the door with her gat trained dead on him. "Don't let the gray hair fool you because I don't give a damn who you be. Get the hell away from my door and leave my goddamn sister alone. She's the nice one, you hear? Not me. I ain't running from none of y'all low-life, drug dealing bastards. I will blow a hole in your fuckin stomach so quick you'll shit out your breakfast before you hit the ground. Y'all caused us enough trouble. Fuck with me, and the next mama to bury her child will be yours."

"I'm sorry," Hood said quietly. His lifted his eyes from the gat and looked at her with sympathy and sincerity in his face. "I came to tell Miss Baker that I'm sorry about Diamond and her kids. I'm Marjay's son. Marjorie Jones from Van Dyke was my grandmother. Your sister knew me all my life. She used to help me and my baby brother out before he died. She fed us. Took us in out the cold. I heard about the fire and everything and I wanted to come by and see how she was doing. That's all. You ain't gotta shoot me because I didn't come for no trouble. I came with love."

The woman narrowed her eyes slightly. She looked him over real good, but never lowered her aim a single inch. Hood stood there quietly, wondering if the old lady was gonna just say fuck it and pop him. Finally, her gaze softened like she could sense he was legit. She nodded and backed up a little.

"Angelique!" she hollered over her shoulder. "You got some company!"

The apartment the women shared looked like it should have been in a private home instead of a pissy project building. It was clean and neat, and pretty curtains fluttered at the windows letting the sunshine in. Miss Baker's sister walked down a short hall and Hood took a seat in an antique armchair and relaxed. He smelled fried chicken and macaroni and cheese cooking in the kitchen. It reminded him of how good Miss Baker's house had made him and Moo feel during those cold, homeless days.

"Monty!" Miss Baker seemed to flow into the living room and Hood stood up with a big grin on his face. Over the years he'd seen her off and on, and the fact that he was a street hustler had never stopped her from treating him like a son.

"Miss Baker," he said as she took him into her arms and hugged him like he was still a desperate, hungry ten-year-old.

"Look at you!" she exclaimed beaming at him. She touched his face and smiled. "You grew up real nice, Monty. You sure did. After everything you and Moo went through, just look at you now. How's Marjay doing?"

They sat side by side on the sofa, and for Hood, a cloud seemed to darken the room at the sound of his mother's name.

"I don't really know. I just got home a minute ago. I guess she's straight."

"I heard they had you out on Rikers Island. That's no place to be, baby."

Hood lowered his head a little bit and nodded, then changed the subject. "I came by because I heard what happened. To your crib. To Diamond and her kids." He looked into Miss Baker's eyes. "I just want you to know that I'm sorry. None of that shoulda happened to you. Your family has been good to a lot of people around here, and I'm just sorry something so bad happened to folks who are so special."

Miss Baker's eyes filled up with sorrow. "It *was* bad, Monty. I still have horrible nightmares about Diamond where I can just hear her and those little babies screaming out for me to help them and I wasn't there . . ." her voice trailed off but her pain was so raw and intense that Hood could actually hear those screams in his soul. "But," Miss Baker seemed to push through her grief as she forced herself to brighten up, "none of us get through this life without our share of pain and loss. God takes who He will, when He will. What's important now is that those who are left living seek His favor."

Hood nodded, but only because he knew she expected him to.

"Look," she said, taking his hand. "I know you had it hard as a kid, you and Moo. I did an awful lot of praying for you boys when you were little, and I loved you for trying so hard to be grown up and brave for your brother. But I'm too old to bite my tongue, and the stakes are too high for me to keep silent. I know exactly what it is you doing on them streets, Monty, and we both know it's wrong. You're not a helpless kid anymore. You don't have to sell drugs to feed your brother, so there's no excuse for what you're doing. Do something else, Lamont. Find another way of life for yourself. I see what drugs have done to our community, and that's why I help as many people as I can, because we all have to fight it."

Miss Baker squeezed one of Hood's hands between both of hers and leaned close to him. "Monty, you be careful, you hear? There are consequences for everything we do in life, and sometimes they can be really harsh. You watch yourself because that poison can slide off your hands and sink down into your soul if you ain't careful. Doesn't matter if you never smoke it, sniff it, or shoot it up. Just touching it can kill you. Your mama wasn't no fool and she wasn't weak, neither. Her heart just got so crushed that she couldn't find her way clear. She was a good, clean-living woman trying to raise her boys all alone, but that poison didn't care about none of that. It still got her."

She reached into her pocket and took out a business card, then placed it in his hand. "Diamond might be gone, but me and my sister have devoted our lives to helping other folks who find themselves in a bad condition. You wouldn't believe how beautiful our people can be when they stop killing themselves through diseases, drugs, and alcohol. Give this to your mother when you see her—or to anybody you know who might be looking for help but just can't find their way. Tell them they can call on me, okay? Night or day. And if they're really searching for healing, between me and my trigger happy sister Ree-Ree who answered the door, we can help them find it."

$ $ $

Twenty minutes later, Hood ran up the steps of a tenement building, then stood outside of apartment 3C, knocking hard. When nobody answered he knocked even harder, then waited as he heard movement on the other side of the door.

"Oh shit!" he heard a female's voice as the eyepiece slid across the peephole. Then, "Egypt! Egypt!"

It was Sackie's sister, Zena, and Hood knocked again as he heard her calling for Egypt. Just knowing that his woman was on the other side of the door had his drawers bricking up like a mother.

When the door opened Hood stood there staring.

"Hi," Egypt said. The way she was standing behind the door, only her head and the top half of her body showed. She had a towel wrapped around her hair and she was wearing a bright-colored bathrobe.

"Sup."

"You're home," she said, smiling like it hadn't been more than five fuckin months since she'd been to see him. Hood forced himself to make his heart go as hard as his dick.

"Yeah. I'm home."

"When'd you get back?"

He shrugged. "I been back a minute. You gone let me in?"

She bit her lip and shook her head. One of her locks fell from the towel and hung down past her chin. "Zena got company—"

Hood snatched her so fast she bit down on her words.

Pulling her against him he kissed her deeply, sucking on her tongue and pushing his hands up under her robe to caress her softness. Her skin was still damp from her shower and she smelled like Coast soap and Johnson's Baby Oil.

Egypt responded immediately, opening her mouth and pressing her breasts against him as he cupped her naked ass. She moaned as she nibbled his lips and touched his hardness through his pants.

"Down here," she said leading him away from the apartment and down the short hall and past the elevator, over to the window. There was no way in hell she could let Lamont get inside the crib. Her and Zena had gotten higher than shit the night before, and the bedroom and dining room were both filthy and littered with empty vials, beer bottles, and blackened dirty stems.

Hood leaned back on the sill and pulled her close, his tongue seeking hers again as he consumed her mouth, moaning because she tasted so good. Finally Hood knew he was home for real. He'd spent about a hundred and eighty long nights dreaming about his girl. He'd seen her perfect titties, long sexy legs, and milk chocolate skin every night as he jerked his dick off in his fantasies. He forced himself to pull back and catch his breath.

His heart was all over the place. He wanted to hold her and hit her too. His dick throbbed and his hand jumped at the same time. He snatched the towel from her head and saw that her locks had grown a lot and they were laying around her shoulders. She was thinner, but still fine. Her big brown eyes pleaded with him from her ebony face. The whiteness of her smile put his heart on lock. Like time had stood still since the last time they'd been together. No other bitch in the world touched his body the way she did and he needed to feel those warm female hands on him right now.

Egypt couldn't believe how good he still looked and made her feel. He had put on some weight in the joint and his frame was solid and cut, like he'd been drinking gallons of muscle milk. He still had clear, smooth skin and that curly light brown hair, but it was his eyes that threw her off balance. Even as he touched her and generated heat in all the right places on her body, his eyes were colder and harder than she'd ever seen them before. Like he'd seen and done shit in jail that had just made him an even harder version of the rock he had been before he got knocked.

He must've gotten fresh for his court date because his hair was freshly trimmed and his light goatee perfectly edged up. His cologne was sexy as hell. She unbuttoned his G Unit shirt and trailed her fingers down his taut stomach, her hand tingling as she skimmed his washboard abs. Fuck a sixpack. Hood had a delicious twelve pack and she couldn't stop herself as she bent down and pressed her lips to his bulging stomach muscles and licked them.

She almost yelped when he grabbed her, his fingers digging into her shoulders. He pulled her up toward him and stared at her with some sure nuff love/hate in his eyes. She could read his confliction and understood it perfectly. He had feelings for her and needed to fuck her. But he was angry too. Furious. He couldn't understand why she'd flaked out on him for five months, and Egypt damn sure wasn't in a position to explain it.

Instead she slid her fingers down past the waistband of his pants and touched the head of his dick. It was throbbing, and slippery with his early juices. She stroked it gently, trying to tame the beast she saw lurking in his eyes.

"Let me go in the house and get dressed," she whispered, trying to get as close to him as possible. "Then let's go someplace . . ."

His body was stiff with anger, but full of need at the same time. She kissed his neck, then reached higher and sucked on his earlobe, biting it gently as she sucked it to a slow fuck rhythm.

Hood couldn't take that shit. He needed some pussy right now. Not in two minutes, neither. Immediately. They wasn't going nowhere.

Moaning, he pulled her closer and palmed her soft, thick ass again. He gripped her cheeks and ground his hard dick all over her, trying hard to hold his head and not bust off in his pants.

"Umm, baby. You feel so damn good. I been dreaming 'bout this pussy. Craving it . . ."

"Oh yeah," Egypt moaned and pushed her breasts against his muscular chest. She touched him everywhere. Tears began to stream down her face as she stared into his eyes. "This is a dream, ain't it Mont? A dream, baby. Yummm . . . Please. Tell me you're really here and this is not just another dream."

"It's real," he said, zipping his pants down and reaching for his dick. "It's real, girl."

"We can't fuck out here," Egypt whispered and pushed against his hips.

"Oh yeah we can." He pushed her arms aside and turned her around until her back was against the window. He kissed her. His tongue was hot in her mouth. Hard and demanding.

She moaned. "Somebody might come out and see us."

"So?" Hood shrugged. He grabbed her hips and picked her up and set her on the windowsill, then reached into his back pocket and came out with a condom. "They come out *here* they gone see a fuck show."

He lowered his head and nudged her robe aside with his teeth. Gasping at the sight, he put his mouth on her breasts and licked them all over.

Egypt got dizzy. The hallway felt like an oven as her body heat went up to boil. Hood unbuckled his belt and let his pants and boxers drop around his ankles. Ignoring the sounds of little kids playing outside, Egypt took the condom he was holding out and slid it on him. Then she grabbed his dick and pressed it to her throbbing clit. She rubbed it between her legs and moaned as her juices flowed.

Hood bent his knees and guided his missile toward her gushy, then thrust his hips forcefully, pushing into her until their pelvic bones smacked together.

Egypt's moans turned into sharp yelps. Hood sank into her, mashing her out, getting in deep. He held himself there and didn't move.

"Yeah!" she panted. "Right there. Oh yeah, right there." Her cries echoed off the walls. Her pussy was nice and stuffed. The head of his dick was killing her deliciously. In as deep as it would go. Only Hood could dig her out like this and she loved it.

Slowly, he withdrew. Watching as his plastic-coated dick slid out of her, Hood cursed and groaned. Her clit twitched visibly. His dick thumped to the same beat.

Squeezing her thighs, he slid his muscle back inside her warmth and humped so hard her head slammed against the window with each thrust.

"Lamoooont!" she screamed in ecstasy. Her body was on fire and she couldn't wait any longer. She wrapped her long brown legs around his back and rode that dick with bronco strokes.

He grunted in her ear and busted. Hard. His dick jerked so violently that she came too. Creaming him up. Gushing like a fountain.

When they finally fell apart from each other, Hood could tell Egypt was scared to meet his eyes. His anger began rising in him. For five whole months his heart had burned with questions and now, standing in front of her with his balls empty but his heart still full, he felt like striking out at her. Punishing her.

Snatching off the condom, he pulled his pants up then yanked Egypt down off the windowsill. The moment her feet hit the floor he cracked the back of his hand across her cheek sharply, knocking her back against the window. Hard. Twice. Then he leaned in close and asked the question that had been dogging him night and day for months.

"Where the fuck you been, and what the fuck you been doing?"

He could tell by the way she had devoured his dick that she had missed him and still felt for him. But why had his baby girl dropped off like that?

He ignored the fear on her face as she cowered against the window.

"I ain't heard shit from you in five months, Egypt. You supposed to be my ride-or-die. But no visits, no letters. Nothing. How was a nigga supposed to take that shit?"

He felt like hitting her again, but when Egypt finally looked into his eyes he could see her true feelings clearly. They were just as deep as they'd always been.

"I couldn't stand seeing you up there, baby," she said, trying hard to explain at least part of it. "After Daddy got murdered I was here all by myself, and I . . . I just couldn't handle that shit. Him gone, you locked up . . . nobody to turn to. Nowhere to stay. Some lawyer told me you coulda been looking at twenty years, Lamont! How was I supposed to sit there in that jail and face you knowing that?" Hot tears fell from her eyes and she turned her head to hide her guilt.

Hood's heart began to soften.

He knew what it felt like to be out there alone in the cold. He had never wanted Egypt to go through the kind of pain he'd suffered. Knowing how scared she must have been after Fat Daddy got popped cut into him deeply and he was sorry he had hit her. He pulled her into his arms.

"I didn't mean to hurt you," he whispered, planting small kisses all over the spot where he'd slapped her. A welt had already begun rising on her cheek, and he tried his hardest to kiss that shit away.

Two hours later his dick was hard again, but by now Hood and his girl were laying up in Cypress Arms, stretched out naked in his new bed, going at it hard. Hood busted a lot slower the second time around, but he was still way off his sex game and full of cum.

They stayed locked up in his phat room all night long, ignoring the sounds of Dreko and his niggas wildin on the other side of the door. Music was blasting and the smell of sticky green wafted under the door. Hood didn't move nothing but his dick. Him and Egypt stayed wrapped up in a blanket getting caught up physically and mentally. And later, for the first time in six months, Hood slept like a rock.

CHAPTER 27

Busted, disgusted, a fiend just can't be trusted!

EGYPT LAY WIDE awake beside her fucked-out, snoring man. Sleep was unthinkable as a mixture of conflicting emotions overtook her. She was a weak bitch. Nothing more than a project ho who was living a big-ass lie. She'd pissed all over her own dreams. Dropped her life goals with a quickness. Just to get on her knees and suck a fuckin pipe. She had become the exact thing that Lamont hated and despised most, and if he ever found out what kind of trash he was dealing with the results would surely be fatal.

She had been so happy to see him when he hit the block. Both of them had changed in those six months, but only he had changed for the better. He had seemed taller, and he was definitely bulked up, but not like one of them career jailbirds who ate fifty-pound weights for breakfast.

She loved it that he was back on the streets, but it scared her too. So much was different about her. Before Fat Daddy died, her and Hood would fuck half the night then lay naked together for hours. Wrapped in each others arms, they'd talk about everything in the world, from his street game and who was hustling who, to the operas she dreamed of one day seeing in France, to the patients in the world she planned to save with her own hands.

Tonight she'd let him fill up her pussy and dig her out as deeply as he wanted, and while she had come over and over, harder each time, the after-sex comfort she used to enjoy with him was missing. Gone. It was all guilt now.

She listened to the music coming from the outer rooms of the apartment and shivered under the blanket she and Lamont shared. Absentmindedly, she rubbed her feet against the hard muscles of his calves and tried to warm them. But the cold she was experiencing was nothing more than fear gripping her heart and spreading out to her limbs. Cold fear. And a cold craving, too.

Lamont turned over in his sleep, facing away from her. He used to sleep with his arm around her spooning her so tight that it could get uncomfortable. But not tonight. There was distance between them in the bed, and she figured he was still in jailhouse mode and it would take him a minute to snap back. Egypt turned over too, her soft ass grazing him. Her thighs were slick and sticky with her sex juices, and even though her mind was worried, her pussy thumped deliciously.

While her thoughts were troubled, Lamont was snoring like hell. Deep in that just-out-of-jail-and-just-fucked sleep. Egypt closed her eyes too and tried to push her guilt and fear deeper into her consciousness.

Somebody knocked on the door three times. It was a down-low knock. Coming on the sneak tip.

Egypt slid out of the bed and cracked the door.

The light from the hallway hurt her eyes.

Dreko stood there grinning. With his hand on his dick. "You owe me something, girl."

He put his head back and laughed.

"Sshh!" Egypt's heart banged. She looked over her shoulder. Lamont was still snoring. "Motherfucker is you crazy?" She tried to shut the door real fast, but he jammed his foot inside stopping her.

"Dreko!" she tried to whisper. "Get the fuck outta here!"

He laughed again. "Nah, you get your ass the fuck out *here*. I need some head baby. Some of that wet-neck. Hood done busted his, now I'm coming to get mines."

Fear crawled up her spine. "Stop playing," she begged him in a hoarse whisper. "You gone get us caught!"

He thought that shit was funny.

"I ain't his bitch, you are. Sheiit, Hood is my nigga. You won't be the first trick we passed around—"

"SSHHHT!" Egypt shushed him so hard spit flew out her mouth. Lamont coughed behind her and almost scared pee down her leg. "Please . . ." she begged. Tears were in her eyes. "Tomorrow. I'll get with you tomorrow. I'll do you good. Now go!"

"Look, bitch." Dreko reached into his sagging pants and extracted his long snake-looking dick. He maneuvered it around until it was sticking out of the waistband of his boxers and pressed flat against his belly. The head was fat and smooth, and he gripped the black shaft and stroked it to a slow rhythm.

"I ain't fuckin witchu girl. Either you gone come out here and take care of this right now, or I might get nasty and fuck around and wake ya boy up and put him down on our little secret. You owe me girl and your credit is already shaky. You could suck my dick morning, noon, and night for a month straight and still be in my pocket."

Egypt cried. Behind her, Lamont snored. She pushed Dreko in the chest as she walked from the room, crossing both the threshold and the point of no return.

"Where you think you going?" Dreko asked as she headed down the hall with her shoulders sagging and her head down.

She turned around and looked into the eyes of her man's best friend.

"To your room, Dreko," she said quietly. There was no fight in her. "To suck your fuckin dick."

He shook his head. "Uh-uh. Not in there. In here."

Three minutes later Egypt found herself in the small kitchen. On her knees. Under the dining table. Sucking Dreko's dick.

"Now you be real quiet down there," he cautioned her, pulling the tablecloth down around his thighs. Concealed from view, Egypt watched as he slid his whole dick outta his drawers. Balls too.

"I got a little business to take care of, so I'ma call my boys in here. If you wanna keep this shit on the low, you better suck it good and don't make me have to stop what I'm doing to say shit to your ass, you dig?"

Fighting tears, Egypt bobbed her head between his legs as he conducted business right above her with some of Lamont's closest boys. His nuts was cheesey and she tried to get away with licking only the head, but Dreko clocked that shit. He started thrusting his hips forward in the chair in an obvious fucking motion, trying to get deeper down her throat.

Egypt panicked when he moved like that, afraid that one of his niggas would realize he was getting his blunt puffed under the table and catch her kneeling between his legs, then bust her out to Mont. She stopped playing games then, and sucked his dick like she meant it. Dreko must have been satisfied with her work, because every now and then he would pause in his conversation with his sons and suck his breath in real hard with pleasure, then pick up with what he was saying like wasn't shit going on under the table.

Please God, Egypt begged. She thought of her father and wondered how her life had come to this. How she could have fallen so low. And why she wasn't stronger. Unable to hold them back, hot tears fell down her cheeks as she held her mouth open wide, sucking Dreko's dick down to his fuzzy nuts. *Please let this be over with!*

It seemed like hours before her prayer was answered. When the last nigga was gone from the kitchen, Dreko turned the whole fuckin table over and grabbed her by the hair, thrusting so far down her throat that her teeth scraped his dick and she gagged in protest.

"Next time," he panted, humping into her mouth with short brutal strokes, "I want my dick sucked, I don't give a fuck who—oh shit yeah, bitch," his whole body shuddered. "Yeah! Suck it like that, bitch!" He rose to his feet, forcing her to crane her neck. Cupping the back of her neck with both hands, he slid his hands up and held her head like it was an ass, then mouth-fucked her standing up. "I don't care who . . ." he managed to say around his sex moans, "you . . . be with . . . you gone . . . suck . . . my . . . fuckin . . . DICK!" His walnut cracked wide open, squirting his hot seed down her throat.

On her knees, Egypt sucked and swallowed, her head still encased in his death grip. Dreko's knees trembled as he humped and grunted out the last of his orgasm, and Egypt's lips and jaw ached so bad it was all she could do not to snatch herself out of his grasp and fall to the floor.

But to her deep shame, just minutes later she was in the bathroom with her lips wrapped tightly around yet another dick. This one was hot to the touch and made of glass.

"Here," Dreko had tossed two vials of crack to the floor after withdrawing from her mouth. "Go on and get ya head right," he laughed, "then gone back in the room and wake my boy up so he can get another shot of that pussy."

With Dreko's seed dripping down her chin, Egypt had grabbed the vials almost before they hit the ground. It didn't matter that she was on her knees, swollen-lipped with a damp pussy. She thought of those vials as payment for what she had just endured, and if she had to blow this glass dick to make herself feel better, then so be it.

CHAPTER 28

I'm well-prepared,
Never sleepin never scared
Keep the lamas for the drama
Mama keep me in ya prayers . . .

OLD HABITS DIED hard, and morning found Hood stretched out on the floor exercising his body and his mind. Spittin lyrics and doing killer push-ups. Egypt was asleep, so he took a quick shower then kissed her and slipped out of the apartment while it was still quiet.

Brooklyn was coming alive, and so was Hood. The streets were calling him and he had work to put in. The air was crisp and clear and he sucked it down like a starving man. Freedom was a blessed fuckin thing, and never again would he take it for granted. He walked through the projects and nodded at a few cats he knew. He was a street favorite and they gave him respect and stared at him with awe in their eyes. All around him there was movement. Squares were leaving for work, rushing toward the train station, while crackheads had finally finished chasing those tan goods, and ballers were just coming in from yanking that doe all night.

The first stop on Hood's agenda was Sackie's crib. He had been out when Hood had gone there to find Egypt, so he banged hard on the door and waited until his boy opened it.

"Whattup, muhfucka!" Hood laughed at his friend standing there half-asleep in boxer shorts with pillow hair sticking up all over his head. Sackie dapped him, then scratched his balls and led Hood into the kitchen. "Yo what it do?"

"Your boy Dreko came through for you, huh?" Sackie opened the fridge and peered inside. "Breakfast?" He reached in and tossed Hood a beer. They went into the living room and Sackie turned on the television.

"Yeah," Hood held the icy can in his hand for a moment, then set it on the floor. "My man's a fuckin soldier. Soldiers always come through for they comrades. Son done good while I was gone too! Nigga got the Arms, a fleet, a whole fuckin army. He done amassed crazy shit! The boy's a fuckin warrior!"

Sackie shrugged. He put his feet up on the end table and crossed his arms. "That depends on which end you lookin at it from. Ask a dun dun and that's what you'll get. But ask some of these real cats out here and they'll tell you a whole lotta shit done fell apart since you left. That fool went and killed every damn thing we built up, Hood."

"It don't look that way to me. Dreko took Xan's grimy ass out and that's why cats is hatin. That nigga was dead wrong for popping Fat Daddy, and if I wasn't on lock I woulda stretched Xan out cool myself."

Sackie swallowed hard, but didn't correct him.

"Xan made a big mistake, man," Hood went on. "He demanded loyalty in the game but he didn't show none himself. Fat Daddy was down with that fool for years. As much as he did for the crew Xan shoulda had some allegiance to the man. But a playa like him didn't know how to be loyal to nothing or nobody."

Sackie pressed on. "But you heard what happened to Big Monk, right? Somebody set his place on fire after Fat Daddy died and he ain't have no insurance. Dreko's the one who fingered that young cat Donahue, and Big Monk got wild and took him out. The cops just caught him a couple of months ago and his wife and kids had to move into a shelter."

Hood nodded. He'd seen Monk on the Rock and knew his boy would be back out on the streets in a quick minute. "Monk cool, man. That shit wasn't nothing but a misdemeanor murder. No witnesses, right? Then after sixty days the charge disappears. Dreko made sure nobody stepped up to snitch, right? Big Monk oughtta be grateful."

"Grateful for what? If it wasn't for Dreko, Big Monk woulda still been feeding his fuckin family instead of getting his cheeks spread and biting pillows on the Rock. Dreko's fuckin up everybody's flow. How do you think he got Ocean Hill? He used Riff to take down Chaos's click, then stood back while Chaos got knocked by the feds. Riff wasn't on top for a good month before he turned up dead over in that used car lot on Linden Boulevard. And Dreko was running shit in Ocean Hill that same day.

"He got Lil Jay going at Hawk's throat, and that cat Amp from Dumont Avenue is gunning for Vandy now. Your boy is planting shit on a crew from the eastside, then blaming that shit on a crew from the westside. Ain't no order in his game. He fuckin with the balance of shit. He's thrown mad chaos in the game and he likes it like that."

Hood shrugged. "Then them niggas is weak, Sack! Anybody who allows Dreko to get in they heads or in they pockets, they deserve it. This is Brooklyn! Only the strong survive, man."

Sackie made a noise deep in his throat, then went for broke. "Then what about Reem? Ya boy Dreko stirred up some nasty shit over in Raw's camp too. Don't forget, Reem *is* the street. Shit gone start stinkin real fast if Dreko try to go for his throat. What about it, Hood? You gone blow that shit off too?"

Hood grew silent as his loyalty was tested. Dreko was a renegade, but fuckin with a cat like Reem was unthinkable. Hood didn't know exactly how much shit had gone wrong, or why, but fury rose in him as Sackie opened his mouth and caught him up on everything that had happened while he was on lock. It took Sackie a minute, but his son broke it all the way down to him with truth. Almost all the way. Sackie couldn't bring himself to tell Hood who had really popped Fat Daddy. He didn't tell him about Egypt neither.

When Sackie was done talking, all Hood could do was burn inside. Dreko musta been smokin his own crack when he went up on Reem's block waving gats and claiming some wild hype about members of Reem's crew interfering in his biz. Reem's boy Robb Hawk pushed back hard and clowned Dreko in front of all his lil soldiers.

"And that's when," Sackie said, "Dreko put word out on the streets that he wanted Hawk's neck. He said Reem could go down with his nigga if he wanted to. But instead of taking that shit to Reem, some say Dreko took it to the man."

"To the cops? That's insanity, man. Fuckin insanity."

Sackie shook his head. "Not really, man. Hot 97 sponsored Reem's tour man, and that shit got cut short last week because of Dreko. Reem was coming off an interview when a kid from Tilden got popped outside the station. Dreko put the word out that Reem's boys did it. The police got the dime and had a big investigation going all over the news and shit, and that's when the station canceled Reem's tour. They tryna beef up their image, ya know? That's why they moved to Wall Street, man. They yanked back those tour dollars from Reem, man, and if Dreko wasn't your son Reem prolly would've murdered him by now."

Dreko was his nig and he was strong, Hood knew. But not strong enough to be going up against Reem Raw and them Bottom Half Boyz.

There was no way in fuck he could win.

$ $ $

The next night Hood rolled up in the Stank Mic, a popular rapper's club Reem had opened up on the border between East New York and Brownsville. He walked inside and greeted the tank-looking dude at the door.

"What it do, Toppa?"

A wide grin spread over the bearlike head of the bouncer. "Hood! My nigga! When they turn you loose, man?"

"A coupl'a minutes ago." He glanced around, noticing everything. "I see y'all changed shit up in here."

"Had to," Toppa shrugged. "Reem and them niggas blasted the whole damn place up a few months ago. Some cats from Crown Heights rolled through and we had to show them lil gangstas how to act."

Hood moved into the club and immediately began bouncing his head to a Joe Wright beat. Joe was one of the hottest young producers on the scene and his beats were sick and distinctive.

But it wasn't just the beat that captivated Hood as he walked into the main room. It was the dude who was up on the stage stankin up the mic as he spit some real nasty shit at the crowd. Hood stood in the back and listened as Reem Raw put his flow game down hard.

Step in the building you can tell they tense!
My whole fam here fresher than that Bel Air Prince
And uhm,

We get money and inhale that piff!
But if it's wood you can face that, I don't wanna taste that!
Your chick face stay below where my waist at,
When I skeet, she straight, I know she don't waste that!
You good? Nigga well I'm great, you should face facts
My flow bringing the N.Y. state back!

Reem was doing it up. He had on a bullet-proof vest for
the haters, but the crowd loved him. That lil nigga was on
his way up the music charts just like he'd always said he
would. He had something about him that spoke the truth
of the streets to music for real.

I got the cleanest, meanest team, N-J, N-J-S
I live and I breathe this!
My weed's greenish, white-haired and seedless
School of hard knocks, check! Reem's on the dean's list!

Reem's lyrics were tight as usual, but suddenly he switched
up his style and it seemed like his mood changed. And that's
when Hood realized his old friend had spotted him. They
eyed each other, talking without words. It was good seeing
his boy. They'd been real tight over the years, loyal G's to
the game and to each other. Hood lifted his chin. Letting
Reem see he came in peace. Showing him he was there to
try and make all the crazy shit Dreko had started right.

Reem responded with a dark look. Then he opened his
mouth and shit all over the mic. Letting his position be
known with much clarity and absolutely no doubt.

Feed fifths to the prick that told!
That's word to the streets and the strip I stroll,
That's word to the heat and the clip I hold,
Cross my fam, and straight to ya chin I go!

Look, I don't know what provoked him,
I don't know what he smokin
All I know is I smoke him
He come around me . . .

Now, I don't know what they told him,
all I know is I fold him
Fuck around and expose him
He come around me . . .

I'll BITE one of them niggas you know
I don't just talk threats!
You gotta see Reem 'fore you come at Hawk's neck!
You ill niggas ain't got a spark yet?
Fuck ya rhymes, you outshined if I get on your project!
My mind set like a nigga runnin in the projects
Brownsville, East New York, you know where I rep!
East side, nigga that vibe, you know I ride that

I'm RAW like sniffin coke lines off the dishes
I'm vicious, and I done been on both sides of the bridges
No signs of giving a FUCK about none a' y'all!
Whoever said you was nice, they was suckin' y'all!

Then Reem grilled Hood hard and spoke to his boy with pure murder in his lyrics. Game time was about to be up for Dreko if he didn't stand his ass down, and Reem broke that raw message down with a mean gangsta hook while staring dead in Hood's eyes.

I'm up next, Gag Order in effect
Drought time for that nigga now
I'm forcin him to stretch!
Yes! I'm 'bout cheese! These niggas is not G's!
Don't want it to jump off?
THEN KEEP HIM FROM ROUND ME!

I don't know what provoked him,
I don't know what he smokin
All I know is I smoke him
He come around me . . .

Now, I don't know what they told him,
All I know is I fold him
Fuck around and expose him
He come around me!

Hood nodded and turned away.

Reem's message was raw and clear: Get ya man in check else I'ma dead him.

CHAPTER 29

I know you wanna see me hit,
Blood leaking on the canvas . . .
But your sister and ya bitch?
They wanna see me in a sandwich!

IT TOOK LESS than a week for Hood to get back on his street grind. Dreko had built their organization up to a level that made it look like child's play back when Xanbar had been on top. Drug money was practically growing on trees and falling out of the sky, and everyone connected with D.W.I.T. was eating lush meals and rolling around with fat knots in their pockets.

"Ya done good, son!" Hood told Dreko one night as they counted the day's take. They had street teams positioned from Ocean Hill all the way down to the pedestrian bridge that crossed over from Brownsville to East New York, and the cake they raked in each day could be stacked real high.

Not only did Dreko commandeer two tenements, he had bogarted a neighborhood church as well. There was an industrial-size safe down in the church basement, and half of the doe that came out of the count room was stashed there until it could be washed through one of Brownsville's legitimate businesses.

The small business owners in the neighborhood were so terrified behind the brutality of Dreko's criminal crew that they paid him a business tax each week and did whatever else he demanded of them with no questions asked. He had a string of shiesty cops on his roll too. They enjoyed the extra food Dreko was putting on their tables so they turned their heads and looked the other way while he did his dirt.

It wasn't hard to see how his boy had managed to dominate and terrorize an entire neighborhood in such a short period of time. Every nigga with a gat was willing to pop one off, but not too many dudes gave less than a fuck about taking a few rounds to the dome too. Dreko was that guy. He was willing to die without a moment's notice for what he wanted. Not many gangstas could say that and mean it.

Since hitting the bricks, Hood and Dreko had ridden out on a lot of missions together, and and twice Dreko had simply walked up on some cat he thought *mighta* been scheming on their action and put his tool to his forehead and pulled the trigger. Just to send a clear message to the rest of the niggas on the block. And both times son had even pulled out a camera and took a picture of his work. Dead dude on the ground, brain juice running into the gutter.

"Look at that shit!" Dreko had laughed. "Nigga messed with the crew and got his forehead smacked!"

All that shit was well and good. The code of the street dictated that when a cat tried to gank you for your money, your bitch, or your status, you cracked him. But turf boundaries were fiercely guarded, and Hood cautioned Dreko against sliding his toe over the line Reem Raw and his team were holding.

"Don't do it, Dre. You got some beef with Hawk? Squash it. This shit can get so much bigger than that."

"Fuck that nigga!" Dreko exploded. A dark look came into his eyes. "Reem ain't the only general wit' a army! I got a whole tribe of gorillas lined up behind me! That nigga's dick ain't the only one long!"

Hood's tone was realistic. Cut and dried. "Son stop wildin for a minute and think. If we got a thousand goonies, Reem and them Bottom Half Boyz got two thousand. And every last one of them is street tested and loyal. Besides, all this beefin bullshit is bad for business. You go off fuckin with Reem's crew and it'll make shit go south with our connects. It just ain't worth the hassle. Business is booming on our side of the yard. Let's not put no cramps in our cash flow."

The mention of money woke Dreko up, and he finally agreed to stay out of Reem's territory, but Hood didn't know how long that shit would last. What he did know, was that if his boy put his toe over there, just one fuckin toe, Reem Raw and his click would rise up so hard that Dreko would surely lose both his legs.

$ $ $

It was deep in the night and Hood was sleeping naked on his back with a silk sheet covering his legs. He opened his eyes in the darkness and immediately he could feel the tension in the air. Shit wasn't right. His hand shot out and slid across the sheets searching for Egypt. When she wasn't there he sat straight up and was surprised to see her sitting on the windowsill.

One of her long brown legs was bent at the knee, and her chin rested upon it. Her hair hung past her shoulders and her eyes were wide in the darkness. They looked haunted and were filled with tears.

Hood checked himself. Instead of rushing to comfort her like he would've done back in the day, he just waited. And watched.

"I'm sorry," she said after a few minutes. She wiped her eyes and got down from the windowsill. "You was sleeping so good, I wasn't trying to wake you up."

Hood didn't say a word. Here she was looking crazy and staring at him in the middle of the night with tears all over her face. It was obvious that the girl had some shit she needed to get off her chest. Even though she hadn't been down for him while he pulled his bid, he still loved her, but he wasn't a fool and he for damn sure wasn't a fuckin herb.

"It's just too damn hot in here," Egypt said like she had an attitude. "I can't even sleep." She stood up and stretched her arms over her head. Her body was long and curvy. She had on a pair of light blue boy shorts and a matching Naughty Girls tank top. They'd fucked before going to bed and Hood remembered her being ass naked when he'd dozed off with her in his arms.

Eygpt pulled up the edge of her top and dried her eyes. She had been sitting there battling with herself as she feened for a hit. Money wasn't the problem right now. Getting out of this damn room was. Mont was paid and as generous as he could be. A few days after coming home he'd taken her shopping and told her to pick out all new shit. Bras, thongs, shoes, everything. Dreko had set aside some big bank for his boy to enjoy when he hit the bricks, and Mont had wrapped her in the best of shit, happily.

But none of that mattered right now and she was almost mad at Mont for coming home and throwing curves in her flow. The neighborhood drug czar was actually standing in her way. Blocking her game. Stopping her from doing what she wanted to do, and what she wanted to do was get high!

Instead, for the past two hours she had been laying next to Lamont listening to him snore while she had the most delirious of awake-dreams. Each time she closed her eyes she fantasized about wrapping her lips around a stem. It was almost like her brain was one big clitoris and she could bust a nut just by visualizing the thick curls of smoke and that sweet, acrid smell of burning rock. She was just too weak, and that poison was just too strong.

Egypt loved Lamont from her soul. She really did. And what he felt for her was pure and true. This she knew. But right now she needed some room to move because she wouldn't be able to hide this shit from Mont much longer. He was bound to find out. And when he did, he was bound to kill her.

$ \quad $ \quad $

Less than two weeks later Hood came face to face with his past once again, and this particular encounter was enough to make his heart thud to a halt in his chest. He was coming out of a clothing store on Pitken Avenue carrying three large bags filled with new gear. Slanging rock was a cash and carry business, and neither him nor Dreko had the time or the patience to be doing nothing as simple as laundry. Both of them shopped for new clothes two or three times a week and tossed their old shit off to the doljahs and dun duns, even their drawers, as soon as they brought new shit in.

Today Hood had laid out over a G for some Enyce gear and a few pieces by Rocawear. He'd bought some new footwear and twenty pairs of silk boxers too. A couple of fitteds, a dope jacket, and he was straight.

Sackie was standing outside the whip, which was double parked, and the horn beeped as he clicked the remote and unlocked the doors. Hood was about two steps from the curb when he stumbled forward, bumped from behind. Hand on gat, he whirled, ready to blow.

"Sorry." The nut who had fallen into him was wearing a long knit dress with all kinds of crazy buttons pinned to it. Not a clear spot was to be found on that shit, and the rusty pin-on buttons of all size, shapes, and colors, clanked and clanged against each other as she moved. She was skinny and tired looking. She dragged a raggedy black suitcase behind her on broken wheels. She was small-boned and she used to be pretty. She was his mother.

Pain squeezed his heart as he looked into her dazed, disoriented eyes. Her drug addiction and mental illness had driven the normalcy from her face and it had been so long since they'd seen each other that there was no recognition in her eyes for him whatsoever. She didn't even know who he was. She was with someone. A raggedy, one-eyed nigga who pulled a suitcase behind him too.

"Mama," Hood said letting his bags drop to the ground. He put his arms on her shoulders and searched her eyes hoping she would recognize him, her first-born son. She wasn't even forty yet but the harsh years of drugs and self-abuse had taken their toll. "It's me, Ma. Monty. It's me."

Marjay frowned, her eyes darting all over his face. She looked just like Moo when she did that, Hood thought sadly.

"I know who you is," Marjay finally said, busting out in a big grin. "You *is* that Monty, ain't you!" She hugged him, squeezing tight. Then she pushed him away and smacked his face. "Boy you s'posed to be round there taking care of your gramma! You out here foolin around in the streets. And where is that Monroe? Is you been watching your brother?"

Her friend laughed and smacked Hood on the back of his head. "Yeah! You s'posed to watch your brother!"

"Moo is de—" Hood almost yelled in his mother's face, but he caught himself. He looked at the nappy-bearded crackhead standing beside her and slammed the palm of his hand square into the man's bony chest. "Nigga if you *ever . . .*" Hood breathed deeply, willing himself not to strangle the cat. "If you ever put ya fuckin hands on me or my moms, I'll kill you where you stand. Straight blast your polluted ass away."

Marjay frowned. "Now you ain't got no reason to do Picky that way! He been helping me! He the one helping me get myself together so I can come to Gramma's and get you and Moo. We all gone live together again soon, Monty. I promise, baby. We gone be together again, all of us. Even ya daddy. You just watch."

Hood had been digging into his front pockets as she spoke. He held a fat roll of bank in his hand and all he wanted to do was throw it at her. She was skinny and she was dirty. She was trapped in a world of confusion and delirium. And even worse, she was a fuckin crackhead.

He peeled five twenties off the top of his knot.

"Here," he said, thrusting the money out at her. He would've given her a hundred times more if it could have saved her, but all she was gone do was smoke that shit up. Besides, he didn't want her little ugly friend to see her with a jackpot then get her somewhere and beat her up and take her money. Hood would really have to kill him then.

He waited while she stuck the doe down the front of her dress, then reached out and held her again. So what she was dirty and she smelled bad. She was his moms, and he loved her. But he was wise to the ways of a crackhead. This was gonna be his last time dishing off cash so she could get high. He was gonna put the word out thick on the corners too. Between him and Dreko, they oversaw every rock slanger in Brownsville and Ocean Hill. Marjay was gone hafta travel into somebody else's territory if she wanted to smoke any more crack because after today them boys in his sector better not sell his moms so much as a fuckin flake. No powder, no fish scales, nothing. If they did, and he caught 'em, he'd kill 'em.

$ $ $

Between Egypt and his mother, shit started fuckin with his head and Hood stayed in a foul mood for the next five days. A trap boy came up forty dollars short one night in the count room and he choked him so bad that the boy blacked out, nearly strangled to death. Four of his dudes had to pull him off the guy, and when they did Hood turned on them in a raging fury, lunging at them one at a time until he sent them all running out the building in fear for their lives.

Hood spent a lot of time guarding his mental state, scared that if he let himself think too deep or slip too far he'd find out that he was indeed his mother's child. He composed mad rap lyrics in his head, putting metaphors and similes together with flawless effort and delivering them with gangsta gusto over at the Stank Mic almost every night.

He battled cats on the mic and got mad props from his boy Reem, who still hadn't quite let that shit with Dreko rest.

"Man," Reem told him as he poured from a bottle of Krug. Hood had just come off the stage and the crowd was still chanting his name. "I got mad love for you, my nig. But your boy is grimy." Reem sparked up a blunt and pulled from it.

"You know, I seen your moms a couple of times while you was out there on that Rock, man. I tore her off some change and shit, but I could tell it was gone get wasted." He looked hard at Hood. "Nah mean?"

Hood nodded.

"I did a little asking around, you know. Wanted to make sure none of my teams was trading favors with her. And ya know what? Nobody on my side of the bridge ever sold to her. And they all know they better keep it like that."

"I appreciate that shit."

Hood had already put the word out about his mother to the slangers on his side of the bridge too, and the whole world was gonna hate it if one of them cats fucked around and violated it.

$ $ $

A couple of weeks later Hood was almost back to normal and everybody around him was breathing sighs of relief. Dealing with him when his heart was dark was dangerous and unpredictable, and not even Dreko wanted to fuck with that.

He jumped back on his grind, ruling the D.W.I.T. empire side by side with Dreko. But some static kicked up when one of their cats slipped on a payoff to the NYPD blue boys who were in pocket, and as a result three of their teams got knocked and tossed out on the Rock. Dreko went ballistic and blamed Sackie for the transgression.

"See? What I told you? That white boy is dumb as hell! He can run his fuckin mouth but he can't handle his business!"

"Nah." Hood rejected that bullshit. "It wasn't Sackie who slipped, it was ya new boy Vince. Sackie gave him solid fuckin instructions. That nigga just failed to follow them."

"How you figure that, man? Was you there when Sackie gave the order?"

"No. But Sackie's a vet, yo. He told me he relayed that shit properly so that's the truth to me. I ain't got no reason to doubt him."

Dreko narrowed his eyes, then opened his desk drawer and got a stick. He fired it up, then sat back and watched the tip smolder and burn.

"I hope you ain't crazy enough to believe everything that white boy say outta his neck, Hood. I'm telling you, that cat will lead you into a cold box."

"Man," Hood stretched his legs out in front of him and yawned. "Kill all that stupid-ass noise, Dreko. Sackie been down for this whole ride. I ain't never had cause to doubt shit that came outta that dude's mouth. He's a hard-body soldier. A true rider."

Dreko dropped his blunt to the floor and ground it out with his Timb. Then he walked over and positioned all six-feet four inches of his frame above his friend.

"But you ain't saying you trust that fool's tongue more than you trust mine, is you? Me and you done hustled a lot of shit together, Hood. *I'm* the one been down with you for the whole ride, remember?"

Hood raised his eyes. Danger was in them.

"Hey man." His voice had ice chips in it. "You might wanna back up off me, ya heard?"

Dreko hesitated, then broke out in a big grin. He took a few steps backward, laughing and grinning like shit was funny for real. "Aiight! Lil nigga you sitting here looking like a fuckin murderer! You got the jailhouse look in ya eye and ere'thang! Chill, partner. We riding the same strip, remember?"

Hood nodded slowly. He gave a *fuck* about all that grinning. Dreko had backed the fuck up, and that's what was important.

"You my nigga, Hood," Dreko said. He came over and held his hand out for some dap. "You know that shit, right?"

Hood gazed up into Dreko's grin. He caught a funny feeling deep inside, and all of a sudden the only thing he could see was that number one platinum emblem on Dreko's front grill.

He held out his hand and gave up the skin. But that funny feeling still didn't go away, and after a moment Hood realized it was because for the first time ever his boy's dap felt like it was leaving shit on his hands.

CHAPTER 30

This is gangsta rap!
And in the hood I got gangsta stats!
So fuck ya lil teardrops and ya gangsta tats!

IT HAD BEEN raining for four days straight, but that didn't stop the slangers. Them niggas was out there on a serious grind. Desperate customers was rolling up like clockwork, fixated on accomplishing their life's mission. Some came on foot with no umbrellas, others pulled up in whips with the windshield wipers going steady and waited as the trap boys ran out and delivered that corner action right to their windows.

Up in Cypress Arms, Dreko had shit bouncing. He pumped the volume on his system loud enough to blow out a speaker and had everything in the joint humming from the bass vibrations.

As usual, the house was full of soldiers. Even more

were in place downstairs on the door, and the sentries were up on the roof keeping their eyes peeled for trouble, even in the rain. A crew of Dreko's most loyal doljahs were high enough on the ladder to be allowed to stay inside and stay dry, and they passed the time playing spades and barraged each other's rap game with battle verses.

Dreko was buzzed and feeling himself. Earlier him and Hood had attended a meeting where they found out that one of their connects was cutting them off. The motherfucker was either gonna up his price to almost double, or completely drop them from his distribution list. Dreko had jumped crazy with the cat and demanded to know what was up.

"Hey, man," the young guy told him. His family was Columbian, but he was straight outta Brooklyn. His tone was easy, with no emotion. "Its about business, my friend. Reem Raw expanded his sector and those Bottom Half Boyz are trappin out more yay than I can keep 'em supplied with. Their shit is economical too 'cause they buying in bigger bulk. You know how it goes. Money is money, homey."

Hood had taken that shit in stride. There were other connects on their roster. This guy could straight suck his dick. Besides, Reem had a much larger sector so it made sense that his demand was higher. But Dreko had taken that shit personally, like the cut-off from the connect had cracked him straight on his chin.

"Them niggas better watch they fuckin backs. All of 'em. Reem, Hawk, Gita, Speedy. Even that fuckin connect. That whole crew gone get took down."

"You mean like you took Xanbar down?" Hood's voice came out quiet, but cold. He'd heard some grimy shit from the old guy Felton who used to work in Fat Daddy's shop back in the day. It seemed like every time he turned around somebody he trusted was buzzing some unspeakable shit in his ear. Shit that fucked with the G in him.

Dreko laughed and shook his head. He lit a cigarette, inhaled, and blew out an *O*. "Nah, nigga. Like *Chaos* got took down. That fool drew twenty years for trafficking and distribution. Shit, there was enough stats on him for them to give him twenty more. He came out lucky."

Hood knew he'd heard wrong. Snitching was something Dreko despised. Both of them had popped niggas dead in the grill for having loose teeth.

"That was you, Dre? You put the blue boys on to Chaos and then put the tool on Riff too?"

Dreko laughed. It came out sounding cold and nasty.

"You know me better than that, Hood. Friend or foe, I'd blow my own fuckin teeth out before I let 'em swing loose. Don't disrespect me like that, man. Chaos was grimy, man. You know that for ya self. He had a shitload of niggas lined up outside the DA's office just itching for a chance to rat on him. But I wasn't one of them."

Dreko had spent the rest of the rainy day getting fucked up, and now he was sucking down Patrón like it was water. Hood had watched his boy pop a few tabs of X that one of his dun duns was passing around. The more he drank, the cockier he got. He got fucked up until he was swole up on his swagger. Evil and on edge.

But all the other cats in the joint was wildin and having a good time. Cheeba was clouding the air, yak was being swigged back, and chickenheads was running around half-naked, jumping in laps and claiming their dicks for the night.

Shit got serious when four young cats pushed a few tables and chairs out the way and then lined up in teams to battle on the mic. Three of them were pretty good, but the fourth one was straight fire. They all shined though, and Hood dug the hell outta their flow. When they were done he leaned back in his chair and bust out with a dark, sinister hook that he had been humming in his mind for a good minute.

Who's pushin that work like me,
Down to go all out, put in that twerk like me, haah?
Who's getting them hoes like me,
Make 'em play that strip, go off for doe like me, haah?
Who carries the strap like me,
Keep one in the head, ready to clap like me, haah?
Who's on the block making traps like me, or
Up in the booth burning them tracks like me?

"Yo, Hood, spit that shit!" Sackie said. "You was resting up on that rock for six whole months. I know you got some tight shit stacked in ya arsenal, man."

Hood waved no, and shook his head.

But then a bunch of other cats joined in on the plea.

"C'mon man! You need to give these young muhfuckas a little rap-a-ma-cation!"

"Shit, I remember when we couldn't pry a mic outta that niggas hands! Now he out the joint and done gone all silent on us and shit."

And then: "Next to Reem Raw, you the best in these parts, hands down. Ain't nobody bars iller, nobody's delivery smoover. It's almost a crime for you *not* to spit."

Moments later Hood had the floor and somebody tossed him the mic. All eyes were on him and what came outta his mouth became the center of attention.

Ay yo, fresh outta state boots,
I'm feelin hateful
'cause livin on the rock will either make you
or break you,
But I was makin moves like A.I. breaking ankles . . .
So you'll never catch the Hood eatin . . . shit
on a shingle nah!
Niggas get mangled,
For fuckin with the squad,
I'm lookin for some pussy and they be lookin for some heart!

Grillin my eyes, yeahhh!
Fake promotion, noooo!
So when it's beef—I'm straight approachin them
Stretchin and poking 'em,
Anything to open 'em,

Raw got the Gag Order, no problem choking them!
I'm tryna blow, I'm the next to do it,
I'm getting doe and I'm the best in music,
And I can show and prove!

Niggas got crazy off that one. But then a buzz went up in
the room and danger sparked in Dreko's eyes. Everybody
knew he carried mad hate for Reem and his crew. It was
bad enough for one of them niggas to say Hood was the
best next to Reem, but for Hood to give respect to Reem's
mixtape *Gag Order* in his lyrics was a crushing blow to
Dreko's image and to his gangsta ego too.

But Hood spit the second verse like he didn't notice
the change in the air.

Who's pushin that work like me,
Down to go all out, put in that twerk like me, haah?
Who's getting them hoes like me,
Make 'em play that strip, go off for doe like me, haah?
Who carries the strap like me,
Keep one in the head ready to clap like me, haah?
Who on the block making traps like me, or
Up in the booth burning them tracks like me?

All day sticky green, rush haze blowing crews,
Twisting dutchies, niggas can't touch me!
And I'm a cannon in the home that I rep,
But keep a cannon when I'm roaming the 'jects,

Them niggas snakes out there—
Gotta grind, get ya cake out there!
But take ya time, gotta break out there . . . but don't slack up!
Drove by the spot, saw the drop, had to back up!
If I think it's sweet, grab the Glock have to act up!

You'll hear the tech spit if you tryta get to my throne,
I will wreck shit!
If you tryta take what I own!

N.Y. state, we oh-so-great, we pop tags,
Got dreams of a foreign estate and drop Jags,
For all you niggas crowdin the place, we not fags,
But you can catch four in the face from Sack's mag!
From this point on, we only fuckin with official dudes . . .
Hop in the cockpit, I'll show you how the missile moves!

The love was thick. Every cat in the crib came over and
dapped Hood out, giving up respect for his superior flow
game. Almost everybody. A kid named Kilo took the floor
next. They put on a new beat, and the kid got it in, showing his shit.

Move over or get pushed over!
I'm in too deep and the waters getting murkier,
I'm in the lead, y'all hurry up,
I been bringing the storm y'all just starting to flurry up!
Homey I been flames, you just startin to turn it up—

Dreko got up and snatched the mic outta the kid's hand.

"Nigga that's all you got? That lil weak-ass shit?" He turned to his boy Black. "Yo, throw that beat on by Game, man. You know that jawn he spit 'Where I'm From' on."

The beat started jumping and Dreko got pumped.

Come and roll with me I can show you how it's done . . .
I'm the shit, you wanna be me but can't!
I'm the MAN, oh yes I AM!
I'm the SHIT!

I'm the shit so go 'head witcha bullshit rap,
You say you gunnin but you runnin,
Get ya old head gat'd!
Go 'head wit' the bullshit, Black!
Soon as he move I'ma clip him and gun-hit him
Till his forehead crack!

Dreko looked right at Hood and spread his arms wide, like nigga bring ya shit. Bring ya shit!

Hood better do what he gone do to me!
I'm here in my community
Riding with all my soldiers and everybody
That's cool with me
Disrespect the I? Shit I gotta put the tool to him!
Leave him outstretched in a box
Now how cool is him?

Most of his lil cats laughed at that one, but that was to be
expected. They was on Dreko's dick hard anyway, scared
they wouldn't be able to eat without him.

I'm on the move again, cash money movin in
So call up your hooligans and tell 'em bring the Glocks,
You ain't got nothing to touch,
You gone catch rounds to the top,
That's another general dead and another open slot!

Come and roll with me I can show you how it's done . . .
I'm the shit you wanna be me but can't!
I'm the MAN, oh yes I AM!
I'm the SHIT!

It wasn't lost on nobody that Dreko was spittin directly to
his boy. But Hood was feeling hateful for real. He took it up
a few notches and slammed Dreko right below the belt.

Nigga all of my tools shoot,
Don't play the crazy role cause I don't give a fuck
If all of ya screws loose!
One shot, it'll blow all of ya screws loose!
Shoot niggas smoke too many L's to shoot hoops!
You?
Just a dirt bag,
Blowing on them dirt bags
Cops rush the door bitch I'm aiming for the first badge!

What had started out lookin like a regular old battle had turned ugly and was now an all out rap war. Hood switched up the beat and spit his next couple of verses to the beat behind Damian Marley's "Road to Zion."

I led a sinister past, but ya'll fag niggas livin a laugh,
And I went straight to war, never been in the draft
I'm a sinner, me and my niggas makin ministers mad . . .

Wasn't no holding Hood back. He had locked his teeth on Dreko's throat and he went in for the verbal kill.

This is gangsta rap!
And in the hood I got gangsta stats!
So fuck ya lil teardrops and ya gangsta tats!

Muhfucka I'm in the gutta blowing bags of the marijuana . . .
And I can feel it in the air when it's bad karma . . .
Round here we rock the flags like a badge of honor
Any beef they gone blast then they crash the corner
Hop out with the hammer then smack it cross ya
Damn face just for acting like you wanted drama!

Hood was straight actin up now and didn't give a fuck. He had taught Dreko everything he knew about runnin niggas on the street, dealing crack, and getting that gwop. That nigga had it twisted all the way around. Hood was number fuckin one on this side of town. Dreko was a distant fuckin number two. On the strip and on the track.

Duckin the N.Y.P.D. jakes,
I understand why this nigga wanna see me break!
He can't imagine what it took just to be this great!
How a nigga say I'm shook, never seen me shake?
He fake!

You want the streets? Yell at me, I'm that guy!
He say he better than Hood? He told you a flat lie!
Mama said when you "the shit" you attract flies!
I clap mine!
So keep my name out ya rap line, nigga!

CHAPTER 31

It's about to be a showdown
Whoaa now . . .
Got me paranoid lookin all around,
Say it ain't nothing to it but to keep it moving,
Or some shit gonna have to go down . . .

ABOUT A WEEK later Sackie sat on the toilet smoking a cigarette and taking a shit. The loud voices on the other side of the door were fuckin with him hard, and he inhaled deeply as he tried to get his temper under control and figure out his next move.

He was itching to crack Dreko's grill.

It was Sunday morning and Dreko was in the spot wildin out on Zena, getting up in her face and scaring the shit out of their daughter. Sackie knew his sister was terrified shitless of Dreko. Plenty of gangstas on the street were scared of him too. But lately Sackie had been getting

a vibe that all Dreko's wildin out on Zena was really aimed
at him instead of his sister. He bonked out on her almost
every time Sackie was in range. Like he was daring Sackie
to G up for his sister or something. And the more Sackie
tried to stay cool on that shit, the harder Dreko rode Zena.
He rode the hell outta his baby daughter too.

The lit cigarette made a quick whooshing sound as
Sackie reached between his thighs and plucked it into the
cold toilet water. He could hear baby Andreka screaming in
the living room, and Zena was crying in her bedroom too.

"Shit." Sackie stood up and looked in the mirror. Zena
was stupid as fuck over Dreko and Sackie had sworn he
was gonna stay out of their biz. No matter how bad Dreko
shit on Zena and Egypt, he was their crack daddy and
they submitted to him at all costs. Zena was long lost,
and Egypt was just as bad. The guilt Sackie felt over Fat
Daddy's murder was the only thing keeping his tongue
quiet about her. If it hadn't been his gat that had smoked
her father, Sackie would have put Hood down on his girl a
long time ago.

Anger burned in his clear blue eyes as he stared at the
reflection of his own scowl and listened to them going at
it on the other side of the door. He was almost sure that
half the shit Dreko was talking was meant for his ears and
he wasn't gonna be pushed but so hard. He was tired of
Dreko and his shiesty stroll. He was tired of watching him
shit on good people too.

It had taken Sackie some thought, but he'd finally figured out why Dreko hadn't tried to take him or Lil Jay out

yet, and why he had gone all out to make sure Hood beat his attempted murder charge and got back out on the streets.

The cat was an actor.

He liked to floss and he had to have an audience to impress. None of the shit he'd amassed was worth jack unless Dreko could flaunt it in the right faces. He gave a fuck about what the dun duns and the doljahs thought. They were real easy to impress. But they hadn't walked the hard roads with him. None of them had been around to bear witness to the bottom rung he'd started out from, and then seen how high he had climbed. Sackie and Lil Jay had known him from kiddiehood and could testify to his upward travels.

And Hood? Shit. Dreko had been running a fever ever since the night all those years ago when Xan had put Hood in charge. By putting Dreko beneath Hood on the food chain Xan had practically sealed his own death warrant. Dreko had waited years for the right opportunity to come blasting out of that number two spot. He had burned every day with the need to show Xan and Hood who was really number one on the block, and he'd done it too. The streets were his. Fuck all the bodies he'd had to lay down just to prove a point. Xan was dead and Dreko was in charge. He'd done it.

Zena's cries were louder. More like shrieks of alarm now. The baby's cries had changed too. She was actually yelping like a puppy whose paw had been stomped on.

"Hell fuckin nah," Sackie muttered, storming out of the bathroom. Zena was one thing. His niece was something else. He entered the living room to find Zena jumping on Dreko's back as he gripped the screaming baby by her tiny wrist. Her naked little body twisted in the air as she dangled painfully by her father's side.

"Yo, muhfucka!" Sackie ran across the room and stopped in front of Dreko. They stood toe to toe, eye to eye. Sackie reached for the baby as Dreko snatched her away. "Man what the fuck is you tryna do? Break her fuckin arm?"

Zena was still screaming and punching all over Dreko's back. He didn't even feel it as he shifted his weight and threw her off with almost no effort. Zena hit the floor and moaned, then rolled over with her teary face upturned toward her brother. Her eyes begged for help and Sackie found it hard to resist.

"Is this your fuckin baby?" Dreko spit, yanking Andreka painfully and thrusting the baby up higher in the air until his arm was above his head. The baby yelped then shrieked louder. Urine ran from her tiny body and trickled down her legs to the floor, splattering her father's new boots.

"Gimme her," Sackie demanded, reaching for his tiny niece. She wailed with her mouth wide open and her terrified eyes were full of tears. Damp tendrils of curly hair clung to her face.

"I said give her to me, you stupid muthafucka!"

Dreko laughed and turned away, pushing Sackie in the chest as he jerked Andreka out of reach again. Then lowering her slightly, he kissed his daughter on her wet, open mouth and chuckled at her frightened screams. He laughed again, and then without warning he tossed her. Hurled by one arm, the baby flew past Sackie and landed on the sofa where she had been sleeping peacefully before all the madness started.

"Man, you is crazy!" Sackie said in disbelief. He rushed over to the baby and picked her up. "Straight fuckin crazy. This is your little girl you throwing around, Dreko!"

"Yo," Dreko warned, "you gone wanna stay the fuck outta my business, Sackie," Dreko said, his voice deadly. He touched the spot on his waistband where Sackie knew he kept his burner. "You run ya mouth too fuckin much."

Sackie's hand went to his side as well. He had his strap on too.

"Oh?" Dreko said, eyebrows raised. He stepped up closer. "You wanna get with me, muhfucka? Come on wit' it. I'll open up ya fuckin forehead right now. Bloody this whole muhfuckin crib up! Let's go!"

Sackie backed off. He wasn't scared of Dreko. He just didn't want no gunfire and bloodshed going down in front of his sister and his niece. He'd be patient and save that shit for another time and another place.

Noting his hesitation, Dreko nodded. "That's what the fuck I thought. If you wanna do something to me, you better do it. Otherwise, go sit your stupid ass down at that computer and stay outta my biz. I do whatever the fuck I wanna do around here, homey. With Zena and with Dreka, because both of them ugly bitches belong to me."

CHAPTER 32

I hope you lil cats got ya game perfected . . .
Don't come around here and get ya gangsta tested!

"SEE YOU NEXT week, Mrs. Ono," Sackie said a couple of days later as he left the Asian dry cleaners through a back door. It was his last stop for the day, and his whip was parked in an alley in back of the store where a couple of corner doljahs waited inside.

The thin old woman smiled and waved real cheery like, as if Sackie wasn't forcing her and her sick husband to wash Dreko's drug money through her busy little shop each week. There were more than thirty small business owners like her in the hood whose laundered funds were funneled to Sackie's uncle Pete, who in turn set up phony accounts and invested in high-yield stocks. But it was Sackie who studied the market and anticipated the trends.

He decided when it was time to buy and when they should sell, and over the past few years he had made so much legal money for D.W.I.T. that he was far more valuable than any trap boy or sector capo.

With the day's work done Sackie dropped the doljahs off and drove off as his mind wandered back to the two problems he had at hand: Hood and Dreko.

Every bit of loyalty he had in his heart went to Hood. There was no doubt about that. Yeah, he had smoked Fat Daddy and if Hood ever found out he was the trigger-man it might bring some awkward shit between them, but these were the streets. Cats did what they had to do to survive, and he hoped if that news ever reached Hood's ears his boy would understand that. Killing a muhfucka was a common thing out here. There was no shame in pulling out a tool and puttin in work. Every one of them had done it at one time or another. But it was that second problem that fucked with Sackie's head the most. The shit with Dreko, and the small matter that had gotten Hood knocked and sent out on the Rock in the first place.

Sackie walked down Pitken Avenue, deep in thought. There was no other way to look at it. Dreko was worse than psycho. He was a fuckin snitch. Sackie had practically heard it from the horse's mouth. In fact, he'd gotten it from the very detective who had cuffed Hood and administered him an ass-whipping on the morning of his arrest. The fat, redheaded cop was dirty, and worked out of the 73rd. Before joining the force he had run hard with Sackie's Uncle Pete, and whenever he got a little extra change from street busts and cash bribes he called on Sackie to help guide his market investments. The DT had told Sackie that the call had come from somebody inside the abandoned house where they busted Hood. And since the only other person who had been there ended up getting away with the entire proceeds of a drug hit, come on. It didn't take a fuckin stock whiz kid to figure out how to add that shit up.

But dropping that kinda bomb in Hood's lap was gonna create some severe consequences, Sackie knew. Hood loved Dreko, for real. They had history, and Hood would never forget how Dreko had run to the hospital with Moo cradled in his arms. That act alone had earned Dreko Hood's loyalty for life, but Sackie had to admit that Dreko had been hard-body and loyal too, dead on point for Hood for a lot of years. No doubt he had some kinda twisted love for his man. But Dreko also had a lot of jealousy and hate for Hood too.

Hood was street smart as fuck, though. Sooner or later he'd be forced to face up to who Dreko really was, and that shit wasn't gonna be nothing nice. Sackie knew his boy was a beast, and he'd come out clawing and biting savagely like one too. Yeah, there'd be some casualties but that was a risk Sackie was willing to take. And hell yeah he had his own reasons for wanting Dreko deaded. If Hood didn't do it then Sackie might have to.

And why not? The cat made a mockery of the G-code and he wasn't fit to live. He brutalized women. He terrorized babies. He was a snitch bitch who had risen to the top the grimy way, and for that alone the penalty he paid had to be most severe.

The corner of Bristol and Pitken was crowded. Sackie found a parking spot and ducked into a pizza shop, bought a slice, then walked down the street eating it. When he got back to Hopkinson Avenue where his whip was parked, he climbed behind the wheel, hit Hood on the chirp and told him to meet him at the crib.

By the time Hood arrived Sackie was on the computer browsing the NASDAQ website and studying Standard & Poor's figures from the *New York Times*.

"Whattup," Hood greeted his man. He dapped him and stepped into the small apartment.

"What it do?"

Hood shrugged, taking off his jacket. He pulled up a chair from the dining table and sat down beside Sackie so he could see the computer screen. "Same shit. Me and Dreko been out there runnin the business. Keeping shit tight. What we looking like in the bank?"

Sackie leaned back in his chair, and put his arms behind his head. He frowned at the computer screen, then turned to Hood. "I don't know what the fuck *we* lookin like, man. But I know how you lookin. Blinded."

Hood cocked his head. "Man what the fuck is you talkin about?"

"Dig," Sackie said quietly. He swiveled his long legs around and turned to face his boy. "You my man, Hood. That's truth. A whole lotta cats out here couldn't even see me as a G until you and Xan embraced me and shot down all that bullshit they was talking. You know I'll pump a round in a cat's throat over you, and there's never been a time when you had to question my loyalty or my heart."

"Man," Hood laughed. "What the fuck is up with you?"

"Ain't shit wrong with me," Sackie barked. "But what the fuck is wrong with your eyes, muhfucka? What happened? You got locked up and went blind? All that fuckin time you sat up on that Rock and you ain't spend none of it wondering how the fuck you got there? How did them jakes know where to find you, Hood? Just how the fuck did they sniff you out and follow your trail straight back to that empty house?"

"I know how they peeped me. It was one of Chaos's boys. One of the niggas his mule was making a delivery to. We had 'em all tied up on the floor and one of them bitches snitched. Dreko got him, though. That cat got handled a long time ago."

Sackie shook his head. "Or it coulda been the muhfucka who got away with the coke too. You ever stop to think of that?"

Hood shook his head too, like he didn't wanna believe it, but of course he had considered everything about his case left and right and from bottom to top. Six months alone is enough time to think. Even longer when you might be facing twenty years more years. In this game every fuckin body was a suspect. But he wasn't about to show his hand to Sackie. Not yet anyway.

"Man what was Dre supposed to do with all that powder? Give that shit back? By the time he got to Xan that grimy bastard had already smoked Fat Daddy! There was nothing else to do but keep it!"

Sackie swallowed hard at the mention of Fat Daddy's name.

He shook his head, praying Hood would see the truth and he wouldn't have to tell it all.

"That's a lie, man. Fat Daddy was alive and well and counting on you to come through. Xan was on time waiting for his package, and if he had gotten it shit woulda been all the way straight. Dreko is lying. Fat Daddy didn't get capped until *after* that dope disappeared."

"How the fuck you know all this, Sack? Was you there? Dreko been like a brother to me. We jumped into this game together side by side, and when that fuckin prosecutor wanted me to face the music in that courtroom, it was Dreko who made sure the tune got changed. I walked outta there a free man, Sackie. If Dreko was dirty, why the fuck would he do that?"

"Because he just had to *show* you man. Letting you sit in jail and hear about it wouldn't have done it for him. He needs you out on the streets so he can show you every single day, man. That's what get his juice going on a daily, man. Pushing it up in you face that it was him who took the top kingpin down, and that makes him bigger and better than you."

Hood shook his head.

Sackie tried harder. "Come on, man! You might *think* that dude got love for you! But who else knew where y'all was that morning besides Dreko and Xan? Which one of them muthafucka benefitted from getting you off the streets?"

Sackie scooted his chair close and spoke fast.

"Dig. From way back in the day Xanbar set up our ranking order. You was always number one and Dreko was always number two. You didn't smell nothin shitty when you came home and seen Dre had a number one plastered on his grill? What? You going to jail automatically meant when you got out he became the boss and you became his bitch?"

Hood stood up and dapped Sackie without another word. He was no fool, and he knew Sackie wasn't no hater and he wasn't no emotional muthafucka neither. Sackie was a loyal soldier and a trusted G. Hood had been weighing his own suspicions ever since the morning he got knocked, and even though he kept them on the low, they had always been there. He just hadn't been willing to bring no charge to the table unless he knew certain things for sure. Everybody's loyalty was liable to be tested in this game. He would make his own moves in his own way. In his own time.

Hood walked out of Sackie's crib spittin what would end up becoming one of his most famous rhymes.

A million dollars in ya hands—
what's power to you?
But if he tellin' on his man—
what's a coward to you?
You on ya muthafuckin grind!
what's a shower to you?

Don't let the money change you
It do what you allow it to do!

CHAPTER 33

So why cry if you live or you die?
Take the F outta life and you livin a lie!

A FEW NIGHTS later Egypt sat up on the side of the bed. She'd lain there for over an hour until she was sure Mont was asleep, and now the streets were calling her and it was time to make that move. It was getting harder and harder to keep him from peeping her game, and Egypt promised herself that after she copped these next few vials she was gonna try real hard to shake her crack craving for a little while because she had a feeling he was starting to get suspicious.

Dreko was making life so hard for her. Not only was he still being tightfisted and sometimey with the drugs, that fool acted like he didn't even care if Hood busted them acting ill. He came around demanding pussy or salad or head whenever he felt like it, and that was usually at a time when Mont was most likely to catch them.

That shit always terrified Egypt. She knew exactly what kind of disgust Mont felt toward chicks who sucked off the pipe, and just the thought that he might find out how low she had sunk terrified her. But none of that meant shit to Dreko. He was the kind of cat who lived for danger. His dick didn't even get hard unless there was something crazy about to go down and he might get caught, like waiting until Lamont got in the shower, then quickie-fucking Egypt right there in his boy's bed. Or walking into the living room with her and snatching his long dick out, demanding she give him three big licks before he would leave her alone. His shit got turned on extra high when there was a house full of niggas present and somebody might walk in and bust them at any moment.

"Put that shit away!" Egypt would beg, wild-eyed and glancing toward the kitchen, hallway, and bedroom doors to make sure nobody was coming.

Somehow Dreko would find that shit real funny.

"Just three licks!" he would laugh. "I'll put it back as soon as you give me three licks!"

Egypt would disgust herself by glancing around again, then running over to him and ducking her head down and licking the tip of his dick three times real quick. But sometimes he was satisfied with that, and sometimes he wasn't.

"Nah, come on now, E. You know you didn't do that shit right. I ain't hardly even feel them last two licks. Hit me again."

Oh, the fuckin torture! These days he kept her nervous and strung out on a crack string, only dishing that shit off to her when she was so gripped by a craving that she was begging and crying. Then he'd either fuck her, beat her ass, or call Zena in and humiliate her by making them eat each other's pussies, or worse, do his back the way he liked it.

Egypt's only escape was the glass dick she worshipped, but getting it was hard when Dreko was acting so stingy with his product. Sometimes even when she was obedient and did what he wanted he'd still only toss her enough for one or two hits, so both her and Zena were forced to go out in the streets to get what they needed from one of his trap boys, who would sometimes look out for them.

Egypt shuddered as she dressed in the darkness, preparing to cop the poison that she needed to survive. She had scraped real low to feed her habit, and she felt dirty all over. Filthy. Guilty. She missed her father. She couldn't even sleep without having horrible nightmares behind the way her life had turned out.

Egypt gazed at Lamont as he slept. He was a true-to-the-game baller. No man's doljah. It was only a matter of time before he found out about her and Dreko and a mountain of shit collapsed on top of both of their heads. And when that day came, Egypt knew both her and Dreko might as well be dead. Because there was no way in hell Lamont would forgive either one of them.

Egypt crossed the room and stood by the door. She glanced at Lamont again and tears came to her eyes. She loved him. God knows she did. But she loved crack too. Maybe even more.

$ $ $

"You want some eggs?" Egypt asked two days later. She pulled off her jacket and opened the refrigerator, scanning the shelves. She had just come in off another all-nighter, and found Hood already awake and moody and staring out the kitchen window into the dawn sky.

He turned around, his eyes cold and questioning. "No. I want some muhfuckin answers."

Egypt sucked her teeth. "I already told you, Lamont. Zena called and asked me to come help her with the baby. She was running a fever and they didn't know what to do."

"They who?"

She shrugged. "Zena and Sackie. Neither one of them know nothing about babies. Just cause I went to Clara Barton they swear I'm a nurse. All I did was give her some Tylenol and a cool bath and she was straight."

"So you telling me that shit took all night?"

"Not all night. We watched a movie too. Some stupid shit. I forgot what it was . . ."

Hood let her talk that dumb shit. She had turned into a big liar and he wasn't impressed by none of it. This was the second time he'd woken up at night to find his woman gone, and wasn't no bitch that slick with her game that she could run it on him.

He stared coldly as she moved around the kitchen trying hard not to believe his heart. She was skinny. She'd lost her ass. Her locks was nasty. She hadn't said a word about college or bragged about all her hopes and dreams. Hood kept his eyes on her as she fixed a plate of fried eggs, ate a mouthful, then threw the rest in the garbage.

Either Egypt was getting high, or she was out there fuckin some nigga. She wasn't the type to trifle with drugs, so she had to be slumming with some nigga. Fury washed over him as he visualized her getting dicked by some cat while he was sitting up in the joint. That's probably why she'd fallen off on him for five fuckin months. Hurt and betrayal rose in him and his eyes were snake-like as he watched her. Just because he hadn't said anything didn't mean Hood wasn't on it. He just couldn't see her doing none of it. Fuckin with drugs, fuckin with some nigga... Yeah, they had been together since childhood and his was the only dick she'd ever had. Maybe she had gotten bored waiting around for him. Decided to sample some new shit and see if it was good. Still, it was all impossible for Hood to picture. He knew Egypt like a book, and his love for her made him give her the benefit of the doubt. But his rage had her looking like prey, and he wanted so badly to pounce on that ass.

He forced himself to be as still as he could. The only thing that moved was his eyes and a throbbing vein on his temple that beat dangerously. Shit had been hard for

Egypt after Fat Daddy got killed. If she had stepped off into some lame nigga's bed because she was hurtin and alone while he was locked up, that was one thing. But to have the bitch getting up outta his bed at night and running into the streets behind some dick now that he was back, oh . . . that was something else.

An image of his mother flashed through his mind and something so dark and menacing pulsed through his body that hot blood wanted to burst through his nose, his ears, and even his eyes.

This better not be what the fuck it looks like, he thought. *It fuckin better not be.*

CHAPTER 34

Honor and respect never gets you no regrets, lady . . .

IT WAS LONELY at the top, but Dreko wasn't complaining. He had shit locked down in Brownsville and nobody could dispute the fact that he had risen to supremacy with nothing but his hammer and his heart, and niggas knew better than to test either one.

You couldn't tell it from the outside, but on the inside Dreko was still furious over that battle rap that had gone down between him and Hood. That nigga wasn't all that on the mic, and any other bitch who came up in his nest tryna rip him with them lame-ass lyrics woulda caught a hot round to his dome already.

But there were other ways to get at that nigga, and Dreko didn't mind going around the back door when necessary. He was out there proving he was large almost every day, whether his boy knew about the greasy shit he did or not. He was still doing it. But despite it all, Hood *was* his nigga and while Dreko *did* have love for him, there was nothing about that fuckin Sackie that warranted an inch of Dreko's restraint. Whether it was about Hood or that skank crack-ho Zena, that ghost muhfucka Sackie had been trespassing on his game for a minute now, and it was time to teach that bitch a lesson in street respect.

And that's why three days later Dreko and his boys were sitting in his g-ride watching as Sackie walked out of his building next to a chunky dude with spiked red hair.

"Bitch-ass muhfucka," Dreko muttered under his breath as the two white cats dapped out. Sackie looked around real quick, then stood outside the vestibule while the dude climbed into a black Mazda and sat there reading something as his car idled at the curb.

Dreko fumed in his seat. It was time to bust a fuckin move and he planned to bust one real hard. Sackie was a white boy with a big fuckin mouth. He'd been whispering shit in Hood's ear ever since his boy hit the bricks, and his loose teeth was about to get him smashed.

The red-haired cat pulled away from the curb and drove toward them as he rolled down the street. Dreko grilled him hard, with recognition in his eyes. The last time he'd seen this cat had been the day Hood went to court and his witness bitched up and caught amnesia. The first time he'd seen him was the morning Hood had gotten knocked and tossed across the hood of a police car.

Gazing at the building, Dreko narrowed his eyes as Sackie turned around and went back inside. There could only be one reason them two white boys was fuckin around in the same airspace, and one of them was gonna catch it bad.

"Yo, who the fuck was dat white guy?" Black asked as the white dude rolled by. He twisted a toothpick around in his mouth, then turned a bottle of brew up to his lips and swallowed.

"Which one?" Dreko asked with a deadly grin. "The cat in the whip is a fuckin jake. A fat-ass DT from over at the 73rd. But the big-mouth fool who just went back in his building?" Dreko chuckled humorlessly. "Oh, that muhfucka is a dead man."

$ $ $

"I'm hooking up with Egypt and we're going out," Zena called out to Sackie as she leaned over the bathroom sink and stared into the mirror. Her face was so skinny it made her eyes look huge. She pressed her tongue to one of her front bottom teeth and wiggled it. The shit was so loose she could have spit it out with one big sneeze.

Zena sighed and made sure her gear was straight. Her cute little Armani jumper had gotten three sizes too big, and the belt she had tied around her waist was on the last notch and still not tight enough.

Before she had hooked up with Dreko and started using, Zena had been a stunna who had all the brothas wanting her. There were a lot of Hispanics in the hood and a couple of Asian chicks too. But there weren't a whole lot of straight up blondies walking around Brownsville, especially one who had an ass like a sistah. Zena peeked over her shoulder at the sag below her waist. Well, she used to have a big ass. That shit was dried up and gone now.

As usual her brother was on the computer playing with some stock charts. The small desk he sat at was only about ten steps outside the bathroom, so she knew he'd heard when she said she was going out.

"You still mad?" she asked, walking over to put her arms around his neck. She hugged him, her stringy blond hair falling over his shoulder. "Don't be mad at me, Sackie. I said I was sorry and it won't happen no more. I mean it this time. I'm through with all that. For real."

Sackie grabbed her pencil-like arm, and pushed her away. "You gotta chill with all that shit, Zena. It's fuckin you up real bad. Egypt too. Both of y'all was too busy getting high the other day to care about where your baby was and what she was doing. What if Dreka had swallowed that fuckin crack and died? Huh? What woulda happened then?"

Zena felt so guilty. Sackie had come home and found Andreka playing on the floor with a piece of crack in her mouth. She was almost walking now, and she must have pulled herself up and grabbed the drugs off the dresser while Zena and Egypt were busy sucking on their stems.

Sackie had picked up his niece to kiss her, then seen what was in her mouth and gone crazy on Zena and Egypt.

"I'm so sorry," Zena said. And she really was. She might not have been the best mother in the world, but she loved her little girl with all her heart. She looked at her brother and bit her lip, on the verge of blurting out her plans. No, she held herself back. Miss Baker had told her to speak up and claim her recovery, but Zena didn't want to tell Sackie about her plans until *after* she had taken that all-important first step.

Zena was nervous, but she was ready. Running into Miss Baker was the best thing that could have happened to her. So much of what was wrong in her life was wrapped up in her self-esteem and her need to fit in and belong somewhere. She'd never been enough of anything in her own eyes. And when Andreka was born HIV positive, that had been the ultimate proof of her inadequacy. Not only had she managed to make all the wrong choices in life, but Zena had given her innocent baby a deadly disease as well, and no amount of getting high in the world could help her forget that.

But then God sent Miss Baker back into Zena's life. The older woman had hugged her tightly right out on the street that morning, holding Zena in her arms and admonishing her for not coming back to the clinic.

"Why didn't you come back to see us? We've been trying so hard to reach you!" Miss Baker said beaming. "I've got some news that I think you'll be happy to hear."

Miss Baker couldn't tell her what that good news was standing right out there on the sidewalk, so Zena had taken the bus with her to Brookdale Hospital and sat nervously in Miss Baker's office as the older woman looked through her file.

"Now normally Doctor Beatty would be the one to tell you this, but since I've finally gotten you in here I don't think he'll mind if I give you the good news."

Miss Baker had taken both of Zena's hands in hers, then paused before speaking softly. "Your daughter's latest HIV test results are negative. She's seroconverted, and there are no longer any HIV viral antibodies in her blood system."

For a long moment Zena could only sit there and stare, wondering if she'd heard correctly.

"Th-th-then I didn't give it to her? Andreka's not gonna die?"

Miss Baker grinned. "You gave Andreka your HIV antibodies, not your HIV virus. She's fine, Zena. She's healthy and just fine."

Instantly a weight was lifted from Zena's shoulders. That haunting, unspeakable thing that had terrified her so unmercifully no longer existed. If Andreka was okay, then everything else in Zena's life could be okay too. There was no longer a reason to run. To live in a constant cycle of guilt, escapism, and destruction. Or to get high.

"Are you sure?" her eyes pleaded with Miss Baker as she wept into a wad of tissues clutched in her hand. "Are you really, really, really sure?"

"I'm sure," Miss Baker affirmed. "I've seen this happen thousands of times and babies like Andreka go on to live normal, healthy lives."

Zena put her face down on the desk and took a few deep breaths. She felt light-headed with relief and for once the high she was riding was all natural.

"But there is something else I think we should talk about," Miss Baker said, her voice suddenly serious. "Andreka isn't the only person we need to be worrying about here. Her mommy looks like she might be having a pretty rough time accepting some things about herself too. If you're ready for recovery I think I know where you can go for help."

Zena was wide open.

"How long have you been using drugs, baby?"

Zena shrugged and briefly closed her eyes. It felt like forever. "Three years. Since I was fifteen."

"Have you ever done things to get drugs that you're not proud of or maybe wish you could forget?"

Zena bit her lip, then slowly nodded.

"Do you want to stop using the drugs? Are you interested in recovery?"

"Yes," Zena said in a strong voice. If Andreka was safe and healthy, then she wanted to be around to raise her daughter and take damn good care of her. "Yes."

Miss Baker smiled. "My sister Aretha attends several Narcotics Anonymous meetings each week where people just like you gather to share their stories of recovery. There's one being held on Watkins Street tonight. If you're looking for people who can show you how to battle the disease of addiction I can call Ree-Ree for you. She'll come by and pick you up and the two of you can walk to the meeting together."

Zena thought about Egypt, and bit her lip again then frowned.

"What?" Miss Baker asked. "Tonight is no good? You need to find a baby-sitter?"

"No, tonight is good, but uhm, is this invitation only for me? I have a friend who needs help too. Can I bring my friend?"

"Oh yes," Miss Baker laughed. "The meetings are open. You can bring as many friends as you like."

$ $ $

Zena's heart beat with excitement as she waited for Miss Baker's older sister to arrive. She had agreed to meet Aretha Baker downstairs and she peeked out the window every ten seconds or so, afraid the lady might think she had changed her mind and leave without her.

Excited or not, Zena's conscience was fucking with her hard. After receiving the best news in the world that Andreka was HIV negative, she'd been wracked with intense guilt all morning because of what she might have exposed her best friend to. It had taken more courage than she knew she had, but she'd come home from Brookdale Hospital and forced herself to sit down and write Egypt a long letter. It was one of the hardest things she had ever done in her life. A little devil on her left shoulder was steady talking shit the whole time she was writing it too. *Don't go telling nobody all ya damn business! Egypt's been out*

*there doing bogus shit too. If she does have it, how do you
know she actually got it from you?*

But there was a voice of love speaking from her right
shoulder as well, and Zena was torn between the two.
*You've gotta tell her. It's only right. Don't mess around
and jinx yourself or your baby, Zena. That shit could end
up coming back on you. Be grateful Andreka is healthy
and do right by your girl. Egypt's been a damn good friend
and she deserves the truth. If it was the other way around
she would have never done something so grimy to you.*

It had taken her the whole afternoon, but between
the guilt and the tears, the remorse and the shame, Zena
wrote the letter. As she signed her name she noticed that
the pages were damp, and in some places the writing was
shaky and smudgy, but it was done and Zena was relieved.
She had managed to get the truth out and tell Egypt exactly what kind of horrors that she and Dreko had been
exposing her to for all these months. Near the end of the
letter Zena had begged her friend for forgiveness and
urged her to get tested immediately.

Zena folded the letter into a small square and took it
in her bedroom and stuck it inside her purse. Later that
afternoon she walked the neighborhood until she caught
up with Egypt outside of the pizza shop on Rockaway Avenue. She could tell Egypt was high, but she went ahead
and told her about Miss Baker and the meeting that was
being held that night anyway.

There'd been some hesitation in Egypt's eyes and Zena
feared her friend just wasn't ready.

"Come on, Egypt. Please. Look at you! Look at *me*! That shit is killing us. We both look a mess and we *are* a mess. Just come to one meeting. Please, E. Do it for yourself, but do it for Hood too."

Egypt's eyes grew even bigger and she glanced around like Hood might jump outta his ride and bust her flying high any minute. "I just don't want nobody to know about me . . . they'll be a whole lot of people there, Zena," she whimpered in shame. "I just don't want nobody to *know*."

Zena took her friend over to a parked car and turned her around until she was facing her reflection in its glass windows.

"Take a look, Egypt. Take a real good look. Baby they already know. *Everybody* knows. But the people at that meeting tonight won't care about what you've done out here or what kind of drugs you might have used. The only thing they're gonna care about is helping us figure out how to stop."

Egypt still looked reluctant, but Zena gave it another try.

"Look, Egypt. Please come. I'm begging you." She reached into her purse and took out the small folded letter. Folding it once more, even smaller, she stuck it in the back pocket of Egypt's baggy jeans.

"I wrote this letter because there's something I need you to know, E, but I could never figure out when or how to tell you. Please read this. Not in front of me, but later when you're alone. I love you, Egypt and I want you to know that I'm sorry for everything. But the only way I know how to make it up to you and help you, or even help myself, is by telling you the truth and then sharing something with you that I think might give both of us a chance to get our lives back. The meeting is on the corner of Livonia and Watkins at eight o'clock tonight, E. I hope and pray with all my heart that you'll meet me there."

A piece of Zena's heart broke off as she watched Egypt cut down the street with the letter in her back pocket, speeding off on her mission to get that next rock. As painful as reading the letter would be for her, Zena just couldn't bring herself to tell Egypt the truth from her mouth, even though she knew she owed her friend that much and more. A lot of stuff was about to go down at one time and Zena hoped she was strong enough to withstand it all without turning to drugs to ease the guilt and the pain. Egypt would have to get tested. The possibility was there that she may have been infected, and that would be one more agonizing burden piled on Zena's back that she'd have to find the courage to bear.

"One thing at a time," she cautioned herself. "Just deal with one thing at a time." First she'd go to this meeting and put a toe down on the road to recovery. Next, after Egypt read her letter, she'd sit down and talk and no doubt cry with her friend. Zena would confess to everything she'd done, and beg Egypt for her forgiveness. Maybe Egypt would give it, and maybe she wouldn't. But Zena knew that was a chance she'd just have to take.

A rush of emotions came down on Zena and she swallowed hard. None of this was going to be easy for her, but it was definitely what she had to do. She had walked back to her building slowly and climbed the stairs to the apartment that held so many bad memories for her. The walls had seen every foul thing she'd done here, and they seemed to mock her and taunt her and tell her she'd fucked up so much in her life that she might as well run outside and catch up with Egypt and get her rock on too.

But then Zena had glanced at her brother as he sat on the sofa playing with her daughter and tears sprang to her eyes. She loved them so much, but her drug use had prevented her from enjoying a life with them. Sackie had always been like a father to her, despite the fact that he only had her by two years. He'd done more for Andreka than her own father had, which made Zena love him even more.

Zena had taken a shower and changed into her sagging denim jumper and combed her hair. She glanced outside again, and saw a stout, black woman standing downstairs gazing up at the window.

"I'm coming, Miss Aretha!" Zena hollered as her heart leapt, then for the first time in a long time, she kissed her daughter and left the house without guilt or reservation. Tonight was the first step toward her healing and recovery. Yeah, she was leaving her baby again to go out in the streets, but tonight she'd be out there doing something good for all of them. Tonight the healing would begin, and so would the rest of her life.

CHAPTER 35

I understand why these niggas wanna see me break
They can't imagine what it took just to be this great!
How a nigga say I'm shook, never seen me shake?
They fake!

"AIIGHT! GET THAT money laid out on the table! Let's get that count going!" The money room was in full motion as Hood walked back and forth down the rows and in between the metal tables. He looked good in his Sean John ensemble and fresh AF 1's. His goatee had been trimmed by Fat Daddy's old friend Felton, and the shine gleaming from his fingers and chest was blinding.

Count time in the money room was every Friday evening. If everything went good with the tally then the teams got paid and everybody on the payroll ate. By nightfall everybody who wasn't working a corner would be getting blasted, getting pussy, and getting ready for a lively weekend.

Hood and Dreko usually worked the count together. It was easier to control shit with both of them watching niggas, scoping for bad intentions and observing their every action. But right before count time Dreko had hit him on the cell and said he wasn't gonna make it.

"Hey my nig," Dreko spoke loudly into the phone. He'd been acting a little cool after that verbal ass-whipping Hood had put on him, but he sounded straight now. Hood shrugged. Spittin shit at a nigga was all a part of the battle rap, and Dreko should've been back to his normal self a long time ago. "I ain't gonna make the count, man. I got a bitch out here wildin and I need to handle that ass. I'll catch up with you later, though. In the club."

Hood was cool with it.

There was one table per team leader, and each leader was responsible for making sure their trap money came to them correct from their corner boys. If that shit was a dime bag short they had to report it to Hood and Dreko, but it was up to them to make up the difference.

Hood used to be an expert at moving dope on the streets before he got locked up, but managing a whole crew of capos was even better. His reputation for being a coldhearted killer was enough to keep these cats straight on their game. These was some hardbody niggas he was dealing with, but they still liked living. Seldom did him or Dreko have any real problems that couldn't be handled with a swift, harsh, and very public lesson. They had taken turns cracking niggas's skulls and demanded complete obedience to the council rules at all times.

Hood watched fifteen pairs of hands move. Shuffling money and stacking paper. He walked down the line and stood looking over Roman's shoulder. Twice last week that nigga had rolled in the spot with a short trap, blaming it on his boy Waheem. Dreko had gave a *fuck*. He'd stuck his gat up under that nigga's chin and told him by the time he sat at that count table his numbers had better be adding up.

"Your shit straight right?"

Roman glanced up, his hands full of money. He nodded, his lips turned down at the corners. "I shoulda been straight both times last week too, man." He set his stack down and stroked his goatee, his eyes narrow. "Something ain't clickin, Hood. You know me, nigga. My shit always tight. I need to holla atcha later, cool?"

Hood shrugged and moved on. Rome was a down cat. They'd scrambled together for Xan back in the early days, but you never knew about a nigga. Hood had seen and heard the craziest of shit, and when niggas started fallin off with the doe there was usually a grimy reason behind it. He'd hear Rome out, but it prolly wouldn't change shit. Either the nigga came correct with them papers, or he paid the fuckin price for running short. It was just as simple as that.

When the money room had been counted down and closed, Hood made sure the doe was recorded and loaded into the safe. Then the safe was locked and the steel-encased office was secured. He was on his way out of the building when he saw Roman laying in the cut. He was sitting slouched down in his whip looking like he didn't wanna be seen.

" 'Sup Rome?" Hood stood at the driver's window, waiting.

"Man," Roman said, sitting up. "I need you to ride with me for a minute, dog. I got some shit to say I think you gone wanna hear."

Fifteen minutes later they were sitting in a parking lot at Canarsie Pier, facing the waves coming in from the Atlantic Ocean.

"Check this out," Roman began. His eyes was locked dead on Hood, without an ounce of deception to be found in them. "Waheem's trap been off. I'd give him thirty, he'd hand over the money for twenty-four. Then the nigga would lie right in my fuckin grill, swearing on his dead mother that twenty-four was all I dished out.

"At first I thought the young cat was smoking," Roman said, then shook his head. "But I watched him real close and I could tell that wasn't it. I started noticing that his shit was never short unless certain people was in the area, ya know? Then the next day that lil nigga would do his turn-in and be short on my money."

Roman put his hand on the steering wheel, drumming his fingers. "So I figured Waheem was passing off freebies, you know? But I just couldn't figure out why. I mean, he wasn't getting no pussy for the product, and he knows the fuckin council rules. We don't work on no credit. And then he told me."

Hood's voice stayed cool. "Told you what, Rome?"

"Now, he ain't wanna fess up on that shit, but I busted that nigga's lip real good for him and made him spit me some truth. Wah swore it was Dreko who had him dishing off vials. He said he got his orders straight from the top. He said Dreko told him don't fuckin worry about coming up short or about nothing I said. Dreko told Wah to just give out as much as he told him to fuckin give out, and that he'd handle any beef that came up in the money room."

Roman frowned then continued. "But that shit just didn't make no sense to me. If Waheem was dishing off for Dreko, then why didn't Dreko just square that shit up on count day like he said he would? Why the nigga let my shit keep coming up short so I could look like a skimming-ass low baller? The only way I can figure it is, Dreko let me take the heat because he wanted somebody to fucking know what Waheem was doing. Like he was counting on me to figure this shit out and make some noise about it to the right person."

Hood shook his head. "That shit *don't* make no sense, man. Dishing off to who? Dreko don't smoke. And even if he did, he wouldn't have to go through a nigga like Waheem to get to his own product. He's sitting on all the weight he needs every day."

"Yeah. That's what I thought too, ya dig? But see, Dreko can't be every fuckin where all the time. Waheem's corner is far enough away from the Arms where the bosses don't peep every damn body who rolls up to cop a package.

And besides," Roman said, his face grim. "Waheem wasn't dishing them vials off *to* Dreko. Just at his command."

Roman frowned again. "I don't know man. That nigga Dreko done stacked at least a million dollars, Hood. And he still ain't satisfied unless he taking and violating. Violating and taking."

Street intuition is a funny thing. There was a reason Rome was telling him all this shit tonight. Hood felt the hammer falling even before it hit him in the head.

"Nigga, I'ma ask you again. Who Dre got Wah dishing off to, Rome?"

His old friend sighed deeply, then looked in his eyes and said quietly, "Dreko's out there feeding shit to your girl, Egypt, man."

Then he added softly, "And if you ask me, I think that nigga is being so loose with his shit 'cause he wanna make damn sure that you find out."

CHAPTER 36

As a man you gotta learn to come to terms with decisions
So pay attention 'cause you never know
What's lurkin within him
Now sing along, if I'm wrong, put the blame on me
But if I let you bite me twice, then it's shame on me . . .

SACKIE TURNED HIS niece onto her back and flipped the switch on the musical Winnie the Pooh mobile hanging above her head. She was almost knocked out, and her sleepy eyes and wispy curls tugged at his heart and made him lean over and gently kiss her forehead.

But then he frowned. Her crib was stank. The whole thing smelled strongly of vomit and old diapers, and when he pulled the covers up over her he discovered four foul, dookie Pampers that Zena had stashed inside the crib after changing her.

"Fuckin lazy ass!" Sackie cursed, snatching the nasty Pampers up with one hand. He tossed them in the middle of Zena's unmade bed and cursed again. Her sheets were filthy and crusted with some of everything. Blood, dirt, and Dreko's cum. The girl was so far gone there was no way she could begin to take proper care of the baby, and just the thought of that scared Sackie.

He bristled. The next time Zena left Andreka home alone, or left her drugs laying around where her daughter might find them, it could mean a bad one for his niece and that wasn't cool. Sackie shook his head as he took in the trashed room. Zena and Egypt were probably out there getting lifted right now saying fuck him and the baby.

He looked down at her. Andreka was already asleep. He touched her cheek and walked out the room. He left the door open but turned off the light.

In the small living room Sackie plopped back down in his chair in front of the computer. He surfed for some tracks to download to his iPod, and listened to a hot new mixtape Robb Hawk and Reem Raw had just put out called *H&R Block*.

He'd just chosen to download a track from Papoose's new jawn when a key turned in the lock and the front door swung open.

Dreko cast a long shadow as Sackie looked up in surprise.

Dreko held the door open as Barry, Flip, and Waffle came in, locking the door behind them.

"What it do?" Sackie asked, then nodded, swiveling around to face his boys. *Fuckin Zena,* is what rushed through his mind. He had changed the lock, but his sister must have given Dreko the new key. It only took Sackie two seconds to smell the cup of lighter fluid Waffle carried, and a half a second after that to dig the murderous look in Dreko's eyes.

"You the one with all the mouth, muhfucka. You tell me what it do."

Instinct drove Sackie to his feet. With four big men in front of him sucking up the air, the apartment felt small and tight.

Sackie shrugged like everything was straight, but in reality his mind was on whirl. His eyes never moved but he sure as hell saw the small pair of art scissors, handle up, in the pencil holder next to the computer.

"You got a bitch mouth, muhfucka. It's time somebody closed it for you."

"What you talking about, man?"

Dreko swung his fist like it was a hammer.

Ducking below the blow, Sackie lunged to the side and grabbed for the scissors, snatching them as he crashed into the computer stand and went down hard.

They were on him then. Feet, fists, however they could get him.

Sackie defended himself like he wanted to stay alive. He blocked with one arm and stabbed out with the scissors with his other hand. The only sounds in the apartment were those of a beating. Sackie was quickly overpowered. He was taking some furious head shots, and fading fast. He realized that if he was going to have a chance at survival then he couldn't be the only mother-fucker down on the floor.

Enduring the stunning blows, he grabbed Dreko's foot in both hands and twisted it sharply, bringing him down to one knee. The moment Dreko was in reach Sackie went for his eye, digging his thumb in until Dreko screamed and twisted away. His boys turned up the attack. Doubling the blows and stomping their boots into his face and body until he cried out in pain.

Blood oozed from Sackie's face and into his eyes. His lips and nose were busted. Numb. He turned on his stom-ach and tried to crawl away, and the weight of a full grown man came crashing down on the small of his back. Some-thing cracked and Sackie screamed once, then laid out flat. Helpless.

They dragged him over to the dining table and lifted him into a chair. Barry ran over to the door and got the lighter fluid and rope they'd brought with them. Sackie felt himself being tied to the chair. His arms were snatched behind him, his feet bound tightly together at the ankles.

Squeezing his poked eye closed, Dreko grabbed one of his daughter's spit rags off the table and balled it up, then picked up the lighter fluid and sloshed the cloth. Grip-ping Sackie by his hair, Dreko yanked his head back then crammed the cloth into his mouth as far as it would go.

"Yeah, muhfucka," Dreko said quietly. He voice was so cold and deadly he didn't even have to raise it. "You thought

Fat Daddy caught a bad one that night you popped him? Well just wait till we get this shit going. Won't be nobody here to put your bitch ass outta your misery."

Digging his intentions, Sackie's eyes grew big. He struggled against the ropes, choking and gagging as the acrid taste of lighter fluid flooded his mouth. He bucked and growled as Flip poured the rest of the fluid over his head and into his lap. The liquid burned as it washed over his abraised facial skin, but that's not why Sackie was suddenly crazed out of his mind.

"Ahkega ih heh!" His words came out garbled as he stared into Dreko's face and swung his head wildly toward the apartment's only bedroom. "Ahkega ih heh!"

Frustrated tears fell from Sackie's eyes. His rage was bitter and deep. Screaming into his gag, he arched his wrenched back and stretched his body, trying to stand. And when that didn't work he bounced in the chair trying his best to scoot toward the bedroom.

No dice. Waffle grabbed the back of the chair and slung it to the ground. Sackie landed with a defeated thud, and when he looked up into Dreko's eyes all he saw was ice. But Sackie didn't give a fuck about himself. All he cared about was that baby girl back there sleeping in her crib. Sackie silently begged. Pleaded. Darted his eyes back and forth, and aimed his head toward the bedroom, desperate for Dreko to get his message.

And then finally he saw it. Understanding. It was right there in Dreko's eyes as he glanced toward the bedroom and grinned. He was reading Sackie loud and clear.

Dreko held up his hand and his boys fell back.

Sackie sighed, silently thanking God.

Dreko bent down and lifted Sackie's chair upright. Then he slid his hand into his own front pocket and came out with a lighter.

"Yeah. You got a big fuckin mouth, Sackie. Let's see how good you can swallow some of this fire."

Sackie really screamed then. His muffled sounds of rage were pitiful as he stared at Dreko with pure hatred.

Dreko laughed, then held the lighter next to the spit rag that was lodged halfway down Sackie's throat and flicked up some fire.

A high flame licked the ends of the cloth and Sackie bucked backward. The pain was instant and intense and his nose hairs singed.

Dreko's boys moved toward the door as Sackie writhed in agony, screaming from the back of his throat and flinging his head from side to side. The next thing Sackie heard was the sound of a baby crying. Wailing loudly from the bedroom. The front of his hair caught fire and he shrieked.

And then Flip's voice cut into his pain.

"Oh shit!" he said to Dreko. "Man, ya baby is in there! What you want me to do?"

Dreko only had two words to say, and they were the last two words Sackie would ever hear.

"Leave her."

CHAPTER 37

With nothing to eat,
And a couple days lack of sleep,
I hear the beat and still craft me a masterpiece . . .

SOMETIMES THE HARDEST thing to imagine is your worst fear come true. Hood didn't believe in karma. The type of life he lived demanded he handle his own destiny and kismet coincidence didn't have shit to do with it. But there was no denying that the thing he had devoted his life to pushing off on others had reared up and claimed victory over those he loved.

There was blood in Hood's eyes as Roman dropped him off back in the Ville. Blood in his eyes, and murder on his mind.

Hood cruised the neighborhood in the ice-blue Mercedes 550 that Dreko had bought him when he came down off the Rock. He sped down streets and whipped around

corners in the luxury vehicle as his eyes scanned the bodies littering the streets for one person in particular.

He drove under the el slowly, glancing from one side of
the street to the other. He spotted a slim figure wearing
jeans and a white sweater, walking fast. He hit the brakes
hard, swerving as he double-parked and quickly jumped
out his ride.

She was striding toward a small crowd on the corner
of Livonia and Watkins, outside of a community center
where a meeting looked like it was about to take place.

Egypt looked up in surprise when she saw him coming,
then shrank back. Busted.

"Get in the car," he spit, even as he snatched her by
the arm and yanked her stumbling into the street. He
threw her in on the passenger side, then got behind the
wheel and peeled out into the street, his tires smoking and
screeching loudly on the pavement.

"I was going in there to find Zena!" Egypt panted, her
guilty eyes wide and scared. "I swear to God, Mont. All I
was doing was looking for fucking Zena so I can *kill* that
dirty bitch!"

"So you's a head, huh? That's why ya ass couldn't hold
me down when I was on the Rock, huh?" He laughed bitterly. "All these weeks I been thinking you was out there
suckin on some nigga's dick, when it was them fish scales
you had on ya brain."

"No!" Egypt denied. "I swear to God I only smoked it
a few times," she insisted. "I'm not addicted to that shit,

Mont. It don't mean nothing to me and I can walk away from it anytime, baby!"

Hood let her beg, babble, and lie. He zipped through traffic and sped toward Eastern Parkway without saying a word. He couldn't even look at the bitch. He couldn't stand the smell of her lying, crack-smoking ass, either. His heart felt cut. Pain seeped from his pores. That poison he'd peddled had gotten all over his hands and under his skin. Hood felt his gat pressed against his side and he longed to whip it out and bust her one right in the grill. If she could suck a pipe then damn right she could suck a Glock.

"Mont, please! Listen to me!"

Hood tuned Egypt out as she cried and apologized, swearing on the soul of her murdered father that she loved him and had never meant to hurt him.

He took Eastern Parkway toward downtown Brooklyn as Egypt begged and moaned. He gave a fuck about any of that noise coming outta her mouth. Her mouth was contaminated. There was nothing she could say that he wanted to hear.

Less than twenty minutes later they were waiting at a traffic light on Tillary Street. Egypt was still crying and trying to explain.

"Mont, please!! You gotta believe me! I'm sorry. I'm really, really, sorry. Oh my God . . . I don't even know how all this happened . . . and Zena . . . I just can't *believe* her and Dreko did this fuckin shit to me! Mont, please say something, baby. Oh God . . . I might as well just *die*. Mont, please talk to me baby. Please forgive me."

Hood never spoke a word until the wheels of his Mercedes touched the metal treads of the Brooklyn Bridge.

"You say you wanna die?" he asked softly.

Halfway across the bridge Hood pulled to the far right, then put on his flashing hazard lights and slowed to a complete stop.

"You wanna die?" he asked again, his voice just as vast and cold as the ocean below.

"Mont, please . . ." Egypt cried, reaching for him. "You don't even know . . ."

He slapped her hand away brutally, then reached under his jacket and pulled out his gun.

Egypt's eyes grew wide as she looked at the piece, then glanced around at the cars speeding past, those traveling in their lane cutting a path around them.

"Mont . . ." her voice came out a dry, cracked whisper. "Please."

Hood cocked the gat, then held it out to her.

"C'mon, take it, Egypt. Finish yourself off, baby. Stick this metal dick in your mouth. It's a whole lot quicker than the pipe and it sure ain't as ugly."

Egypt broke down sobbing even harder. Mont had never once called her anything close to ugly. She cursed herself for being so weak, and cursed the drugs for being so damn strong. She cursed Hood too.

"Well where the fuck was you when I needed you?" she screamed. "You think I wanted to fuck with that

shit? Huh? You think I just went out one day and decided to cop me some rock and sit back and let it ruin my
whole fuckin life? *I'm* the one who had the dreams, remember? I'm the one who stayed in school and worked
damn hard to reach my goals! But I was hurtin, Mont.
I was in so much fuckin *pain*! My father got murdered
and I had to come home and find his dead fuckin body!
So where were you, Lamont? Huh? Where the fuck
were you?"

Out there trying to save your life, is what Hood would
have said if his heart wasn't hurting so bad.

He held the gun out to her again, his hand cool and
steady.

Egypt gasped. She searched his face and found a cold,
brick wall. Unwaverable. She trembled as sweat ran
from her hairline, between her breasts, and down her
back. Her heart fluttered, and any hope for forgiveness
she might have had dissipated into the air, gone. The
look on Mont's face said it all. She was foul and worth-
less. Her life had turned into a garbage can full of dirty
regrets. A quiet sob tore from Egypt's throat as her soul
cried out for mercy. Mont would never, *ever* forgive her.
It just wasn't in him and she knew that without a doubt.
But he *was* offering her a chance out, and she saw no
reason not to take it.

Her lower lip shook as she reached for the heat and took
it into her slippery hands. Zena's letter of confession was in
her back pocket burning a hole into her contaminated flesh.
The thought of having to tell Mont about all the nasty, per-

verted sex with Dreko, Zena having the virus, and how she had laid down with both of them and opened herself up to all that . . . Egypt shuddered. She'd rather die. Because one more fuckin thing she had to be afraid or ashamed of would just break her back. She didn't have that kind of strength left in her. Only weakness and fear.

Egypt slid the barrel of the gun between her lips and the cold metal clicked against her bottom teeth. She took three deep, heaving breaths and blinked her eyes against the sting of her sweat. Snot ran from her nose and she sniffed it back, then with one last sideward glance that was filled with love, remorse, and sorrow, she pulled the trigger.

$ 　 $ 　 $

Click.

Hood's whole body jerked. The sound of a misfired gat sent an echo through the whip, and then there was silence. His eyes bored into Egypt. She was trembling violently and drenched in sweat. Her lips were slack, the barrel of the gun still clenched between her teeth.

"Girl . . ." he whispered, then swallowed hard in disbelief. What should have been certain death had been reduced to her ragged, desperate breaths and the hollow sound of a jammed pistol held in the trembling hands of a hopeless crackhead.

It all fell down on Hood at that moment. The craziness of it all. The senselessness of the life they were living and the agonizing need to get away from it all and save his own life. It was over. He was done.

"Get out," he whispered.

His own hands were shaking as he snatched the tool from her wet grasp and tossed it under his seat. His face was harder than stone as he took a business card from the ashtray and pushed it at her. Then he reached over and pressed a button on the dashboard and unlocked the car doors, and turned to face Egypt one last time.

"Get out."

Cars whizzed past outside and she stared at him pitifully through her tears.

"I said, get the fuck out."

Egypt's lips parted and a long, tortured moan fell from her soul. Moments earlier she'd been ready to die, but where there was life, there could also be repentance and forgiveness, and more than anything Egypt wanted that second chance. A galaxy of pain was in her eyes as she gazed at Hood and whimpered, "Don't do this, Mont. Please. Don't do me like this, baby. I'll do anything to make this right. Anything."

"Cool. Prove it. Get outta my ride."

"And do what?" Egypt shrieked. "Look where you putting me out at, Lamont! What the fuck do you want me to do?"

"First I want you to get outta my ride. Then you can either walk over to the edge of that rail and climb ya ass up on it and . . . jump."

Hood was silent for a long moment, then he turned his back on her. He faced completely away from Egypt and said, "Or . . . you can walk back to the Brooklyn side of the shore and call the number on that card. A lady named Miss Baker is gonna answer the phone, and she'll help you get your shit together, if that's what you wanna do. Either way, you gotta get the fuck up outta my life."

Egypt whimpered. "Baby, you are all I got in this *world*. All I got! What do I have to do? You want me to kill myself? Huh? Then gimme the gun back, Mont. Is that what you want me to do? Look at me!"

Hood refused.

"You're already dead," he spoke quietly, his forehead pressed against the cool glass of his window. "Your weak ass died the day you chose to get down with a pipe."

The sound of the car door opening then slamming shut cut through him like a sword. And only then did he allow his tears to fall.

Don't never let nobody know you got a sweet spot.

Xan had been right, because predatory niggas and bitches would fuck with that sweet spot every time.

Hood signaled and pulled off slowly into traffic. He glanced in his rearview mirror only once, and when he did he could have sworn he saw Egypt climbing over the fence and heading toward the outer railing.

Hood's heart lurched but he forced his eyes forward. He kept them that way as he drove toward the Manhattan side of the bridge and he was proud of the fact that despite the anguish burning in his heart, he never looked back again.

$ $ $

Back outside of Cypress Arms, Hood checked his piece and made sure the clip was full and there was one ready in the head.

His mind in a homicidal tunnel, Hood hit the streets and went looking for Dreko. If he had ever feared for his sanity before, there was no doubt about it now. He was past crazy. He was a raving fuckin beast. Lyrics raced through his head at mad speeds as he boiled over a cat who he had once loved like a brother, yet turned out to be lower than a fuckin worm.

Fuck fame, fuck glory!
When they bury Hood let my niggas tell my story!
Tell 'em 'bout the orgies
How I never snitched up! How I never bitched up!
True to my dudes, refused to ever switch up!
My band of brothers, haters plannin to slug us
Death before dishonor no traitors stand among us!

Hood rounded the corner on Rockaway Avenue and stormed into the pizza shop. The look in his eyes was enough to make niggas stop chewing as he scanned the crowd, searching for Dreko. He had held that nigga down

during the early years. They ate off of each other's forks
and guarded each other's backs. But one of them was a
fuckin slug and a snitch, and that nigga was gone hafta die
tonight.

Every step a nigga take, God tests a nigga's faith
Ever notice the nigga kept a weapon on his waist?
Maneuvering thru the block, no hesitation in his pace
A chip on his shoulder and desperation in his face! What!

Hood stormed down the city streets on a manhunt. The
el roared overhead, and it sounded more like a whisper.
There was nothing louder in the universe than the kill bells
ringing in his ears. No matter how much territory Dreko
had conquered on the streets of Brooklyn or how many
niggas he'd struck down with his grimy sword, he still
wasn't satisfied. He'd had to go and shit on his boy too.

I'm the pride of the hood! All these other niggas fall short!
Heard a nigga stuck Hood? It was on the ball court!
If he ain't a G then DON'T match him with me!
I'm so strapped it's silly! I sold packs to willies!
Dre can have the jewelry, throw backs and fitteds!
Get knocked he gone rat like Po, Cat, and Nicky!

A million dollars in ya hands—
what's power to you?
But if he tellin on his man—
what's a coward to you?

You on ya muthafuckin grind!
what's a shower to you?

Don't let the money change you, it do what you allow it to do!

Hood hunted for Dreko in every rat hole he could think of in the vicinity of Cypress Arms. But that grimy nigga had misted up from the neighborhood, nowhere to be found. Everywhere Hood went he left a clear message for his partner in crime. "Tell that nigga I'ma dead him." He wasn't even tryna sneak up on that bitch. He was coming straight at his boy, Glock on cock, aimed for his heart.

Midnight found Hood searching a joint on Blake Avenue where Dreko liked to chill. He stomped through the whole place. His eyes crawled all over the back rooms. He even bust up in the bathroom looking for him. That nigga wasn't there, but his homo thug friend Frenchie was. Hood caught him standing in front of a urinal holding his dick in his hand.

He stepped up and cracked his Glock up against that nigga's nose.

"Where he be?"

Frenchie was shook. "I don't know, man. I swear to God, I don't know."

Hood forced Frenchie's head back, the barrel of his piece pressed center mass to the cat's forehead. "I'ma ask you that shit again. Where—"

The 911 signal sounded on Hood's cell. He gun-mushed Frenchie in the grill and stepped back.

"Yo."

He heard deep gulping sounds. Heaving cries. Panic and grief.

"Hood . . ." It was Zena. "They got 'em Hood . . ." her voice was weak. She was moaning like she had been tortured.

"Who?" Hood demanded. "They got who?"

Zena sobbed. Her cries were bottomless. Drug up from the pit of her soul.

"My baby . . ." she wailed. "Oh, God. They . . . killed . . . my . . . *baby*. And my brother . . ." she whimpered. "They got Sackie, too, Hood."

Hood listened, growing cold as Zena gulped and panted, trying to catch her breath. "They burnt both of them up," she wailed pitifully. "My whole fuckin family is dead!"

CHAPTER 38

With my brain on another terrain I'm tryna muffle the pain,
'Cause me and the hood is one and the same . . .

"AH, SHIT . . ." FRESH rage rose in Hood as he stood across the street watching the firemen and paramedics coming in and out of Sackie's building. He forced himself into a zone, steeled against the aggression and fury that swelled in his heart.

The coroner's crew had just brought out two body bags. One tiny and one big. Zena was sitting in the back of a police car with a woman Hood recognized as Miss Baker's gun-packing older sister. They were crying and hugging each other as a female officer wrote down some information on a pad.

The streets had been full of onlookers when Hood rolled up. He saw families with small kids wrapped in blankets, bigger kids standing around crying in pajamas, and elderly people sitting on benches and clutching each other while they wondered about their life posssessions that remained trapped behind the walls of the smoky five-story apartment building.

Hood had moved quietly and slipped through the crowd, blending in easily with everybody else. By listening to the chatter around him, he learned that the neighbors had gotten worried when they smelled smoke coming from Sackie's apartment. Knowing that a baby lived there, several men had rushed to the door and tried to open it, but they were forced back by intense black smoke. By the time the firemen arrived, flames were already shooting from some of Sackie's windows and everybody in the whole damn building had to be evacuated.

"What you know 'bout this?" Hood asked, turning to Lil Jay, who had spotted him and come over to stand beside him.

Lil Jay shrugged. He looked shook in the face. "Nothing except that it's fucked up. I bitched with Sackie all the time man, but on the real I had love for that cat. He wasn't no herb nigga. He was the real truth."

Hood nodded then squirted spit through his teeth and thrust his hands in his pockets.

"Man," Lil Jay complained, "shit ain't the same as it was when the niggas of old days was running the Ville. Xanbar and Kraft and them down-ass cats. Remember how we used to do it up in Fat Daddy's shop? These niggas out here now ain't no gangstas, money. They just crazy. Niggas so scared of this *one* muthafucka they do anything they told. Pussies runnin on pure fear. Even me. That's why everybody was so glad to see you back on the street."

"Fear?"

Lil Jay laughed. "Nigga you know. Why you think so many dudes was out here living the shook life when you came down off the Rock? Ya boy's a fuckin psycho! If Sackie fried up in that crib then your partner was prolly the one who lit the match. He gave a *fuck* about his own baby being up in there. That's how that nigga be. He ain't nothing like you, Hood. Just cause he'll kill a nigga don't mean he fit to run no street business. There's rules for everything you do man, even out here. Dreko just ain't never followed none."

Then Lil Jay added quietly. "He better watch his head though. There's a whole lotta cats who wanna see that shit get rocked."

"Then why ain't none of them niggas step up then? Dreko ain't been hiding nowhere. He been playing this game right out in the open. Just like always. What the fuck them niggas been waiting on?"

Lil Jay laughed bitterly. "We been waiting on a street savior man. Somebody ten times badder than Dreko to ride in and save all our shook asses. Shit. You don't know? We been waiting on *you*."

$ $ $

Ten minutes later Hood was back on the streets. Back on his hunt.

He'd run across a lot of young D.W.I.T. soldiers on they grind, and since Dreko wasn't nowhere to be found he knew his boy was traveling light. He prolly had two, no more than three gorillas rolling with him. That would put the battle odds at roughly four to one. Light shit. Hood could come out way on top.

He walked all the way through Baller's Paradise with no luck. Dreko liked to get his dick sucked in the back rooms, but hadn't a soul seen him come through the door tonight. Crossing Livonia Avenue, Hood zipped toward the Stank Mic and stepped inside the vestibule fifteen minutes later.

"What it be like?"

Reem Raw was coming out of the main lounge. He dapped Hood with love, then looked at him and grinned.

"What's good? You ready to shit on the mic tonight? We got some good—"

The fury on Hood's face stopped Reem cold.

"Yo, nigga, what up? You got a fuckin problem?" Reem swirled his fitted cap around backwards and touched his piece. "Well tell ya boy where it at! We can take care of that shit real quick. Just gimme the name. Tell me who it is and ya boy is straight airing that ass."

"Dreko been through here?"

Reem snorted, "Dreko?" A sinister mask fell over his face. "Man, I'll *bite* that bitch snitch if he ever sticks his grill anywhere near here. You gunning for *that* nigga then he's as good as dead. But I'll tell you what," Reem said, craning his neck as he signaled his boys who were standing on point in the main lounge, "Why'on't you bless the stage for me and stank up the mic right quick. Lemme send one of my crews out on that mission for you. Me and my boys'll take care of that little problem you got on ya hands, man. We'll do it for free, too. No charge. All love."

"I'm good," Hood said, dapping his boy then heading for the door. This fury was way too big to pass off. Hood was getting this one in for himself.

Back on the streets, Hood's rage was reignited. He swung back past Baller's Paradise again and this time he saw a white Range Rover parked outside. "Yeah, nigga," he growled, pulling up beside it and double-parking. Inside, the music was banging and the lights were low. Waitresses in T-shirts and thongs walked around in high heels, serving drinks. Ballers chilled in booths running game, and strippers worked the poles selling that used gushy.

Hood walked through the club moving like a panther, gun in hand. Dreko was nowhere to be seen. Hood had just ducked into the hallway that led to the back rooms when Black stepped in front of him, grinning.

" 'Sup, Hood. What you know good, boss? Ya boy a lil busy right now, man. He gone need a few minutes."

Hood nodded and turned away, then whirled back around and cracked Black square in the temple. Twice.

That nigga folded like a card table. Hood stepped right over him and swung the door open, and what he saw froze his heart.

Dreko's back was to him. He was standing spread-eagle against the wall, naked. He was deep in the pat-down position, but there wasn't a cop in sight as he moaned out loud and his body trembled.

Hood stepped inside then cursed in surprise, and Dreko glanced over his shoulder.

Their eyes locked and both men froze.

Hood stared as the buttons on the chick's skirt and blouse clanked against each other, her neck jutting like a pigeon's as she tongued and licked outta Dreko's ass, tossing his salad for all she was worth.

"Shit!" Dreko screamed. He whirled around and almost knocked her to the ground. Hood cocked his pistol and Dreko was on the move. Hollering, he snatched the female up by her hair, holding her against him and using her body as a shield.

"Wait muthafucka!" he yelled. He kicked his pants aside and cursed again. Yoking the woman, he kept her close, his head directly behind hers. He pressed his back to the wall as he inched toward the door.

"Hold up, man! Let's talk, my nigga! Lemme tell you about this shit!"

The woman reached back and grabbed Dreko around the waist. She hugged him close to her, defiance in her mad eyes.

"You put that gun down, Lamont!" Marjay demanded. Her face was sweaty and one of her breasts jiggled as it hung outside her shirt. "I will *whip* your ass! This boy been helping me! He gimme everything I need so you just leave him alone!"

Hood was blinded. "Mama," he muttered. She stood there glaring at him and looking just like Moo used to look with that little red dot beneath her eye.

Pain was on him as his eyes shifted to Dreko. "You grimy fuckin bitch. Nigga you gots to die!"

Hood aimed to fire, but there was nowhere safe to hit him. Everywhere he could have tagged Dreko, his bullets would have also struck Marjay. But when the sound of gunfire boomed in the room, it wasn't because it came from Hood's gat.

The round hit him from behind, in the top of his left arm and below his shoulder, spinning him around.

Hood went down to one knee. He turned and fired with his right arm extended. He dropped Black with one shot. But before the doljah hit the ground Dreko was out the door backward, still gripping Marjay in front of him.

Hood pulled himself up and staggered out the door behind them. The music was loud and his arm was dead. He let it dangle as he ran, following Dreko through an exit door.

"Hold the fuck up!" Dreko begged him, one flight up. He was going up the stairs backward, close-yoking the now terrified Marjay. He ran up another flight, still begging. "I been taking care of this bitch all because of you! If it wasn't for me she'd a been dead by now!"

Hood chased him, mindless. Marjay yelped and hollered as she struggled to keep up with Dreko. Her titty jiggled. Her feet back-pedaled. His forearm dug into her throat. Hood took another flight, and then another, and was almost on their asses.

Dreko burst through a doorway at the top of the sixth flight of steps. Blood streamed down Hood's useless arm and dripped from his fingers. He felt the cool breeze sweep down the stairs even before he made it to the top. The door slammed just as he reached it. He pushed it open and stepped out onto the roof, then aimed his gat again.

"Man!! Can you put that muthafuckin shit down so we can talk about this!?!" Dreko was pissing scared. Breathing hard. Stink sweat ran down his naked brown body and glistened under the moonlight. He wiped his eyes in Marjay's hair, then gripped her tighter with his left arm and held out his right hand, pleading. "C'mon, Hood. We brothers, man. We always been brothers. We can talk about this!"

Hood fired.

Dreko yelped, taking a bullet straight through his palm.

"Yo what the fuck is you *doing*?" he screamed. He backed up, shaking his bloody hand. "She's just a bitch man! Just another fuckin bitch!"

Hood moved closer and aimed again.

"Don't fuckin shoot me!" Dreko cried out. He gripped Marjay and crouched behind her, bending his knees. "Man, just don't shoot me!"

Hood fired again.

The bullet whizzed past Marjay's head.

"Bitch!" Dreko ducked down much lower and cursed.

Hood glimpsed his silhouette and fired again. Dreko flinched. The round passed through Marjay's thigh and sank into Dreko's right shoulder.

Marjay screamed and they both went down on the pebbled rooftop bleeding. And then Hood was on Dreko's ass. He stuck his gat in his pocket and smashed his fist into Dreko's nose, breaking it.

Blood ran from both men as they fought on the roof like wild animals, both of them wounded but both still fierce.

It was hard fighting a naked man, but Hood put in work.

Dreko did too. They threw down with a death wish.

Dreko fought to drag Hood over toward the edge of the roof, than grabbed the front of Hood's jacket and slung him over the low railing. Hood sailed clean over, but with his good arm locked around Dreko's neck the momentum carried his boy over with him too.

They struggled briefly on the narrow ledge. Ignoring his wounded hand, Dreko clutched Hood in the chest and tried to push him over.

Hood held on tight to the metal rail and stomped down hard on Dreko's bare foot. Then he lifted his leg high and thrust his boot deep into his boy's groin, sending his dick and balls way back toward his asshole.

Dreko shrieked like a kicked dog. He grabbed for his dick and went down, his sweaty feet slipping off the edge of the roof. His knees scraped against the side of the ledge and he lunged for the pebble-laced tarpaper in desperation. Panting, he braced himself on one elbow and grasped Hood's limp arm with his good hand, then held on and tried to save his grimy, useless life.

"Please, man," Dreko begged. His eyes were wild and scared. Fear ran off him in stink, sweaty waves.

Hood grunted in pain, his dead arm now alive with agony.

"H- h-hold on," Hood panted. The weight of his boy almost pulled his shoulder out of its socket but there was no way in fuck he was letting go of that metal railing. "Just hold on, man . . ."

Grimacing against the fire burning in his shoulder, Hood lifted his right leg and swung it over until he was straddling the rail with a foot on both sides. Then he slid his right foot between the bars and hooked the toe of his boot halfway back in.

"Don't let me go," Dreko grunted in a voice trembling with fear. Sweat dripped from his body as he gripped both the edge of the roof and Hood's injured arm. "Don't fuckin let me go."

"I won't," Hood promised.

Squeezing the railing between his knees with just the strength in his legs, Hood released his hand-hold and slid his fingers into the front pocket of his hoody. He came out holding his gat and he pressed that shit right against Dreko's forehead.

"Yo!" Dreko cried out, his body straining as his legs dangled six stories above the pavement. "Man what the fuck is you doing???"

For a brief second Hood wondered the same thing. The platinum grill in Dreko's mouth glinted as his boy grimaced in fear.

He slid the barrel of his tool down between Dreko's eyes, and over the bump of his nose. Hood pressed that shit dead against Dreko's trembling lips, then raised it up and slammed it down hard, cracking the cold metal against the glimmering number one on his left front tooth.

"What you doing?" Dreko screamed through a mouthful of blood and broken teeth. His words came out sounding like he was sucking a dick, but Hood still heard his boy loud and clear.

"I'm doing what it takes," he spit down at him.

And then he fired.

A million years seemed to pass before Hood heard the sickening thud of Dreko's body as it slammed into the concrete down below. And then Marjay was screaming and dragging her leg across the pebbly tar and making horrible noises that touched his soul.

"I'm coming, Mama," Hood muttered. He unhooked his foot and let himself fall down onto the roof side of the railing. "Just chill out, Mama. I'm coming."

AND AT THE END . . .

No Regrets!

THE HOMETOWN CROWD was wildin as Reem Raw ripped the mic in an outdoor area of Van Dyke projects known as "The Hole." Touring was some exhausting shit. Twenty-four cities, a sweat-drenching show almost every night . . . the schedule was brutal, but who would ever give it up?

The crowd was throwing up a mad chant for the Bottom Half Boyz. Reem had blessed the projects with this complimentary performance of his latest chart topper and people were hanging all outta their windows trying to be a part of it.

"Yeahhh," Reem said as he grinned into the screaming crowd. "Brownsville! We home, goddammit. Been all over the world, but I can sure tell we back home!"

A sick beat dropped from the mounted speakers and Reem's chart-topping single, "No Regrets," kicked in hard.

Reem laughed as the crowd started illin.

"We 'bout to give y'all something spectacular, ya dig me? Reem Raw! Robb Hawk! Hood! Speedy! Yeah! You know how we do ours!"

His Bottom Half Boyz were flowing with the crowd on the edge of the stage. Security was having a hard time keeping niggas back, and chicks was giving up that groupie love as they flung phone numbers and love letters up in the air like crazy.

Reem broke in and kicked the first verse with his distinctive, born-for-the-mic voice.

Tears I shed for the years I bled,
Thought I'd die in the slums when I took my pledge!
Hell is waitin tell Satan he can book my bed,
Looked Death in the face and he shook his head!
Wasn't ready for me.
So now I'm here, y'all ready for me?

Screams of love flew up from the crowd and rose into the air. The folks who were hanging out of their windows had a bird's eye aerial view of the show and were spittin that brutal shit right along with Reem.

Peep the scene! Niggas wanna be the king!
If they think they seeing Reem's flow? Need cre-a-tine!
Homey, step ya strength up, press the bench up,
Yes, I'm the shit! Can't cover the stench up! Yep!
Shit! What a gift God graced me with!

So the number one spot, they gotta place me in, my nigga!
So make room, let the race begin!
I'll meet you at the top, my foundation is the block!

Then the whole crew cut in with a hook that was so banging and uplifting that it had become a ghetto national anthem in housing projects and urban centers all over the nation.

No regrets cause life is sacred! Never let go of what you put your faith in! Times get hard, gotta keep your patience! Hold on till your dream comes true and embrace it! Face it!

The crowd was getting crazy swole. People were streaming over from Brownsville Houses, the Plazas, Riverdale, Tilden, Marcus Garvey, Seth Low, and Langston Hughes. Everybody who was close to the stage was straight wildin out. They were amped up and starstruck at the sight of their local boys who had made it out of the hood and done it up real good.

A tall, shapely young sistah stood quietly in the midst of the chaos watching one performer in particular. She'd arrived extra early to make sure she had a front and center spot. Every so often some crazy chick screamed real loud in her ear, or bumped a gangsta booty up against her hip, or elbowed her in the back as she got her freak dance on, but the pretty, chocolate-skinned sistah didn't seem to mind.

It had been a long time since she'd seen him. Fourteen months, to be exact. She tucked her small purse under her arms and allowed her eyes to get full on him. He looked good. Better than ever. She'd seen him grow from a boy into a man, and she couldn't be prouder of him for achieving his dreams. She had purchased the CD he was featured on, so she knew the second verse was his. She smiled as he grabbed the mic and banged up the stage.

Count the bars! Can't count the scars!
And I plotted a better plan when I found my flaws!
Now I put it down of course, so I'm crowned the boss,
Do what I feel, so fuck it if it's frowned upon!

Now I got my craft mastered,
On tracks I spat acid,
Check my past hits I smashed the last bracket!
I'm in a whole 'nother league/whole 'nother speed,
With my man on the stand that's a whole 'nother breeze!

The crowd was loving him. How could they not? He'd been working toward this dream his whole damn life. Lyrics had always rushed through his head. His lips had always moved. Trying not to lose his words, he used to say. Well, by the way the crowd was responding to him, the words he spit today had come straight off the pages of his life. He hadn't lost a single one.

Trip? Please! I can show you the highlights!
I shoulda did me, I can see it in hindsight,

Shoulda went left when everybody done flew right!
This is not just a song it's the soundtrack to my life!
I do it for my niggas, they can shine in my light!
Ticket out the hood? They can fly on my flight!
Yeah! No regrets! Just living my dreams!
Reem, Hood, Hawk, Gita, and Speed, ya'nah 'a 'mean?

Oh, they was feeling him. She smiled as he strode around the perimeter of the stage skimming hands with the fans who loved him so. She tried to step back as he neared her, but the dancing crowd pushed her right back out. Their eyes met and she inched out her hand. His fingers skimmed hers and they both knew. He hesitated just for a moment, then moved on. Giving up the love to the screaming fans who were dying for his touch.

Her fingers tingled from his energy and she took a deep breath as Robb Hawk came up for the last verse.

Her road to recovery had been rough and lonely. She'd gotten her GED, enrolled in community college, she was making meetings . . . and she was clean. But she'd been wrong to come back here so soon. Her heart was still open. The wounds still tender.

She opened her purse and pulled out a much-folded piece of paper as Hawk put his flow down on the third verse.

Son of the slums, my block ain't got Jags on it!
Just crack, gats, and deadbeat dads on it!
Young bucks like to wild out and spazz on it,
Every other hour there's another body bag on it!

Egypt unfolded the letter and stared at the single line of writing before her.

You have tested negative for the virus that causes HIV and AIDS.

It was her third test in fourteen months, and each one had come back negative.

Egypt sighed, reaching inside herself for her newly gained peace. So much had happened that it still seemed unreal. Sackie and baby Andreka gone. Hood turning his back on the drug game and going for his music career full force. Zena living on the streets and smoked out, totally crazy with grief . . .

Robb Hawk was onstage cutting up, and she refolded the small sheet of paper and stuck it back in her purse as she turned her attention back to the show.

She was drawn to him, of course. And he was drawn to her. Their eyes met again. There was still a lot of love there. And a lot of pain too.

Egypt let go first. She turned away, sparing him.

His eyes were heavy on her back as she pushed through the bouncing crowd and quickly disappeared from sight.

Hawk was finished slaying his verse and it was time for the hook again.

Hood lifted his mic to his lips and joined his boys. Spitting with hard-body fire, he tore the hook all the way down, reciting the words that he'd written from his heart . . . for the woman he would always love.

No regrets cause life is sacred! Never let go of what you put your faith in! Times get hard, gotta keep your pa-

tience! Hold on till your dream comes true and embrace it! Face it!

"Stay strong, E," Hood whispered softly. He nodded in her direction with mad love shining in his eyes. "No regrets, baby. Just hold on to your dreams."